W9-CEC-943

Pix

PIX

Bill James

THE COUNTRYMAN PRESS

Woodstock, Vermont

ISBN 978-0-88150-882-6
Library of Congress Cataloging-in-Publication Data
has been applied for.

Published by The Countryman Press, P.O. Box 748,
Woodstock, VT 05091

Distributed by W. W. Norton & Company, Inc.,
500 Fifth Avenue, New York, NY 10110

Printed in the United States of America

10 9 8 7 6 5 4 3 2 1

Chapter One

When Mansel Shale looked into his personal soul – and he did that now and then, though not making a big thing of it, for God's sake – yes, when he looked into his personal soul he saw that the main reason he ran a business was so he could use the good profits to buy good art. Manse liked the neatness and the wholesomeness of this thought – good profits, good art. It made the profits seem more worthwhile, not just a crude, grab-all chase for money. In discussions with certain friends Manse often mentioned he could not be more in favour of art. He considered that those words – 'could not be more in favour of art' – got his feelings exactly, and he stuck with them. So, when he returned one afternoon after golf to the ex-rectory where he lived and found nearly all his paintings fucking gone from the walls, it truly knocked him.

Above all, Manse loved pictures known as Pre-Raphaelite, being a tremendous team well over a hundred years ago. One of these pictures, in a very suitable frame, was by a great artist called Arthur Hughes, and until now it had covered the wall safe where Manse kept all his Heckler and Koch 9 mm pistols and ammunition. Obviously, the frame of a picture did not amount to anywhere near as much as the picture itself, but he thought frames should be suitable. Sometimes, when he bought a picture, he would have the frame changed, finding the original one what Manse referred to as 'off-key' or 'at variance'. Mock wood for frames Manse detested. If you had a genuine picture, surely the frame should be just as genuine. He disliked seeing the safe exposed – unkempt for it to be glinting at about his eye level, so plain and metallic, very much in that way of safes. When the picture hung there, it had been full of grand, bright, but also soft, colours. Manse operated the combination and opened up. Everything looked all right inside – the three automatics and bullet boxes. He relocked and decided he had to check all through the house for any more troubles. And this turned out wise, plus significant, really. Near the top of the rectory's main stairs, with his throat cut and four bruises to the face, lay a white, dark-haired man of about thirty-five, wearing a very decent Paul Mixtor-Hythe, three-piece navy suit, the lowest button on the waistcoat undone, as always recommended by style people for waistcoats so as not to seem stuffy. In fact, he was very obvious from below in the rectory entrance hall, his limbs haywire, but Manse had been focused on the ground floor empty wall spaces, first in the hall itself, then the drawing room and the study-den, and didn't at first look at the stairs. Naturally, nothing in any of the suit pockets gave an identification, though a quiet label sewn *on to* the inside breast pocket did identify Paul Mixtor-Hythe as the tailor. Manse knew that label, of course. The suit was messed up now, but you could still see it had been custom-made in terrific material, a sort of total rightness.

In their time, the Pre-Raphaelites had what grew famed as a Brotherhood. This idea always thrilled Shale. He wished he could belong to a Brotherhood himself, not necessarily to do with art, because he realized he had almost no talent at that, but a *commercial* Brotherhood, instead of this damn barbaric competition lately and out-and-out turf warring in the substances industry. The traders' understanding Manse had with Ralph Ember could not really be called a Brotherhood. It was an arrangement – a fine arrangement, but still, just an arrangement. And, of course, all the time people wanted to get in on it, newsters to the game in this area. The media sounded off non-stop about Nottingham and Manchester getting rough through commercial rivalry in the drugs business, but they ought to take a look here.

Although his safe had been put on show now, all the other bared bits of wall stood blank except for hooks and dust lines, and Manse felt like this blankness took over his own personal soul, especially as the paintings had no insurance, because information on value might leak, followed by possible questions on how he could afford them. This would be about £3.5 million, Pre-Raphaelites plus others. People *knew* how he could afford them, but that was different from being asked straight out how he could afford them. Shale always tried to dodge that kind of head-on quizzing. Too much definition helped nobody.

The Arthur Hughes used to talk to Manse – that's how he often described it, like a spoken, one-to-one message – and he felt wonderfully in touch with the work and with the painter. In fact, he felt in touch with not only the painter hisself but with the period he lived in and the Brotherhood. This connection delighted Manse, going back to the middle of not just the last century but the one before. He was in favour of history. Also, art had a spiritual factor and he approved totally of that. Manse considered spiritual things in general should get a better chance. A safe and the guns and rounds it contained could be very important, definitely, but not in a spiritual manner at all. As Shale regarded this present situation in his home, there'd been a troupe stealing the pix and a fight started over something. Or possibly an execution had been schemed as extra to the robbery somewhere private and quiet, such as on his property. He felt so damn relieved nobody dear to him was around the house at the time these savages intruded. That might of been grave.

For instance, he enjoyed letting a girl move in and cohabit here now and then, although this house had been a rectory before Manse bought it. A girl might remain for weeks at a spell, or even a couple of months if he didn't have much else going on, and Lowri or Patricia or Carmel could easily of been here when this break-in happened. Fortunately, though, Manse had arranged a couple of weeks for hisself without one of the girls while he did some wide thinking. He believed in a pause now and then.

But these girls meant something deep to Manse. Never would he let more than one stay at a time because he would of regarded that as poor, unkind behaviour to the girls theirselves, and confusing for his children. He did not choose these girls just anyhow, and not only to do with features and body. He knew Carmel kept quite a deal of contact with her parents, which Manse considered a credit. All these girls gave him pleasant companionship and so on for spells since Sybil, his wife, left Manse to live in Wales with that chef or anaesthetist.

And this produced the grandest and happiest piece of fluke today – Manse's children, Laurent and Matilda, were away on a routine half-term with their mother. Otherwise, one of them, perhaps even both, might of got pulled into this foul violence. Luckily, Sybil did not want the children with her non-stop, or, if she heard of the rotten mischief that hit the rectory today, she might argue the children was in danger with Shale, due to his ongoing career. Occasionally, they'd be in the house alone. Sybil and Manse had never divorced, and he considered it would be wrong for another woman to live with him on a permanent arrangement, particularly as this house used to belong to the Church and was, clearly, the home of rectors, very much one up on ordinary vicars. It had a good driveway behind trees and hedges and seven bedrooms. He liked to think of rectors trotting to the front door in a pony and trap after visits or a service and pouring a pick-me-up from a silver-embossed decanter. As soon as Manse bought it, the house had become a *former* rectory, yes, but he did refer to it now and then as 'the rectory' and he felt he must respect its past up to quite a point. Some of his writing paper had 'St James' Rectory' printed on it as Manse's address. People joked sometimes about Manse in a rectory, manse being the word for a Nonconformist minister's house, but rectories was Church of England. Also, of course, some thought it amusing that a rectory had been bought with drugs money, though Manse did not go along much with that kind of humour.

When he saw what had happened, then looked right

through his place and around it outside, he naturally got on the phone at once. 'Chandor, you fucking evil lout – have you been here? Of course you been here.'

'Manse, that you?'

'This got your mark on it,' Shale said. 'No sign of a break-in anywhere. This got your mark on it. And in daylight.'

'What's happened?'

'Don't –'

'Honest to God, Manse.'

'Or if not you as you, your people, running a-fucking-mok.'

'What – some trouble at your home?'

'This got to be put right, or as near as can be,' Shale replied. 'Soonest. I need to wash – well, you can believe it following that kind of contact! – then I'm going to pick up my kids, after access days with their mother. I don't want them coming back to a house in this state. That cannot be helpful.'

'Which?'

'Which what?' Shale said.

'Which state?'

'Don't piss me about.'

'The house – in a poor state? Some intrusion? Is that what you're saying, Manse?'

'You know the state it's in, you sodding smarm prince,' Shale replied. 'You know about intrusions.'

'Hang on a minute, Manse, will you?'

Shale heard Hilaire Wilfrid Chandor call to someone, maybe in a different room, possibly his name. It sounded like Rufus. That would be the kind of name someone who worked for Chandor might have. Then Chandor's hand went properly over the mouthpiece and Shale got nothing but a mumble, what could be an *angry* mumble, or put-on angry for Manse to pick up the tone of, a performance they'd most probably rehearsed, him and this sodding Rufus. After a minute, Chandor took his hand away and spoke to Shale again: 'I'm not getting a clear answer from

9

these two fuckers here but I think they might have improperly targeted your –'

'Which two fuckers? Was there three, then, at first?'

'Absolutely improperly. Look, Manse, you go on and pick up your children. That's at Severalponds service station, yes? The usual swap over? It's going to take you, what – four hours there and back with an interlude for cold drinks and possible muffins? Ample. I'll see things are absolutely fine at the rectory in time for your return with Laurent and Matilda. Guaranteed. Don't worry. An error. I acknowledge it. Anything that's been taken will be replaced, I assure you, and undamaged.'

'It's not just possessions missing. There's this . . . well . . . another aspect altogether.'

'What's that, Manse?'

'Another aspect altogether.'

'Right. I think I'm getting the outline, Manse. I'm learning more from you than I've got so far from these two fuckers, but that's going to change, believe me. They have their own damn rivalries and venom. Who can tell what they'll get up to?'

'Which two fuckers? Was there three of them? More?'

'They assume they can read my wishes, Manse, and they go ahead crudely, grossly, and *very, very* wrongly. Yes, amok, you've got it. You –'

'Why was they in my place at all? I mean, why?'

'No sense of what's appropriate.'

'In a Paul Mixtor-Hythe suit, not reach-me-down.'

'Well, yes,' Chandor said. 'That would probably be right.'

'Black slip-ons, Charles Laity by the look.'

'You know how it can be with staff. They imagine they're being helpful but fall into excess.'

'This is the kind of thing that could upset children not just now but lifelong. They see something bad and also a sudden lack on walls where they're used to beauty, vividness, warmth. And so they'll come to regard disappointment as normal.'

'You can relax, Manse. The rectory will be just as you

like it and a credit to you. Kids of their age ask damned embarrassing questions, I know. Sharp-eyed. They notice things.'

'Well, of course they fucking notice things. If there's something like that dumped here they're going to notice, aren't they? It's unusual.'

'Point taken, Manse.'

'I don't understand how you got people like that working for you.'

'I'm going to think about them after this, believe me, Manse. Staff reappraisal annually under seven main headings, including Balance and Tact. Well, have we been getting any of that? Hardly. They mean well, but –'

'Mean well to who?'

'Your place will be perfect,' Chandor replied. 'Or something in lieu.'

'In fucking *what*?'

'In lieu – instead, Manse.'

'There's no instead for them items off of the walls.'

'I meant if they've already gone, or something like that.'

'What's that mean?'

'What?'

'"Something like that."'

'Suppose they've been moved on.'

'Moved on how?' Shale replied.

'Like sold. If they've been sold to some middleman already, perhaps for freighting abroad, collectables. In that case, the absolutely total money will come to you, Manse. I'll get it out of the two fuckers, I promise.'

'I don't want the money. I want the items.' That business colleague, Panicking Ralphy Ember, had taught Manse never to be clear on the telephone because of intercepts, and to use general words like 'items' or 'aspect' when things was sensitive. And Manse did not have no doubt – these things now *was* sensitive. Chandor seemed careful, too. Even landlines could be tapped, especially if you thought of someone like that fucker, Assistant Chief, Iles. He did what he wanted.

'Or, if they've taken a knock-down price for them on

11

account of haste, I'll make it up to you from my individual funds, Manse,' Chandor said. 'You quote me the average cost from any auction catalogue within the last six months and that's the price you'll get from myself, no haggling, plus five per cent for disturbance. I wish to avoid the least grievance on your part at this juncture.'

'Which?'

'What which, Manse?'

'Juncture.'

'This moment in time.'

'But why is this moment in time a juncture?' Shale replied. 'That's what I'm getting at. What is it makes this moment in time a juncture? Why are you in my place at all? You're someone who's hardly been set up in this region for any duration, but you're into my property. This is a fucking *rectory* for Christ's sake. Do you know rectories? I say this operation got your mark on it, but I don't really know your mark because you're so new, but I'd just guess it's your mark not to leave a mark because that's the sort you are and coming here from London.'

'I wouldn't want to upset you at this juncture or moment in time, or any other, Manse – I wish to avoid causing you grievance ever. That goes without saying.'

The sod *did* say it, though. He wanted friendliness. His people had done everything wrong, or that was his tale. Chandor would try to put patches on. Shale said: 'How can I get the price from catalogues? They never been sold. They been here all the time since I bought them. They're not going to be in no catalogue.'

'The equivalent, Manse. Things that match them more or less for age, type and distinction. The internet will tell us. It's the same as if you wanted to price a certain 2004 Bentley, you would not need to have the actual car itself there, you could look up what models of that year and type were going at.'

'What fucking Bentley?'

'As an illustration, Manse.'

'It's not like Bentleys. Every one of them items is different from every other one. This isn't carburettors and

12

handbrakes. There isn't no *equivalent*, not for me. That's what I'm telling you. These items are items. They got a particular value, especially one of them, and this value is not re money. Spiritual. Historic.'

'In its way, this is really touching,' Chandor replied.

'What's that mean?'

'What?'

'"In its way".'

'Yes, in its way. When I say "touching", I have in mind the warmth of your evident commitment to these articles. And a further snag, you say? Well, you can really relax, Manse. I've got this rectory situation very much in hand.'

'Shall I leave a key somewhere?'

'To what, Manse?'

'The house.'

'To the rectory? That's a kindness in you. But I don't think they'll need it, will they? As you said.'

'And keep them away from the safes.'

'Two, aren't there?' Chandor replied. 'Study-den, drawing room – which is the armoury. I don't want you to fret about these at all, Manse. Out of bounds. I'll tell them – "Study-den safe, drawing-room safe right out of fucking bounds." Both Chubbs? Combination, not keys? Study-den safe for cash and private accounts?'

'When you say "in hand" does that mean you'll be there to control your maniacs – you as you, not just fucking Rufus?'

'Rest assured, I want to look at this constructively,' Chandor replied at once.

'There's considerable stains,' Shale replied.

'Often a way to deal with that kind of thing as a stopgap remedy is actually to *over*stain with, say, coffee or Horlicks, as through an accident, and then redecorate at leisure. Disguise. The chief, short-term objective now is to account to the children for the discoloration, you'll agree. Or sauce. Might you have been carrying a sauce bottle with a loose top, or no top at all, in that area and stumbled? This kind of treatment makes the original stains a nuisance still, but unsinister. We'll see to it.'

'Which area?' Of course, Shale knew which area, but asked in case the gabby sod gave himself away by saying the snag with his throat snagged was on the staircase. 'The area of the staining,' Chandor said.

'Another thing I don't get.'

'What's that, Manse?'

'How come you know about the safes and Severalponds, and the names – Laurent, Matilda? You building a dossier? What the fuck for? You been here no time, but you got a file on me?'

'These are great child names,' Chandor replied. 'A royal dimension to "Matilda". She nearly had the English throne. A warrior lady. Twelfth century? But why am I telling you, Manse? This would obviously be in your mind when you and your wife picked that name. I always think names are significant. You've got a bird called Lowri, haven't you? That's Welsh. And your wife, Sybil, is over in Wales on an alternative lifestyle, right? One can come across all kinds of odd links and connections through names. But Lowri's second name, Billsborough, not Welsh at all. Weird. You eat late on these Sundays, don't you? Look, the least I can do in view of all this – if you give me your order on the mobile when you're, say, an hour from the rectory with the children, I'll get meals sent over from the takeaway, Chinese or Indian, simply decide and let me know – chutneys, garlic bread, anything.'

Shale often drove the Jaguar himself these days following the extremely problematical death of his chauffeur, Denzil.* He'd have to speed a bit to make the Severalponds meeting at six o'clock. That search of the rectory and then the conversation with Hilaire Chandor had been necessary but they messed up Manse's timetable. He always liked to be at Severalponds ahead of Sybil and the children, as a courtesy factor, and because he did not want them wandering unaccompanied in the service station building.

He went back to the naked drawing-room wall safe

* See *Easy Streets*.

before starting out and fully loaded one of the Heckler and Koch automatics, then waist-holstered it. Lately, he'd begun to prefer this to shoulder harness. Unless you had some shapeless bloody anorak on, a shoulder holster would generally produce a bulge and scream 'Gun aboard!' But a jacket covered the waist weapon without no evidence of it.

He liked to dress in decent style when going to Severalponds. It gave a ceremonial flavour. As a matter of fact, he had a couple of made-to-measure Paul Mixtor-Hythe suits himself. Sybil and the children must not see he came armed on a family occasion such as this. That would brand him so damn thuggish and jumpy, like someone who had a job with Hilaire Wilfrid Chandor. Manse always did go armed on these Severalponds runs. This was no exceptional precaution tonight – not brought on only through that trouble at the rectory and the call to Chandor. Shale never felt at ease in service stations. The crowds and the wide-openness of the car park and the restaurants worried him. That had been so even before Chandor showed off all his dirty research earlier. And so, tool up as standard. They had put a jolly sort of country-scene name on this place, Severalponds, because in old times there must of been several ponds here and maybe tadpoles and ducks and other Nature elements, but that did not make it harmless now. They wanted to seem relaxed – not Threeponds or Eightponds, but Several, like 'Who's counting?'

The regularity of these rendezvous – a mistake. Manse had known that. But he would hate to scare Sybil or the children by suggesting they should constantly switch venues, which would have been wiser. Severalponds it must be. Otherwise, he could imagine Sybil going back to that potter or vet she lived with and saying in bed, when winding down and canoodling in a domestic style after intimacy, yes, telling him how right she had been to quit someone in the illegal substances trade whose profession made him frightened all the time that he or she or the children might get wiped out, or all of them. Tears seriously blurred Manse's eyes as he visualized that bed scene

15

and imagined the conversation, and he brought the Jaguar down to 40 mph for a few miles on the motorway.

Of course, he had to think what might be behind as well as ahead. Chandor's information on the Severalponds meetings must of come by someone tailing the Jaguar previous. Manse realized he had been so dreamy and slack about watching the rear-view mirror on these trips. That was something Denzil would never of done. He really knew the tricks of driving, although sometimes he refused to wear the chauffeuring cap Shale bought. Manse did a lot of mirror now, but what point? There'd be no need to tail him today. Chandor knew everything, didn't he, even though he'd had such a short time to discover it. Shale thought he could understand part of Chandor's game, but not all. Why put on display in that phone talk so much of what he'd dug out re Manse and his family? And then that disgusting raid at the rectory. Had some of Chandor's animals really gone wild, beyond his instructions and wishes, *against* his instructions and wishes, thieving and, as an extra, attacking each other, resulting in a death? What *were* his damn instructions and wishes? How far beyond them? 'Get into the house and –' And then? Hilaire Wilfrid Chandor seemed to say people on his staff had mistaken what he wanted. True? Or just a ploy, a tease? What *had* he wanted? How could they mistake it? Did he employ idiots, drunks, addicts? Or had he talked so vague to them that he knew they'd go miles out of order once they started?

Always there were firms like Chandor's longing to get right in on the dealing scene locally – Brits, Albanians, Turks, all sorts.* Did Chandor think he could act sweet now, but actually frighten and cow Manse into making a place for him? *I know where you live, and where your kids go at some weekends and school breaks, and where you do the handover, and where your safes are, and what your women are called – first and second names – and where your beloved pix hang, hung. So, how about some pleasant cooperation?* Manse

* See *Girls*.

16

felt nearly certain Chandor had Lowri's surname right – Billsborough, or it could be Nettlethwaite or Margerison, but definitely something not at all Welsh. Was the offer to clean up the rectory as to the body, and restore what could be restored, then bring a choice of takeaways with additionals for Manse and the children, meant to settle Shale and make him forgiving and helpful to Chandor's outfit in the commercial sector? So many of them new firms eyed up this city and envied the trade cooperation between Manse and Ralphy Ember. They struggled to be part of it. They would try all sorts of dodges and pressures. They'd heard of the happy, sensible arrangement with Assistant Chief Constable (Operations) Desmond Iles, and wanted to be part of this, too. That slob Hilaire might be saying, *Here's what we're able to do to you and yours, Manse, whenever we like, so get intelligent and matey, mate. We turn kindly now, and, oh! big apologies for the deado, but you'll understand from this that we can also get really bad if you force us to it, can't we, Manse?* Even if Chandor put them Pre-Raphaelites etcetera back undamaged, that would still be the message. And no need of a key. The rectory didn't have no alarms. He would not want police all through his home in response and doing an ogle, would he?

Only Sybil and the children came to Severalponds for the transfers, never the jockey or schools inspector or whatever he was she lived with. They also had a Jaguar. That annoyed Shale. It was older than his and not top of the range, but he still felt irritated. For privacy, a sliding glass partition divided the front from the back of Manse's, but he had hardly ever closed it, even when Denzil was alive and chauffeuring. It would of seemed a bit majestic, and Shale detested pomp. Most likely Sybil said to this partner they better have a Jag because Manse owned one, and she didn't want to go down to a Ford or Skoda, because of appearance. Pride. If they'd bought something else he might of offered to pay off the hire purchase for them, but not when they offered deliberate disrespect and rivalry by picking a Jag. Total anger he did avoid. Manse almost always tried to understand Sybil. He told himself she might of chosen the Jaguar so the children would not feel the change too strong and sudden of being with her after him and vice versa, like going into a pressure chamber when leaving a wrecked submarine. Now and then he thought he *would* do the hire purchase for them, regardless. Manse hated petty vindictiveness. Although living in Wales might be quite all right really, Shale considered he should be very kindly to her to make up for it.

Sybil pulled into the next car-park space just after he arrived, the children grinning and making faces at him through the side window. One thing Shale favoured as much as art was fatherliness. He believed he had a flair for this. Matilda and Laurent jumped from the car and ran together ahead towards the restaurant and gaming machines. They went out of sight. If he'd been masterminding here he would not of allowed that, but he knew he should try and keep things cheery. 'They behave all right this time, Syb?' he said.

'As much as they ever do.'

'And they still get on all right with . . .?' He could never actually speak the name and always left it for her to fill in.

'With Ivor? Oh, yes. He's very easy-going.'

'That would be his training, I expect.'

'What training?' she said.

'I always forget which job he's in. Holiday camp red-coat? Supermarket cashier?'

'He'd tell you if you asked him. Or if you didn't. And he'd go on and on about it. And things at the rectory?'

'No changes. Just this great feeling of a good history.'

'Serene?'

'Serene, yes. That could be the very word, Syb.' He had the feeling suddenly then that she might like to be there with him again, and fuck Ivor. Or *not* fuck Ivor. Never at these Severalponds meetings had he sensed this before. Perhaps he'd been wrong to think of her happy and conversational in the Welsh bed. Then, despite them near-tears on the motorway, he wondered if he wanted Sybil back.

'No purchases?' she said.

'Purchases?'

'Paintings?'

'Not at this juncture,' he said.

'What's that mean?'

'Not at this moment in time.'

'I do miss them. The Hughes,' Sybil replied.

'Oh, the Hughes, yes. I couldn't be more in favour of art.'

'Lights up the wall, the room.'

'It does, it does.'

The children rushed back. They had some winnings and went into the shop to blue them. Afterwards the four sat with soft drinks and sandwiches in the restaurant. 'They've got leaving pressies from Ivor in their overnight bags,' Sybil said. 'Not to be opened until you're home. Things to wear. Modish – or *he* thinks so.'

'But it's kindly.' Shale wondered why he wanted to defend Ivor – to persuade her to stay with him?

'Oh, yes, he can be kind.'

She made it sound like nothing, or a disease. Although Shale waited for her to give kindness a slagging she left it there.

Manse, Laurent and Matilda were back at the rectory by 9.30. Manse felt hellishly tense, terrified about what they might find. In the drive, he said: 'I'd like you to wait in the car for a minute.' He prepared to go first and check. That bastard Hilaire Chandor was so keen on merrymaking and pressure, the downstairs room and stairs might be as they had been, or worse. They said he'd been named after some joker in the writing game or a circus clown.

'Oh, cars we've had enough of, dad,' Laurent said. They dashed from his Jaguar as they had dashed from the other. Both had keys to the rectory in case they came back from school or youth club in the week and Manse was out.

Shale yelled: 'For God's sake wait. Let me go ahead, will you?' He unfolded from behind the wheel and sprinted himself but was too late. Lights went on and immediately he heard Matilda give a long, appalled scream. She shouted: 'Oh, oh, what's happened?'

'Come back!' Shale cried.

'Oh, terrible!' Matilda howled.

19

'Don't look,' Shale bellowed.

'Dad, why have you done this? Awful! Awful! Awful!'

'Oh, yes,' Laurent said. 'Horrible.'

Shale called out: 'Why didn't you wait? Stay where you –'

'You've moved the pictures around on the walls. I don't like it a bit,' Matilda said. 'They look *so* wrong.'

'Oh, is that all?' Manse said. Them Chandor apes – they would not remember which went where. To that crew pictures was pictures and hooks hooks.

'All!' Matilda replied. 'All!'

'I thought a change might be interesting,' Shale said.

'Not interesting at all,' Matilda said. 'A mistake.'

'Yes, bad,' Laurent said. He took his bag upstairs to unpack and try on the Ivor present in his room. Laurent was touchy about clothes. He wouldn't want to be seen in gear he didn't like. He paused near the first landing. 'What happened here, dad?' he said.

'What?'

'A mess on the stair carpet and wallpaper. Did you spill something?'

'Oh, yes, some sauce. A stumble.'

'Sauce?'

'Yes.'

'You were carrying sauce on the landing?' Matilda said. 'You move the pictures around and were carrying sauce on the landing? What goes on, dad? Have you gone a bit loopy through loneliness?'

'It doesn't come out very easily,' Shale said.

'No, it doesn't,' Laurent said.

'Dad, put the pictures back right, will you?' Matilda said. 'All of them – hall and drawing room and everywhere.'

'It was just an experiment.'

'This experiment went wrong, *so*, *so* wrong. As if it's someone else's house, not ours.'

'Why don't you unpack and have a look at your pressie while I pop down to the takeway?'

'Indian,' Matilda said. 'Can we have some chutneys and garlic bread?'

'Absolutely.'

'And please, dad – the pictures?' Matilda said.

'Yes, of course. All as they were. Tonight.'

'I'm trying to work it out,' Matilda replied.

'What?' Shale said.

'The sauce. Spilling it. Were you going *up*stairs with a bottle of sauce or coming *down*stairs when you stumbled? If you stumbled when you were coming *down*stairs you might have fallen all the way and that would have made a real mess with the sauce from top to bottom of the stairs, the carpet and the wallpaper until the bottle emptied itself. The top of the bottle was off, was it, or loose? Plus, you might have been hurt. But what I don't understand is why you had a bottle of sauce on the stairs at all – it doesn't matter if you were going up or coming down. What did you want a bottle of sauce upstairs for? A picnic?'

'Or if you like I could get Chinese,' Mansel said. He shouted up to Laurent: 'Chinese or Indian?'

'This is real rubbish,' Laurent replied.

'What?' Shale said.

'This rubbish present from Ivor. I'll never wear it. Oxfam. Oh, Indian. With chutneys. Garlic bread. And is there any sauce left or did you spill it all? Get some more?'

During the meal, Manse thought of asking them whether they would like to see their mother back in the rectory, but then decided this might not be wily. If they said yes, it meant he must say yes to her, suppose she asked. One of the things with fatherliness was you had to take notice of what your children said about their mother even if she was shacked up with someone else. But if Manse did not ask them, and stayed uncertain about how they would answer if he *did* ask them, he could stay uncertain hisself, and he would prefer that for now. If they said no, they didn't want her back, this would mean he'd have to be chilly to her if she even hinted at it, like today, and he thought that might be cruel. It could be important for her to have at least a vision of getting out of a place like Wales, and away from a partner called so-and-so. Wouldn't it be heartless to crush the hope? Of course, one child might say he or she

21

did want their mother back and the other might say he or she did *not*. That would bring Manse a lot of suffering and anxiety. He always tried to treat them with exact equality, and this could not be if they had different opinions about Syb.

Whatever the children thought, if Sybil did come back as permanent he would clearly have to say a complete good-bye to Lowri, Patricia and Carmel. This could make them feel like they been on the side only. Hurtful. They might turn bitter and start talking around the city of what they'd seen of his special commercial interests while living at the rectory. They would know the haulage and scrap metal side of things was only part of it. Kiss and tell, times three. This could be deleterious. Also, the children grew fond of Lowri or Patricia or Carmel while one of the three lived here on a stint, and might get upset to know none of them would ever return, because of Syb.

When the children went to bed he put the pictures back as they should be. Matilda had it right and the rectory *did* look like *his* rectory again now. Shale went up to the first landing where the slaughtered man had lain. There was still bad staining but, as Chandor had said, it could be just from an ordinary kind of accident, Manse thought. Could it? He examined the stairs leading down to the hall and found no spotting. They must of brought some kind of efficient body bag. He did another systematic tour of the house inside and out with a flashlight, and this time thought he found where they got in. A utility room window at the rear of the rectory looked to Manse as if it had been forced, though properly closed again afterwards. He could see small scratches in the paintwork, and even a little splintering. It puzzled him that he missed this previously. But perhaps shock had a hold on him then, and he'd been careless. Or, of course, they might not have entered by that window first time. Why would they change, though, if the earlier break-in had been so easy and undetectable? Did Chandor send different personnel for the second visit? Perhaps he was genuinely angry with the original people and replaced them. Manse remained mystified. He'd have all locks changed, but did not really believe this would make things fully secure. The children would ask why they needed new keys, and he'd find some answer that didn't frighten them, even if he felt frightened hisself.

Manse went and sat down with a coffee in the drawing room and really enjoyed that Hughes over the safe. Clearly, it was much, much more than a picture for hiding safes with, and Hughes would not of announced to the Brotherhood one day in the Pre-Raphaelite times that he'd just finished a work great for concealing someone's gun store. But it *did* conceal the gun store brilliantly. Laurent came in wearing pyjamas. He said: 'You'll really have to get new wallpaper and new carpet on the stairs if mum is coming back, dad. She'll be able to see right off it's blood. That would bother her because she's used to an ordinary sort of life now with Ivor. He's got an ordinary job.'

'Who said mum's coming back?'

'Did you change all the pictures around, so that was what we would notice, like Matilda did, and not the stuff on the stairs?' Laurent replied. 'It's sort of funny, isn't it, dad?'

'What?' Shale said.

'Mum wants to come back, being fed up with Ivor *because* he is so ordinary. But she wouldn't like it if she came back and something that was not ordinary at all happened, such as blood all over the stair carpet and wallpaper. Was it to do with the commercial side or –'

'Your mother never said anything to me about coming back,' Shale replied.

'I mean, was this a death? It's a lot of blood.'

'Your mother seems to me all right.'

'If Matilda or myself talk about Lowri or Carmel or Patricia you can see mum get like really sad and ratty. Well, it's jealousy, isn't it? Oh, yes, she's wondering about coming back. This wasn't Lowri, was it?'

'What wasn't?'

'On the stairs. Did she turn up while we were away? Or one of the others? Did Lowri or Patricia or Carmel get awkward – such as showing she'd noticed too much about the trade? Women – everyone knows they'll do some blabbing if they think they have not been treated right. In school we're studying a play that says,

> 'Heaven hath no rage like love to hatred turned,
> Nor hell a fury like a woman scorned.

'Everybody has to learn those lines.'
'I've heard of them,' Shale said.
'If Lowri, or Carmel or Patricia thought mum was coming back –'
'Why should anyone think it?'
'If you said.'
'I wouldn't say, because I don't know if she wants to.'
'But you might have said something that Lowri or Patricia or Carmel *thought* sounded like she was coming back,' Laurent replied.
'I never talk to Lowri or Patricia or Carmel about your mother. That would not be right.'
'Or it could be that, couldn't it?' Laurent said. 'You never talk about her so they might think, Hello, something secret's going on and you'll give them the push soon. Did you have a bad squabble with one of them and –'
'I don't want you telling Matilda the staining looks like blood. It would fret her, Laurent.'
'It *is* blood, not just looks like it. Blood under sauce. You see, dad, it isn't the kind of thing that happens in Ivor's house. Oh, they've got sauce there, but it's for food. If mum came back and saw the staining she'd say, "Can the leopard change his spots?" That's another thing from school – the Bible – meaning you, you, dad, the leopard – you can't change because you're into that kind of life. I worry that that blood might be from Lowri or Carmel or Patricia owing to a quarrel.'
At breakfast, Matilda said: 'That's blood at the top of the stairs, isn't it? '
'Blood?' Manse said. 'Oh, really!'

'And someone's been in my room. I can *feel* it,' Matilda replied.

'Tomato sauce looks just like blood,' Laurent said. 'Often they use it when they're making films and want to do wounds. In that one about the shower when the woman is stabbed by the mad guy – you know that tall mad guy at the motel – and you see the blood mixed in with the shower water running down the plughole, they used tomato sauce to imitate blood. When I looked at those marks at the top of the stairs, I thought at first they could be blood, but now I think definitely only tomato sauce.'

Matilda said: 'Was one your friends here while we were away, dad – Lowri, or Patricia, or Carmel?'

'Not a bit,' Manse replied. 'I had some ideas I wanted to run through in my mind, you know. Concentrating. I needed to get solo for a while.'

'Did you tell one of them mum wanted to come back, and this made her angry I mean, Lowri or Patricia or Carmel, and there was a terrible fight?' Matilda asked.

To Manse it seemed like she wanted to continue, *And Lowri or Patricia or Carmel got killed?* But, no, that would be too much for her.

Manse said: 'I haven't heard your mother wants to come back.'

'It's obvious,' Matilda said.

'Norman Bates,' Laurent said. 'He dresses up as his own dead mother and kills Janet Leigh.'

Shale considered it really strong and kind of Laurent to try to soothe Matilda. That's how a brother should be. But Manse saw both of them was very badly hit by what had happened here, or what they *thought* happened here. Although Matilda showed it the most, Shale spotted plenty of strain in Laurent, too. Manse hated the thought that suddenly the rectory had come to seem a threatening, dark place for them. This was not how a rectory ought to be. The house had a history of goodness and calm and order – one reason Manse bought it, and an important reason. Somehow he had to give back to the children that sense of goodness and calm and order. Matilda's feeling about the jumbled-up pix, and her strange belief that someone had been in her bedroom, brought Manse a fine notion. He thought what he would do was buy her her own picture to hang in her own room, and a good picture, a real one, not some fucking wishy-washy watercolour or a production line print. This would create a really settled and steady feel to things. When she looked at the picture she would be able to think, That lovely picture is always there and wipes out for keeps by its true beauty the idea someone been in here lurking. Of course, he would do similar for Laurent. You had to behave equal. In any case, Laurent might need it as much as Matilda. Boys thought they must act hard. A wise father should look behind this cover, though.

Chapter Two

Iles said rather movingly: 'An admirable and really mature thing about Manse Shale, Col, is the civilized arrangement for their children he has with his wife. They're separated, you know – Manse and Sybil.'

'Well, yes, sir, it's in his dossier, ' Harpur replied.

'Mutual tolerance.'

'You've been doing some research,' Harpur said.

'I aim to take an interest in folk like Manse Shale.'

'It's one of your major strengths – this all-round awareness.'

'What are the others?' Iles said.

'The other what, sir?'

'Strengths. My other strengths, major or minor. List them, would you? Indicate which you regard as major, which minor. I don't like the sound of "minor strengths". Are these *your* sort? Another term for weaknesses?' They were in Iles's suite at headquarters, Iles standing behind his desk, head half turned towards the window so Harpur would get the granite of his profile, but not a full outline of the Adam's apple. Iles regarded his Adam's apple as a bad let-down. He wore uniform today. He said: 'I listen in to Shale now and then. And similar, of course.'

'Listen in?'

'Oh, yes, it's the least I can do.'

'Unauthorized intercepts are –'

'*I* authorized it, jerk.'

'Yes, sir, but you're not actually –'

'I think the sod knows.'

'What?'

'That I'm listening. Or that I've got someone listening. Shale talks code. A transcript here.' Iles bent to the desk and picked up a thin sheaf of stapled papers. He glanced at them. 'Manse can't put two fucking words together properly and his head's a jangle, but he's crafty just the same. Well, of course he's crafty just the same. Would anyone who can't be crafty just the same get so he's drawing £600,000 a year untaxed from substance trading?'

'What kind of code?'

Iles read some words aloud: '"Items". "Every one of them items is different from every other one." What items? We're not told. Just that "these items are items". Is this communication, Col? And then, "possessions". What possessions? We're not told. Or "another aspect". "Not just possessions missing. There's this . . . well . . . another aspect altogether." What other aspect? We're not told. But I'll crack it, of course.'

'Many would confidently expect that of you, sir.'

'Who exactly?'

'What, sir?'

'Who would expect it?'

'Oh, yes, many, if not most.'

'Humane. Adult,' the Assistant Chief replied.

'What is, sir?'

'The way they share duties to the children, Shale and Syb. The decencies.' Iles's voice began to move towards an enraged scream, as it would sometimes, when he and Harpur were alone and the word 'decency', singular or plural, came up. Occasionally Iles would drag it in if it didn't come up naturally. 'I mean the way the family structure is respected, even though, technically, and more than technically, Shale's family has fragmented. Do you know what I think to myself when I witness this considerate, sensitive, *decent* approach to things, Harpur?'

Yes, Harpur knew, and also knew he would be told, anyway. He said: 'I feel you'd admire this care for children even from two people who –'

'I think to myself, Harpur: Here's an out-and-out,

through-and-through, titanic villain, Mansel Shale, yet he still exhibits a certain propriety and decorum.'

'Yes, that's what I –'

'Whereas I, I, Desmond Iles, have a colleague, a moderately high rank police officer – Detective Chief Superintendent – who might be expected to live by certain standards, have certain decencies, yet who, on the contrary, contemptuous of all such propriety and decorum, decided regardless, utterly regardless, that he would pursue and have, have repeatedly and in varied locations, Sarah Iles, the dear wife of his superior, and –'

'Who was he talking to?' Harpur said.

'Who?'

'Shale. When he said "items" and "possessions" and "another aspect", who was listening – beside yourself on the phone tap, that is? Perhaps his main listener already knew what the "items" and "possessions" were and the "other aspect" and didn't need anything more specific. A kind of shorthand.'

'Now, when Sarah looks back on that short chapter, that furtive interlude, with you, Harpur – and that's what we term it, "a short chapter", "an interlude", nothing more substantial or meaningful – when she looks back on that interlude she fails to understand how it could ever have taken place,' Iles replied. The scream thickened to a shout. 'She can't. She can't. I tell you, she can't, Harpur.' The door to the Assistant Chief's suite was closed but these traditional agonized sounds would get out into the corridors and cause fond smiles. Such froth-flecked denunciations of Harpur by Iles had become familiar to staff. They'd be reassured by the consistency – would know the ACC was still the ACC and could fall effortlessly into one of his agonized fits. 'To tell the truth, Harpur – and *she*, as well as I, calls you Harpur, no first name recognition – to tell the truth, we enjoy an amazed chuckle over it together, Harpur, commenting on your appearance and clothes and the fact that you're at your career ceiling because, if for no other reason, I'll make fucking sure you're at your career ceiling,' Iles said. The shout had now slipped down to a frenzied, hysterical hiss. A kind of forecastable progress of tones governed these performances, like an over-rehearsed symphony.

'That right, sir?'

'What?'

'"An amazed chuckle". Which would be the main component?'

'In what sense, Harpur?'

'The amazement or the chuckle?'

'I had an experience at Severalponds, Col,' Iles replied.

'Ah.'

'I've been out there, you know.'

'No, I didn't know that.'

'Oh, yes.'

Harpur said: 'Some of these service stations boast interesting names, don't they, and are worth a visit to see the landscaping and fluorescent billboards?'

'This came up,' Iles said.

'What did, sir?'

'Severalponds.'

'Came up where? During your phone tap? Shale said he was going to Severalponds?'

'And I thought, This is an opportunity. I'll get out there and observe unobserved.'

'That would be like you, sir – getting out somewhere and observing unobserved. This is hands-on. People know you for that. I've heard folk say at a mention of your name, "Oh, Assistant Chief Constable Desmond Iles, he's *very* hands-on."'

'Which?'

'Which what, sir?'

'Which folk said it?'

'Oh, yes, quite a few.'

'Obviously, at that stage, during the phone spiel, when Manse spoke of his children and a transfer at Severalponds from his wife to him, I couldn't tell whether he was lying like the damn full-time degenerate and dodger he is, or really meant it. But once I got out there – everything, so admirable. The wife, the children, Mansel himself – harmonious. A benign ritual. That's how it struck me, Col. I felt privileged to be present, despite the crummy crowds you see cross-legging in for a piss at these places, entirely unashamed of their market stall clothes and roughhouse skin. And the men are worse.'

'Shale has his complexities.'

'I left very satisfied. That's why I refer to it as an experience. They were still there when I decided to return, so happy in one another's company, husband, wife, children, even though the wife is, in fact, having it off with someone else. In Wales, is it? Tranquil. Amiable. Soft drinks. Expensive, hygienically wrapped snacks of palpable freshness. Manse magnificently dressed, probably carrying something at waist level, but no upper-body holster to spoil the jacket line.'

'Grand. But Severalponds wouldn't be the chief element of the intercept to interest you, would it? It's the cryptic "items" and "possessions" and "other aspect", that are the challenge. You revel in challenges, don't you, sir?'

Iles waved the papers. 'Col, it's quite possible I'll show you this transcript. Oh, yes. I *could* treat it as in the Most Secret category, but I do notice you around the place and to a significant degree accept you're part of operations here.'

'Thank you, sir.'

'But you wouldn't be able to make sense of it. I'd have to do that for you.'

'Thank you, sir.'

'You're head of CID, after all, Harpur, and deserve some basic consideration as a colleague, despite that disgusting, now risible, betrayal with my –'

'Who was he speaking to?' Harpur replied.

Iles threw the transcript pages over the desk. Harpur read them quickly. 'This is about his house being stripped of pictures,' he said. '"Collectables" and so on. Shale buys art. He's a sort of connoisseur. It's in the dossier.'

'Oh, God. *Of course, of course*, it's about his house being stripped of pictures,' Iles replied. '"Items" equals pix, yes.

31

But, more important – considerably more important, obviously – the murdered body on the stairs.'

Harpur reread, more quickly: 'Which murdered body on the stairs, sir?'

'The "other aspect", isn't it?'

'How can you tell that?'

'A Paul Mixtor-Hythe suit, non-reach-me-down. The Laity shoes. What else could these mean, Harpur?'

'What else but what?'

'This dead man on the stairs.'

'I don't get it, sorry, sir. There's no mention of a body anywhere. Why do you speak of that? Is this transcript a full account of the conversation? Am I short of something?'

'I don't know if you're into art at all, Col,' the ACC replied, 'real pieces, not pink rose petals with a raindrop on.'

'Art? Well, I –'

'People get very bound up with their art. Why he says "spiritual".'

'Also, when he refers to the children noticing a "lack on walls where they've been used to vividness, beauty, warmth", he's obviously talking about art in a serious style,' Harpur said. 'I think he goes for a lot called the Pre-Rastafarians.'

'Don't play more fucking philistine than you actually are, Harpur. Pre-Raphaelites, as you know.'

'Someone called Hughes? And Prentis. We've got notes on them. Quite possibly genuine canvases, I'm told.'

'"Beauty, vividness, warmth" is the order he spoke of. Yes, naturally, he's talking about art,' Iles replied. He paused, then said: 'I can visualize it myself – the blankness and possible cobwebs and dust lines where previously hung immensely distinguished works. You're a Bible man, aren't you, Harpur? Ex-Sunday school. You'll know that Old Testament cry of –'

'"Ichabod."'

'"The glory has departed." Yes, I see it, I see it now at the rectory. Mere dust on the walls where fine works had been displayed. I have that kind of ability, Col – the visualizing kind. At Staff College I was known as Mind's-eye Iles. Most likely he used one painting to cover a wall safe, its blunt unwelcoming features made suddenly evident.'

Harpur considered and tried some face-reading on Iles, always ineffective. The ACC's face was not expressionless, but the expression never accurately told what malice or absurdity or kindness he had lined up. Harpur said: 'Christ, you've been into Manse's place for a look, have you?'

'Those empty, emptied, walls. So bereft, so void, Col.'

'You broke in, did you, you crazy fucker, sir,' Harpur said.

'Manse has built up a little personal gallery and sees it suddenly pillaged. Heartbreaking.'

'You'd know they were all still at Severalponds and nicely settled for a while,' Harpur said. 'Why you left them? So you actually *saw* the stripped walls and body on the stairs?'

'Look at the transcript, Col – quite early on. I wondered what he was getting at when he said, "I need to wash – well, you can believe it following that kind of contact." See those words? "I need to wash – well, you can believe it following that kind of contact" – as if his listener would entirely understand why Mansel needed to sluice himself, because, of course, his listener was party to something that had gone on at the rectory.'

'What answer did you get when you wondered?' Harpur said.

'Blood.'

'Blood how?'

'Manse has been searching a body,' Iles said. 'Perhaps a savaged body. Throat-cut, for instance. Shale is bloody from contact.'

'You've been in there and observed this, without being observed – the throat-cut body?'

'Manse would require identification of someone discarded like that, wouldn't he? A trawl through the made-to-measure Paul Mixtor-Hythe suit pockets.'

33

'You did a window catch, did you, sir? No alarms, of course. Alarms bring outsiders and Manse wouldn't want them poking about, especially police outsiders. As far as I remember, though, your breaking and entering skills are damn low. True, a writer my wife liked did say the mind and instincts of a burglar were similar to the mind and instincts of a police officer, but . . .'

'Conrad. *The Secret Agent*. We've spoken of this before. It's the only book you've ever read, isn't it – except for the Bible?'

'. . . but you're a useless burglar and will have left traces, not like the first lot who entered.' Harpur went back to the transcript. 'What is it he says? Here: "This got your mark on it. No sign of a break-in anywhere. This got your mark on it." An amusing contradiction, really, wouldn't you say, sir? It's got the mark on it because there isn't one!'

'It makes me hellish nervous when you turn paradoxical, Col. Shall I tell you how I imagine events went?'

'You don't have to imagine. You've damn well seen it, haven't you? Did you try the safe?'

Harpur realized Iles might admit to organizing an illegal tap, not to illegal breaking and entering. An intercept was electronic, devilish and clever-clever – worthy of him. Breaking and entering was artisan. Occasionally Harpur did a break-in for purposes of an unofficial search of some suspect's place. Iles would not wish to be bracketed with Harpur. And, of course, by claiming only to have 'visualized' events at the rectory, Iles could hang on to the identifying details of the body on the stairs and use the knowledge as he wanted – and as he wanted would mean fucking up Harpur.

The ACC said: 'A raid to snatch Shale's pictures – presumably stuff of worth. Someone's pressurizing him, maybe. They want his cooperation. We can understand that, Col, can't we? They're saying to him, "This is what we can do if we feel like it, so get friendly, get commercially amenable, Mansel, dear." The body's extra, I'd suggest. Some sort of inter-crook fight there. Manse immediately knows who's responsible, of course, and gets on the phone. The intercept shows it's Hilaire Wilfrid Chandor. A coming name? Here from London fairly recently, as mentioned by Manse. We've been taking notice of Chandor? No convictions up there in Metroland but lots of rumour? Nordic-looking?'

Iles fancied himself as being Nordic-looking and would not like competition from Hilaire Wilfrid Chandor. Harpur said: 'Yes, we've had a bit of quiet surveillance on him and done some crafty photographs and informal inquiries. The stuff has probably crossed your desk.'

'Well, I'm glad some stuff you instigate does, Col. And, of course, Chandor was aware Manse would know who'd done or ordered the rectory incursion. He acts the chief enraged by mistakes of his men and promises to put things back to normal while Manse is away at Severalponds. Suddenly, you see, Chandor ceases as Vandal and becomes the white knight. He's going to look after Manse, naturally having first flattened and trampled him. It's choreographed. Chandor will expect gratitude in the trade scene. When I say "visualize", Col – what I visualize above all, figmentalize above all, is the return of Chandor's people with the pix, a step-ladder, cleaning fluid, several bottles of tomato sauce, and a body bag. Perhaps Chandor himself. That's my scenario. That's how I visualize. How I posit. At my rank you have to think creatively, make, as it were, one's own pictures about pictures. Don't fret that you'd never be able to manage it yourself, Col, because you're not going to get to my rank.'

'You saw all this? Where were you – in a bedroom or bathroom watching through a part open door? A kid's bedroom? She or he will know it. They can sense such things. They're like animals. I don't know whether it's residual odour or something more mystical. I can't say I've noticed residual odour off you, not lately, sir, but children are sharp. Subliminal.'

'It would be a hellish worry for poor Mansel when he came back from Severalponds.'

'What?'

'In case the body is still there and the pictures still

missing. Can he rely on Chandor's promise to replace and clean up? If no change, how does Manse account for something like that to the children? This is a tender father, with a throat-cut corpse on the stairs and all that cold, unoccupied wall.'

'But everything was as promised in the transcript, was it? Back to status quo?'

'Certainly it would be interesting to know if that's so, Col.'

'You *do* know it, don't you, because you were bloody well there, peeping, sir – at least when Chandor's return party arrived? You'd have been expecting them, though, because of the tap – could get out of sight in good time.'

'All we have is this transcript, Harpur, with its baffling, ambiguous hints. "Items" that are "items". A revelation!'

'No, that's not all we have. Or not all *you* have.'

Iles sat down at his desk, unstapled the transcript and fed it to the shredder. His eyes grew mild and reminiscent. Harpur tried to gauge whether venom or idiocy or venomous idiocy would emerge next. But Iles's voice took the mildness route: 'Sometimes, you know, Col, my mother used to say I had an imagination that ran away with me. Yes, this was her phrase – "Desmond, your imagination runs away with you." Not harshly spoken – bemusedly.'

'Mothers often make remarks to their children, now and then bemusedly. It's a motherly sort of thing. They think they have a right. I don't know how it comes about. As a matter of fact, *my* mother would sometimes say –'

'But what's happening, Harpur?'

'We know what's happening, don't we? Aspiring firms fight for a way in and will try to squeeze or squash anyone obstructing them. It's constant – this unrest, this ruthlessness. The drugs game here is Wall Street in miniature. Private enterprise imperatives. And it's everywhere, not just our domain. The head of Nottingham CID is compelled to move with his family into a safe house because a drugs gang have decided he's a threat and should be taken out.'

'I read about that. I thought this over and concluded it

would almost certainly be a loss to the Force here if some gang got *you*, Harpur.'

'Thank you, sir.'

'Mind, anything that compelled flight from the déclassé, dogshit street where you live now to some spruce, safe house in a wholesome district must be a plus, and beneficial for your daughters.'

In the evening, Harpur had one of their routine, scheduled meetings with Jack Lamb up at the old anti-aircraft gun site on a hillside overlooking the city. For a while they had abandoned this spot because Jack considered it no longer secret and secure. Now, though, he seemed to have decided it would do again. He liked places with military connections and often dressed to harmonize, or in what he *thought* harmonized. Harpur accepted without question whichever location Lamb chose because, obviously, he had all the risk, and risks to informants were big. In fact, Harpur would accept rendezvous conditions laid down by any informant. There was another, special, condition when dealing with Lamb. Jack liked it to be known that he only informed when he considered the cause good. He did not grass for money or as a natural stooly. That kind of finking he thought base and contemptible. He liked to explain this conscience matter to Harpur each time they met. And Harpur always listened. Patience paid. He knew no informant to match Jack.

'I'm talking because there might be children in danger, Col,' Lamb said at once.

'That's bad.'

'I get this from a contact,' Lamb said.

'Yes, I thought so. Which contact is that, Jack?'

This kind of question, Harpur always asked, though not expecting a reply. No informant named *his* informants, or there wouldn't be any. But today Jack said: 'There are scores of locksmiths in this city.'

'Certainly.'

'So, if I say my contact is a locksmith, this is not to put the finger on him/her. But it's necessary you should know his/her work.'

37

'Right.'

Lamb had on what might be a 1930s-style Norwegian army despatch rider's hard-winter, black leather greatcoat with a heavy fur collar, also black. With it he wore a British, plum-coloured, Parachute Regiment beret and desert boots. Jack stood 6 feet 5 inches and weighed over 250 pounds. He and Harpur both liked this spot on the hillside. They could look down over the city and feel they might offer it guardianship, not with the anti-aircraft shells and searchlights of the Second World War now, but through smart use of what they already knew, and what extra they might find out. It was a warm, hazy night and the street lights far below seemed feeble, shrouded. The enormous greatcoat and its fur collar must be oppressive but Jack did not wilt. Probably it wasn't in the character of Norwegian army despatch riders to wilt, because 1930s despatches had to get through. 'I would never identify someone who talks to me, you know that, don't you, Col?' Jack said.

'Certainly.'

'In a sense a locksmith is like a priest or solicitor and has a duty of confidentiality to clients. Matters of property.'

'Right.'

'But in this case he/she spoke to me,' Lamb said.

'Because of the children?'

'Because of the children,' Lamb replied.

'Where?'

'There are two involved.' Lamb and most other informants liked to give their material slowly, in dribs and drabs. They believed this echoed the difficulty and rewardable skill in obtaining it, and made the material appear more. 'A boy and a girl.'

Harpur wondered then if they were Manse Shale's.

'The father is a dubious figure, but his children deserve protection the same as anyone else's.'

'Clearly.'

'Some would dispute it.'

'Do I know him?'

'The mother is to quite a degree out of the reckoning,' Lamb replied.

Harpur began to feel sure the children were Manse Shale's. 'Out of the reckoning in what sense, Jack?'

'Happy for him to have custody most of the time.'

'That's unusual.'

'How it is,' Lamb said. 'I expect from this you can work out the man we're talking about.'

'I'd need to think a while,' Harpur said. Lamb would be upset if Harpur found a short-cut to the answer.

'Shale,' Jack said.

'Mansel?'

'Laurent and Matilda. Most of the time they live with him at the rectory now he and his wife have split.'

'It'll be in the dossier, I expect. You think the children are in danger? Or your informant thinks the children are in danger? '

'New locks throughout, internal and ex. Improved catches on the windows, though I don't know what that can do. The contact thinks a break-in at a utility room window giving complete access. That's why Manse wants effective, lockable internals as well as on main outside doors. You'll see why I have to declare him/her a locksmith.'

'A break-in, but nobody hurt?'

'The contact says he/she got the notion the house was empty at the time.'

'And what purpose? Robbery?' Harpur said.

'Not clear. Shale didn't say anything was missing. But then he might not want to tell a locksmith.'

'But he/she noted the break-in scared Shale?' Harpur asked. 'Did he/she install Shale's safes?'

'Has Shale got home safes?'

'I wonder.'

'And some kind of bad staining on the stairs – carpet and wallpaper,' Lamb said. 'Naturally, the contact had to go up to look at first and second floor windows.'

'What kind of staining?'

'Quite extensive. '

39

'But what nature?'

'Shale told him/her he'd stumbled while carrying an open bottle of sauce and pitched forward, causing a jet. It's possible. People carry open bottles of sauce upstairs? Apparently, both the children repeated this explanation several times, really hammered it, said they'd seen it happen and found it almost comical, except that Shale nearly fell down all the way and could have done himself damage. They explained that Manse often took sauce upstairs for breakfasts and suppers in bed, being "a very sauce" person, the girl child said.'

'These are loyal kids. What did the contact think of the sauce aspect?'

'He/she thought he/she'd better tell me in case I thought it should be passed on.'

'Do you pay the locksmith?'

'Shale's having the carpet replaced and new wallpaper,' Lamb replied. 'Immediately.'

The old concrete road, laid by the Royal Engineers for transporting troops, supplies and ammunition, could still be used and Harpur and Lamb had parked their cars a little way down the hill. They began to walk back to them. Harpur said: 'Manse has some valuable pictures in the rectory, hasn't he? I seem to recall that from the dossier. Perhaps he's worried about them, too.'

'I've sold him some works, yes, most probably genuine.'

Lamb ran a fine art dealership. Not too much was known about this, and Harpur never pressed to find out. Jack looked for no informant fees, but he appreciated tact. 'Manse favours the Pre-Raphaelites. You probably know, Col, that there are a lot of very high quality fakes of Pre-Raphaelites about, some as good as the originals. People make careers at it. Judgements can be difficult. I give Manse a call now and then if I hear of something up his street. He likes girls in rich colours and with tresses, generally auburn. His wife used to call them his "wank women". That might help explain the cooling between Manse and her. '

'Sad.'

'But, Col, isn't Shale's enthusiasm for pictures heartening? I feel a sort of bond to him, which is why I knew I must talk to you about his problems. Always we find this impulse in people, even crooks like Manse, towards the wholesome and estimable. It's a sign, surely, that humanity is basically good, not evil. Here we see dirty money put to high purpose. Shale deals drugs and with his profits buys a one-time Church of England rectory, no doubt happy and proud to immerse himself in the religious ambience. He also goes in for fine art, some of which might be authentic, and for which, in any case, he gladly paid an authentic price. Similarly, the Kennedy family purchase the White House with J.F.'s dad's bootlegging loot and so the Cuba missile crisis can be defused and peace maintained. Or then again, Ralphy Ember hopes and strives to refurbish and transform his for ever unchanging and unchangeable lags' and slags' club, the Monty, into the Athenaeum.'

'Policing depends on a belief in all people's search for virtue, or at least eventual virtue. Sometimes, it will be very bloody eventual. And there might be slips back.'

'You can be so philosophical, Col.'

And as to the Monty, on his way home, Harpur decided to drop in there and sniff some atmosphere. Perhaps, and treble perhaps, Ralphy's club would one day become as selective and professionally glittering as he wanted, but for now it could occasionally give hints and glimpses of what might be going on, or might be about to go on, among the present, generally unglittering membership. Harpur often called at the Monty, alone or with Iles, on the pretext of spot licensing check-ups. It probably worked better without Iles, because the Assistant Chief frightened everyone shitless and made helpful conversation difficult. Iles didn't really go there for conversation or intimations. He went to dominate. As he'd explained to Harpur: 'I show the flag, Col, and *am* the fucking flag.' Iles adored these visits. They were his monkey gland. They told him he could still quell a room by will and stare and unforgiving, know-all grin, despite his Adam's apple and gone-grey quiff.

It was early in the evening and Ralphy himself might

be absent. Generally, he arrived around midnight and stayed to oversee shut-down at 2 a.m., or later when the club hosted some special celebration of, say, a birth or parole. Harpur thought he'd stop off there, anyway. If big upheavals in the substances scene threatened he needed to get some inklings – more than came from Iles's tap and 'visualizing', more even than Jack's lock and stain despatches.

To guard against assassination by contracted marksmen, Ember had arranged for a thick metal shield to be fixed high on one of the club pillars, blocking any direct line of fire from just inside the Monty main door to where Ralph sometimes sat doing accounts or dreaming of his projects at a small shelf-desk behind the bar. As a way of softening its appearance and disguising the harsh function, this steel screen was covered with a collage of illustrations. Ralph had mentioned to Harpur that they came from a book called *The Marriage of Heaven and Hell*, by a poet, William Blake, famous also for 'Jerusalem'. Ember knew such things. He had started a mature student degree course at the university down the road, though he suspended it not long ago because of business demands. These included his tricky mission to get the Monty's social standing considerably up, plus new and persistent uncertainties in the drugs game because of government legislation, and because of constant invaders, like Chandor.

Once Harpur had passed under the shield he could see Ember was at his usual place, working on some papers. 'In early tonight, Ralph,' he said.

'Catching up, Mr Harpur. The Inland Revenue won't take delays, you know.'

'But think of the extra work if you had to tell them about all the *real* money.'

'Mr Iles not with you this time?' Ember replied. 'Off sick? Yet it's wonderful what they can do with just one course of pills these days. He's still seeing that girl who works the streets around Valencia Esplanade, is he? Honorée? I'm sure he'll be back to his usual form very soon.' Ember fixed Harpur a gin and cider in a half-pint glass and poured himself a Kressmann armagnac.

'I was in the area,' Harpur replied.

'That's the function as I see it of a club like the Monty,' Ember said. 'Somewhere to stop off at a whim and recoup.'

'True.'

'It might be a marginal role to the main matters of life, but a necessary and worthwhile one, I feel.'

'True, indeed.' At the other end of the bar near the pool tables Hilaire Wilfrid Chandor and a few friends stood drinking shorts. Yes, Nordic. Harpur would have liked to stroll over and see if Chandor and/or the others smelled of cleaning fluid, and/or of incendiarized Charles Laity shoes, and/or of an incendiarized Mixtor-Hythe hand-tailored suit, and/or of incendiarized flesh. There were few other people in the club yet. Harpur had wondered whether Manse Shale would be here and available for a general chat, but Ember did not like his close, outside business connections to use the Monty. Most likely Shale *was* a member but realized he shouldn't show up here too often. Ralph treated the club as very separate. All right, it could be regarded as a sink, but a legit sink, acknowledged fully to the Inland Revenue, and perhaps about to set off towards social eminence. Yes, very *perhaps*. Ralph might not object to Chandor and/or possibly one or more of the others having membership. After all, Chandor had not really got into the substances trade scene properly yet – which would be why he had targeted the rectory and Manse's art. Of course, Chandor might be thinking of something comparable against the other great and enduring figure in that scene, Ralph Ember. Did Ember appreciate this? Generally he was quick to detect menace. Had he become casual, convinced he'd soon be kicking out virtually all the present membership, anyway, and replacing them with cardinals, professors and ITV board chairmen?

'Sometimes I wonder about the shield, Ralph,' Harpur said.

'Shield? Which shield is that, Mr Harpur?'

'The Marriage of Heaven and Hell. Fine against someone shooting from the door. But useless if he or they is or are actually inside the club.'

'Oh, you mean the air-conditioning baffle board.'

'No, the two-centimetre-thick steel slab.'

'Yes, an air-conditioning baffle board, ' Ember said. 'The engineers maintained it would give me I don't know how many per cent better heating or cooling by deflecting air currents. They drew diagrams – looked like the wind direction maps on a TV weather forecast. I thought it worth investing.'

'Chargeable against tax as a business expense? How do you describe it to the Revenue – "William Blake anti-hit-man rampart"?'

'And definitely my electricity bills are down,' Ember replied.

'You let all sorts in here.'

'Many a droll comment I get, as you can well imagine, Mr Harpur, when I tell folk where the illustrations come from. Couples remark they could have posed for pictures with that as the title – each claiming to be the Heaven side of their own marriage, of course,' Ember said. 'I've heard that a hundred times but I feel it kindly to laugh. This seems to me a duty of one who presumes to run a club – kindness, bonhomie.'

'How do you vet people?'

'Which?'

'Members.'

'A definite and proven procedure.'

'Being?'

'I couldn't tell you how many applications we turn down, Mr Harpur.'

'It's the ones you *don't* turn down that worry me.'

'And how's the big scene, city-wide?' Ember replied.

'I was going to ask *you* that. Things shift, Ralph.'

'Constantly.'

'But you manage to keep ahead, do you, you and Manse?'

'"Ahead"? I'm not sure what ahead means in that context. The club continues. And, obviously, even if I did know what ahead means, I couldn't answer for Manse.'

'You're pals. You'd probably hear if he had problems, wouldn't you?'

'Would I? What kind of problems, Mr Harpur?'

Chandor and his party turned to leave. Chandor gave Ralph a small nod and a small smile. Ember nodded back.

'Yes, things shift,' Harpur said. 'It's hard to keep up.'

Ember refilled Harpur's glass and then went off to another part of the club. Harpur sat on for a while with his drink but talked to nobody else, learned nothing and *had* learned nothing, except that *The Marriage of Heaven and Hell* might be only a placebo, and he'd known that already. When he reached home, his daughter, Jill, came out into the hall and said: 'People here, dad. One's the Press. Both ladies.'

'Oh?'

'Looking for you. To do with someone missing.'

'Oh?'

'A man. They've come on here from headquarters. We've been taking care of them.'

Harpur didn't always like it when Jill and his other daughter, Hazel, took care of callers. The two girls could be very considerate, hospitable and deeply nosy. 'Thanks, Jill,' he said.

She went ahead of him into the big sitting room: 'Here's dad now,' she said. 'He'll sort things out.'

Harpur thought he recognized one of the women, not the other.

'Kate, of the *Evening Register*,' Jill said, waving a hand towards the younger woman. 'She's Crime.'

'Ah, yes,' Harpur said, 'I've seen you around the courts, haven't I, and at press conferences?'

Jill waved again, this time indicating the other visitor: 'Meryl Goss, from London,' she said. 'She's on a search for someone. Well, her partner.'

'Searching where?' Harpur said.

'He's in this city,' Jill said. 'Not findable yet, though.'

'He definitely came here,' Meryl said, 'but suddenly he's not in touch. That's entirely unlike him.' She'd be about thirty-two, tall, frizzed fair hair, fresh-faced, wearing jeans and a three-quarter-length navy fabric coat.

'So, she's arrived from London, looking,' Hazel said.

'Of course, someone who's grown up and seems to go missing – well, your people at headquarters wouldn't think much of that, would they, dad? They'd think he can do what he wants.'

'This is different,' Meryl said.

'Yes, it sounded different to me, Mr Harpur, ' Kate said. 'That's why I –'

'Kate was around Reception at headquarters, dad,' Jill said, 'waiting to see one of your officers about an article they're doing in the *Register*, and heard Meryl report this missing person, and obviously upset.'

'I expect Kate can tell me herself,' Harpur said.

'Yes, we talked a bit,' Kate said, 'and I felt it sounded like something that could be . . . it could be something that would need a senior officer to look into. Not routine.'

Meaning, Kate wondered whether it might make a news story for her. He would have liked to ask Meryl whether her partner wore Paul Mixtor-Hythe suits and Charles Laity shoes, but didn't.

'I knew you were in the phone book, so we came out here and waited,' Kate said.

'We told them you'd be glad,' Jill said.

'Of course,' Harpur said.

'Her partner's in property development,' Hazel said. 'Kate believes he came here to see some intermediaries.'

'Yes, intermediaries,' Jill said.

'Do you know who they are – the intermediaries?' Harpur said.

'No,' Meryl said.

Harpur would have bet on it.

'And then silence,' Kate said.

'It's a worry,' Meryl Goss said.

'Meryl works in a big London office but she's taken some days off because of this search,' Jill said.

'We'd better have a name and description,' Harpur said. 'And pictures?'

'Graham Trove,' Meryl said. 'Thirty-five, middle height, dark, short hair.'

'They live together in Camden Town,' Hazel said.

'He nearly always wears a suit,' Jill said.

Harpur would have bet on it.

Meryl was sitting in an armchair, a cup of tea provided by the girls on the carpet near her and alongside her handbag. She bent down to the bag and produced two photographs. Harpur, who'd remained standing near the door, crossed the room and took them from her.

'And Meryl left one with Reception at headquarters,' Kate said.

'Have you got one, Kate?' Harpur asked.

'No.'

'I didn't want that,' Meryl said. 'I'd rather not have anything in the Press at this stage.'

'Right,' Harpur said.

'We probably couldn't publish yet, anyway,' Kate said. 'It's not really a story so far.'

But Harpur saw she sensed that soon it might be – how good reporters got to be good. He looked at the pix. In one Graham Trove stood alone smiling outside what appeared to be a front door, perhaps the entrance to the Camden Town house. He wore a suit and collar and tie. Harpur tried to stop a vision of him with his throat cut supplanting the actual snapshot. The other picture showed Meryl and Trove conducting a comic kiss in a garden, perhaps at the rear of their house. They stood far apart, both bent over from the waist and stretched forward, like a couple of doves billing.

Hazel said: 'Graham has phoned her several times, saying he'd arrived and so on and that things were going well. If he used a mobile these would be traceable, wouldn't they, dad?'

'Not all. Depends on the phone and how he pays. But then they stopped?' Harpur said. 'So, what happens when *you* ring *him*?'

'Nothing or voicemail.'

'We thought this might trouble you, dad,' Jill said.

Yes, it troubled Harpur. In the morning he went up to Iles's suite and put a photograph of Trove in front of him. 'Yes, I've seen that,' the ACC said.

'How?'

'A routine missing person inquiry came to us.'

'Do you always look at routine missing person material, sir?'

'I looked at *this* routine missing person material.'

'Is that because you think you might have seen a missing person dead?'

'Am I being interrogated? You must be a detective, Col. So, how do *you* come to have the photograph?'

'I like to keep you up with what I'm doing, sir.'

'That right?'

Chapter Three

Now and then, of course, Manse Shale had wondered about installing closed circuit television in and around the rectory. So far, wondering about it was as far as he'd gone. He did not really like the idea of cameras. Chilly things, staring, reporting back. Although CCTV might be fine at a bank or petrol station or jail, it did not seem to Manse suitable for his and the children's home – and Patricia or Carmel or Lowri's home, during their joyful, allocated spells as residents. And to Mansel it did not seem suitable for an ex-rectory, either. He prized this religious connection and wanted nothing to taint it. A rectory, when it was still a working rectory, would not have had CCTV. God watched over it, not fucking cameras. People visiting the rector might of felt snooped on, might even of got put off coming here, if cameras tracked them. This would be the wrong kind of treatment for church members, like they was enemies, whereas they might want to discuss raging soul problems or hand in decent garden produce for the harvest festival.

It's true that if he'd had CCTV filming, Manse would of known straight off who lifted the pictures and what went on at the top of the stairs. But he *had* known by brain power, anyway, who ran the raid and who, like ultimately, was responsible for the corpse in the great suit near the first landing.

But with CCTV he might of had a security camera at the front door to check callers and show them on a monitor. Someone rang the bell now, giving it heavy pressure, it seemed to Manse – a true let's-be-having-you-Shale blurt.

He was in his den-study, maybe Manse's favourite room, although it had Dutch portrait paintings here, not Pre-Raphaelites. He hated narrowness, and art certainly existed before and after the Pre-Raphaelites, he knew that – well, so obvious, think of them cave drawings or David Hockney with swimming pools. Manse sat at what was known as a 'partner's desk', made of mahogany and with a leather top, going through some bank statements. You had to watch them sods in the banks.

These days, a partner at the head of a company would not have a big desk like this, most probably, but a 'work station' for his computer, surrounded by comfortable furniture, such as what were called now, sofas, not settees, where discussions on company policy would take place in a relaxed mode, also 'brain-storming' sessions, meaning where they tried to think of ideas a bit new. Manse's study needed something different from a work station, though. The great size of the desk and the red leather top and the magnificence of the wood suited so well this big, square, high-ceilinged room. The bell continued to call and harass. To Manse it sounded like the police – non-stop, bossy. Lacking CCTV he could not tell who it really was, but he got some greasiness and kow-tow smiles and sharp thinking ready in case it did turn out to be police. You could never be sure what them fuckers knew or thought they knew or had made up. As Ralphy Ember said once: 'Always try civility first, Mansel, but never count on it.'

When he went to open the door he saw it was Sybil. 'My damn key doesn't damn well work,' she said. She waved it at him like a little spear. This must be what started the anger.

'I've had the locks changed,' Manse said.

'Why? To keep me out?'

Yes, it was anger, but also fear, sadness. He decided he still did not want her to know why he'd ordered new locks. If the children seemed at risk here, she might insist on taking them to live with her and lover boy. Such a decision by Syb was not likely, but possible. She definitely felt some connection at times with Laurent and Matilda, he'd noticed that. She did know about motherliness and fell into it now and then. Manse said: 'A girl who stayed here a while grew rather clingy and wouldn't leave. I'm not one to get violent over something like that, am I, Syb, so best just quietly keep her out? She'll find another place, most likely.'

'But why did you open the door, then? It could have been her.'

'I had the idea it might be you.'

'How?'

'I don't know. Like sixth sense?' Shale said. 'Maybe the special way you rang the bell.'

'Special how?'

'Like a personal message. Like saying, "It's Syb, please answer."'

She moved into the hall and he shut the door. 'Did you *want* it to be me?' she said. 'Is that why you thought the ring of the bell might be *my* ring of the bell? The thing is, you never knew until now how I do ring a bell because I didn't need to, having a key.'

'It's something mysterious, yes,' Mansel said.

'I've heard of these girls – Patricia, Carmel, Lowri – from the children, damn it,' Sybil said. 'Which one grew clingy? Had you said something to her that would make her get clingy? Promises? Implications? What about the others? You give them all a key to our . . . to your home?'

'It was a lovely surprise, Syb, when I opened the front door,' Shale replied.

'But you said you could tell it was me.'

'Still great to find I had it right.'

'Suddenly, I wanted to see the old place – and you, naturally, although it's not long since Severalponds. I jumped in the car. Impulse. An hour, maybe two, and I'm on my way back. Perhaps I'll wait for the kids to get in from school. Has Laurent chucked out that crap thing Ivor bought for him?'

'You've always had impulses, Syb. They made you wonderfully unpredictable and exciting.'

'Yes, well . . . history. What's going on, Manse?' Decorators were preparing to paper the stairwell walls, and the stair carpet had been removed.

'I thought the place could do with some freshening up,' Shale said. They went into the drawing room.

'Ah, the Arthur Hughes and the Edward Prentises,' she said. 'You're very faithful.'

'They deserve it,' he said.

'Yes, they do, they do,' she replied. 'But you could sell and restock on the profits. If you're into freshening up the house.'

'I'd miss them. These particular ones.' Syb did not understand about collectors, their love for certain special items. She thought deals. 'Tea or a drink?' he asked.

'A drink.'

'Good.' He mixed a couple of gin and tonics and went into the kitchen for ice and sliced a lemon.. '*Our* home.' He'd noticed that. And then the jealousy and suspicion about the locks. It all meant something? She wanted to come back permanently to the rectory and him, did she? This visit was her way of testing how she might feel if that happened. She had boldness, or call it cheek. What if her key *had* worked and he was here with Carmel or Lowri or Patricia? Lowri would do it anywhere. They might of been on the rug in front of the Arthur Hughes. That had happened with her occasionally. Manse did not regard it as disrespect to art. This was a totally natural act and many great paintings focused on Nature. Think of Van Gogh and the cornfield.

Manse still could not be sure how he would feel if she proposed coming back for keeps. Would he like to settle for someone permanent again? Did he still love her enough? Definitely it hit him very, very bad when she left. He would say wounded. Plus it had to be wrong for a rectory wife to go scampering off with another man to a place like Wales. Perhaps he owed it to the children to give them a returned mother, who would bring a more settled flow to their lives. Yes, he did owe it. Any of them marriage counsellors etcetera would tell him that. Her nice words about the paintings seemed meant to woo him. She didn't call the girl models his 'wank women' no longer and stand in front of the pictures and look like she was going to spit. Manse enjoyed getting wooed, and enjoyed feeling the Pre-Raphaelites had won her over, even if it was only a bloody ploy. She said 'damn' a lot but that would be show.

He returned with the ice. Sybil had remained standing near the bigger Edward Prentis, though not looking at it but staring around the room. 'I don't know where to sit,' she said.

'You mean for the best view of the pictures? It *is* a dilemma,' Manse replied considerately.

'No, I don't damn well want to sit where one of *them* has sat.'

Manse thought this rectory was like full of people from the past. He himself wondered about how it would of been when clergymen lived here, mulling over the Old Testament and making a list of church wardens. And, not so far back in the past, he remembered that body on the stairs. Now, Sybil could imagine Lowri or Patricia or Carmel in one of the drawing-room chairs and wanted to shun that, whichever it might be. This would not be a hygiene thing. A pride thing, a wife thing. She had to be different from them, even if she did live with someone else now.

Probably she guessed that if she sat in the big armchair near the Hughes, for example, Manse would be eyeing her and thinking, *Last time I looked over at that big armchair when a woman was in it, it was Patricia, or Carmel or Lowri. Today, it's Syb. Well, swings and roundabouts.* Maybe she'd wonder if he was comparing her legs with Lowri's or Patricia's or Carmel's, or all three's. Women had their worries. Often they did not add up to much at all, but Manse tried to regard them seriously.

'Here's one *I* always sit in, ' he said, pointing to another of the chairs. 'Take that, will you, Syb?' On the whole, Manse considered this not a bad solution to a pretty tough problem. Tact – he always felt he had quite a bucketful of that. Offering this chair was like putting her in the main seat, the master seat. Although she came back unexpected and cool out of nowhere from closeness with some other man she still got this spot. Quite a few these days supported equality of the sexes, yes, but he'd bet not many men would be willing to listen without no violence at all to a woman bleating on about not putting her damn arse on some cushion because another woman's, or other women's, damn arse or arses had been there, and then offer her instead the room's best perch, his own. He spooned ice and a lemon slice gently into her drink. She sat in his chair. He did not mind. For some men it would be like having their balls cut off to see a woman in the chief place. But Manse would regard that as ignorant. Women certainly had a right to a reasonable chair, this being the new millennium, for God's sake.

'The stair carpet wasn't old, was it?' she said.

'It had become very 1990s, I thought.'

'What's that mean?'

'Yes, very 1990s,' he said, the new millennium being in his mind and probably good, although, of course, 9/11 was in the new millennium, so you never knew what might come.

'Where is it?'

'The stuff that was taken up?' he said.

'Yes, what did you do with it?'

'Burned.'

'Oh, Manse! Many people would be glad of a carpet of that quality, even a bit worn. Hotel standard.'

'I don't like the idea.'

'What?' Sybil replied.

'Other people walking over carpet that used to be in my family's home. Does that sound sentimental? I'm sorry.'

'And the new carpet – have you chosen it?'

'Oh, yes, to be put down when the decorating's finished.'

'Who helped?'

'Helped what?'

'Who helped you choose?'

He felt like saying that Chandor or Chandor's people

didn't exactly *help* him choose but made damn sure he *did* choose, and fucking fast. 'I picked it myself.'

'No advice from Carmel or Lowri or Patricia?'

'I decided something not too vivid, yet with a colour theme that impressed,' Shale replied. 'The same sort of . . . well . . . *mood* as the Pre-Raphaelites.'

'Do you know what I thought, Manse, when I failed to get in?'

'It would be confusing, I can see that,' he replied.

'I thought, he's changed the bloody locks so I can't just roll up and catch him screwing one of those cohabit dames on the rug in front of the splendid Arthur Hughes,' Sybil said, 'or more than one.' It angered him that she could add those last few words. His rule about one woman at a time in his home had always been totally firm. He felt insulted. Manse tried to remember whether he'd ever screwed Sybil on the rug in front of the splendid Arthur Hughes. If not, she must be second-sighted to some extent, though he'd never noticed that before. He had for definite bought the Hughes before she left him, or she would not of referred to his 'wank women'. Shale thought it was the kind of generous thing he might of done at some time – screwed Sybil on the rug in front of the Arthur Hughes – so as to show her that regardless of the glorious Pre-Raphaelite models he still wanted *her*. But, if he had took the trouble to bang her there, it did not do the trick, did it, because she still left him for that greengrocer or psychiatrist, whatshisname?

'It would of been an even more lovely surprise, to meet you inside the rectory, Syb – like suppose your key still worked and you'd come in and found me in my den,' Manse said. 'Just the way things used to be.'

'I wonder if you really want that, Mansel.'

Well, yes, he did wonder himself, and felt ashamed. There was quite an area of Manse that believed a husband *should* want to see his wife around the house, even a wife who bolted, and particularly in a rectory where the family should surely be a true solid example. He considered the behaviour by Chandor and his people had been a one-off – or a two-off, if you counted bringing the art back, taking the body and trying to spruce up the place – yes, a one-off or a two-off, so a wife in this house probably wouldn't never come across anything shocking like that in the future. Probably, Carmel or Lowri or Patricia wouldn't, either, if he resumed them, instead of Syb, but it seemed more important for a wife not to have to put up with that sort of trouble, he didn't know why. When women took part in their wedding ceremony and made the promises, they would not expect their home to get a deado left on the stairs and all the art cleared.

Shale thought she looked excellent today and at Several-ponds, no greying yet – or terrific dye – her skin youngish, eyes dark, full of fight, yet also friendly, her legs as good as Carmel's and better than Lowri's and Patricia's. He didn't think she seemed content, but he would not expect that, being over there in Wales with someone. Well, she would not of turned up now if she was content there, would she? Did him over there know she'd come?

Manse regarded as definitely possible a rug screw in front of the Hughes today, although decorators worked on the stairwell and now and then went into the kitchen to make tea. They had no need to come into the drawing room. Manse did not want dungarees and that sort of thing in the drawing room, anyway, regardless of whether he was screwing Syb on the rug. Shale would never regard himself as snobby, but he believed in decorum. Obviously an artist, when he worked on a picture, might wear dungarees, because of the splatter. But art hanging in the drawing room of an ex-rectory needed respect.

'Which one wouldn't leave, Manse?'

'They all get attached to the place, you know. It's understandable, maybe – the conservatory and high ceilings.'

'I damn well don't like it.'

'No. Awkward. Unpleasant.'

'Proprietorial. A woman who carries on like that shows she believes she has entitlements.'

Manse said: 'I hate being forced into measures. The locks. Against the grain. And yet what else?'

'Her clothes and so on – did you have to put them outside?'

'Unpleasant.'

'And the children?'

'What, Syb?'

'Do they become fond of these people or, say, of one of them more than the others? These are still my damn children, you know. Oh, yes. These women, if they've captured the children by cleverness, subtlety, deviousness, well, they've captured you as well, haven't they?'

Increasingly it seemed to Manse that only by making love to her in here could he hope to ease her bad anxieties and jealousies and help her cut down on the 'damns'. Women lived for these glowing little signs. If a woman drove here from Wales, this showed a true itch. And Mansel felt the start of a throb come on as he watched Syb there, very solemn and bullyboy in his personal chair. No, that was wrong – 'bullyboy' – not just because it should be bully*girl*, but because he could tell that, really, she looked for love and longed to give love. Ivor didn't rate no longer? He found he could think the name now because he must be a failure instead of a menace. Kidology – that's all the dim bits of anger in Syb added up to. Her pride would not let her act sweet, not yet. 'It's a sort of "welcome home" message,' he said.

'What is?'

'The redecoration and new stair carpet.'

'Who for – this welcome home?' she said.

'Have a guess, Syb.'

'Well, which is due on rotation here – Patricia, Lowri or Carmel? But you've kicked one of them out and I imagine won't let her back in. So, you're down to two, or have you recruited a damn replacement?'

Manse could see, of course, that she knew he did not mean one of them girls. He would not be redecorating and getting new stair carpet for a sleep-with lodger. And if it *was* for one of them he would never say so to Syb because he'd realize it must hurt. He could feel the hope and satisfaction in her now as he smiled to show he did not swallow her bluff – the way she pretended that she thought the only women he cared for were Lowri, Carmel and Patricia, or two of them because one had turned difficult. Oh, yes, she had undoubted picked up he meant her, Syb, when he spoke about them refurbishments and who they was in honour of.

Naturally, she could not pick up they was not really to do with *any* woman – not Sybil, nor Lowri nor Patricia nor Carmel – but only with Chandor and his sodding staff, and the disgusting mess they made of an historical rectory. Manse knew that rectories had never been blessed, the way a church building was, but rectories required decent behaviour all the same. He thought he would ask the kids not to mention the sauce story and especially not their blood story about the staining. They would probably agree to play along with that, and he'd give them a couple of twenties to make sure, with a promise of another each if they stuck to it.

'Oh, Mansel, you're saying the new look on the stairs is for me?' Sybil said. 'For me?'

'They're only at the scraping-off stage, but I can show you the wallpaper sample. And I do think you'll like the carpet.' In fact, as he watched her, he decided her legs were better than Carmel's, and so better than all the girls' legs. But what did it mean, good legs in a woman? Manse faced up very square to this poser now, and thought the legs should be rounded but slim, if possible long, and clearly very ready to move apart for the right man at the right time, disclosing that fine invitation-only treat and worthy of it. This was the chief point, in Manse's opinion – the legs should be worthy of it. Where legs became thighs, they began to reach their full duty, in his opinion. Thighs should have some bulk, yes, but not too much, just so they could offer a frame and protection. Women's thighs was tricky. If they was too fat you wondered if you would ever find anything, through overhang. If they was skinny, they made you feel coarse and brutal getting between them. Sometimes, he wished he didn't have this need to ponder matters but instead could just go ahead like so many men probably did.

Sybil said: 'A welcome home – how could it be a welcome home when you don't know whether . . . what I mean, Manse, is I live somewhere else? A welcome? It doesn't make sense. You could not even know I'd ever be inside the rectory again.'

'"Make sense"? I think it made sense because . . . well, because I could *sense* something, Syb.'

'Sense what?'

'At Severalponds. I could spot a wish. I could spot regret. This is not boasting.'

'It's a settled, adequate thing I've got with Ivor.'

So, Manse crossed the room and bent down alongside what would usually of been his own chair by tradition. She turned her head away, which he reckoned was part of that game she had to go on with, because of dignity. He put a hand gently on her cheek and pushed her head around towards him. He kissed her on the lips. She was ready for that, keen for that, Manse could tell. He did not mind the rigmarole, the suggestion that she had not arrived here for this. That was a delicacy thing, and he approved of some delicacy in women. For instance, Manse hated to hear a woman belch although some did these days as a sign of equality and heartiness, and thoroughly enjoying their grub in a healthy style. Without taking her lips from his, she stood, so she could put her arms around him properly and get her body hard against his. When the kiss ended he said: 'That was *such* an idea of yours, Syb.'

'What?'

'On the rug in front of the Hughes.' He wondered if he should say 'On the rug *again* in front of the Hughes,' in case they *had* done it there before, but decided this would be dangerous, because if they had *not* done it there before, Sybil would think he was mixing her up with one of the girls, or more than one, and this would be deadly injurious. Holding each other they stepped over towards the rug. It had black, silver and yellow leaf-like patterns. Afghan. He sat down first and then she lowered herself beside him. He considered it important to be first so that she could see his excitement and would not have to blame herself for being pushy when she set up the idea of having it off beneath the Hughes, or *thinking* she set up the idea of having it off beneath the Hughes.

And he really was excited and eager. That throb stuck with him, the way a throb ought to, and she let the back of her hand brush sort of accidentally across his zip to check it was there and had not gone into malfunction because of her and Ivor. 'You could give it more,' he said.

'More what?'

'Knuckles.'

'Oh, that,' she said, and made the sweep with the back of her hand again, then turned it the other way so she could take a proper, meaningful hold on him through his trousers and pants. One of his own hands was up her skirt, giving a happy rub to those spot-on thighs and dawdling over the triangle of thong pouch. Manse did not care about the laid-down procedures of foreplay, starting high and progressing down, like through an agenda. He believed in priorities and today's priority was that tufted, tucked-away area, but not tucked away from him. He eased the bit of silken cloth to the side and tenderly slipped two fingers into her enthusiasm. She smiled, and her eyes had no fight in them now, only hormone response. Could women turn that on, or was it just Nature, like the juice? In other words, would Ivor get it sometimes in Wales? Often?

The screech sounds of the wall work on the stairs did not bother Manse, nor the occasional talk between the men and some whistling – quite old tunes, mostly, like 'It's Not Unusual' and 'Yellow Submarine'. These noises let him know things went ahead all right and they would not be coming to him with queries. Luckily, he'd got the lock-smith to take care of internal security and when he stood to take his clothes off he went to the end of the drawing room and turned the new key. Vertical slat blinds covered the windows and prevented any spying from outside.

Sybil did not undress. That was normal. Always when they used to make love somewhere other than in bed she liked Manse to strip her. He had found quite often that tough, domineering women wanted things to go this way during rough sex. They seemed to like switching off all the control and trouble-making they usually went for and become offerings to be unwrapped, like weak and past resistance. Patricia was the same and Cordelia Matin-Domo, who had a lot of personality and drive and often went on street protest marches, sometimes with her husband, the famous ITV man, sometimes not, depending which cause. She liked blouse buttons not just to be undone by Manse but made to pop off through clawing. God knows how she explained the wrecked garment when she got home.

Manse did not mind taking care of Syb's kinks. Although he was very ready now, he made a grand, slow ritual of removing each item, as she had taught him when they were together. That sort of coaching he knew he would never forget. As garments came off, she did some very noisy, passionate-growl breathing which Manse felt could be genuine. Tragically, he did not have any women's underwear fetish, a terrible lack in the kind of programme under way now because it would of brought extras to something already brilliant. He wished bra cups and strapping got to him or knicker gussets. Manse believed in fullness of experience, and he knew life had many aspects, besides artistic works.

He tugged a cushion from one of the armchairs and jammed it under Sybil's hips because although they was on the Afghan rug it might not be comfortable for her otherwise and a cushion helped with angle. Then he started to give it to her, slowly to start, as slow as undressing her, and she came up to meet him and force him deep with the same natural rhythm. She deserved steady, unhurried loving after a long drive from Wales, across the Severn Bridge, and then having such a rotten shock with her key. The whistle performance outside went even further back, to 'Stardust', occasionally moving into a short croon session of the words. Manse loved that song and it seemed right as they began to quicken beautifully together, reminding him to a useful extent of days 'when our love was new', as 'Stardust' said, and no Ivor anywhere in fucking sight, not any need of him.

Manse really tried to focus everything on her now, but still managed to hear the front door bell ring, then ring again – twice that sort of heavy push Sybil had given when he thought, police. The whistling and singing stopped. The decorators must be puzzled. They would probably of expected Manse to go from the drawing room and answer. After a while, he heard one of them click-clack down the bare stairs and open the door. Somebody spoke, though Manse could not get what he said. Then the decorator answered. Shale pulled away from Sybil and went to the drawing-room door to listen better.

Iles said: 'Perhaps he's asleep. The drawing room, yes? That's here, isn't it?' A fist hammered the door. 'Are you all right in there, Manse? It's Harpur and Iles on a visiting spree. We wouldn't like you to be left out. Manse? Is this locked?' Manse saw the handle turn. 'Oh, new lock here, Manse? And I thought maybe on the front door, too. Some recent carpentry. Been having trouble?'

Harpur said: 'Is he alone?'

The decorator said: 'With a lady.'

'Who've you got in there, Manse?' Iles said.

'Is that you, Mr Iles?' Shale replied. He could half see Sybil dressing behind him to his left.

'And Col Harpur,' Iles said. 'We looked in, Manse. Having works done around the rectory, are we? Locks, wallpaper, stair carpet – you're giving the full treatment, are you? New look.'

Sybil brought Shale his clothes and he began to put them on. 'Mislaid the key for the moment, Mr Iles,' he said.

'New locks can stick, can't they? Harpur will break the door down if you like,' Iles said. 'He loves a challenge. "Show me a door and I'll show it some shoulder." You know the thug sort, Manse.'

'Sybil and I were going over some property papers,' Shale replied.

'Well, you'd have to lock the door for that, obviously,'

Iles said, 'and take the key out. Oh, yes. Sybil, is it? We all miss her.'

'Ah, Sybil's found the key,' Shale said. He smoothed down his hair and replaced the cushion. He opened the door and reminded himself about the way to behave – politeness first and even a crawl, but other reactions ready, too, such as brickwalling, some silence, some fly footwork. Iles had called it a visiting spree and said they'd just 'looked in' – supposed to sound *so* fucking casual. These two didn't do nothing casual, and especially not Iles. These two knew things, but you could never know *what* they knew. They most likely did not know what each *other* knew, not complete. These two was high police officers.

'Sybil,' Iles said. 'Wonderful! Dare I deduce from this that you and Mansel are once more –'

'Some business matters,' Shale said.

'Oh,' Iles said. 'Well, it's grand to see amity and mutual understanding continue between you despite the –'

'I do think couples who part should still try for a reasonable relationship,' Shale said. 'Maturity.'

Harpur stood in the drawing-room doorway looking up the stairs to where the work went on. He was wearing one of them suits he got from somewhere, but nobody else knew why. He kept the jacket undone, maybe because the fit would not look too comical like that. 'Yes, I'm giving the place some facelift,' Shale said. 'Routinely.'

'Do you know my first thought when I noticed the redecorating and most likely fresh carpeting planned, and then heard Sybil had come back?' Iles said. He paused. 'But, I suppose I'm inclined to get too romantic. Harpur often reproaches me for that, don't you, Col? Anyway, I decided in my fanciful way that these domestic improvements were a sort of welcome home gesture to Sybil – a big gesture which would be so in keeping with your character, as we know it, Manse.' Iles also had on a suit, but a real suit, grey with a darkish stripe in it, not less than two grand's worth, a tie from some club, most probably, more stripes but brighter – red, silver, yellow, offensive, so maybe upper class.

Sybil said to Iles: 'Why are you here?' She could be like that – out with it, too blunt. She did not know the procedure for dealing with this pair, or she knew it but did not care about it.

'We do these little tours of pivotal people,' Iles replied.

'I don't remember them,' Sybil said.

'Harpur likes to call on prominent folk now and then – gets the feel of the city that way, eavesdrops on the buzz. Policing's about more than point duty.' Iles moved across the room to look at the Hughes.

'Is Manse prominent?' Sybil said.

Iles chuckled: 'A unique Pre-Raphaelite collection on his walls!' He bent to look harder at one of the canvases. 'Some of these could be genuine, you know. Unquestionably. I'd say that brought some prominence, wouldn't you, Sybil? And the rectory.'

'But why are you here?' Sybil said. 'To see the art?'

'Ah, the children have arrived, ' Shale said. They came home from Bracken Collegiate, their private school, by special bus in the afternoons. Harpur stood to one side, so they could get into the drawing room.

'Mum!' Matilda said. 'Such a lovely surprise!'

'Exactly,' Iles said.

Matilda gazed at him, mystified 'This is Mr Iles and this is Mr Harpur,' Shale said.

'Mr Harpur is police, isn't he?' Laurent said. 'I've seen him on TV News, interviewed when there's trouble.'

'He loves getting his face on the screen regardless,' Iles said.

'Are you police, too?' Laurent said.

'Don't blame yourself for asking – many people can't believe it, because I don't at all look the type,' Iles replied.

'What's wrong?' Laurent said.

'Wrong?' Iles said.

'Why are police here, dad?' Laurent said.

'Exactly,' Sybil said.

'So what do you think of your dad getting the house all smartened up, Matilda, Laurent?' Iles replied. 'Isn't it going to look great?'

'It's just that now and then things have to be changed,' Matilda said. 'Everybody does this in their houses.'

'Right,' Laurent said.

Shale thought them kids would really deserve the two twenties each, or even three. They went up to their rooms to get out of school uniform.

'A missing person inquiry,' Iles said.

'How do we help?' Shale said.

'You're an Assistant Chief Constable, aren't you?' Sybil said. 'And Mr Harpur's something high, too. You actually do missing person inquiries at your ranks?'

'Harpur likes to be what's called "hands on",' Iles said. 'Also referred to as engaging with "the nitty-gritty". I go along.'

Harpur brought a photograph from the inside pocket of that suit and put it on the circular rosewood table. Shale gave this a full inspection. 'No,' he said. 'Sorry.' That was what he had meant when he told himself to get ready with some dazzling footwork, as well as slimy mateyness. The dark-haired, smiling man didn't have his face bruised or throat cut at the time of the photograph, of course, but was still too recognizable. 'Can't help you with him. Who is he? As Syb says, an ACC and a Detective Chief Super – it must be important.'

Oh, yes. Didn't all this show you could never tell what them two fuckers knew? But how *could* they know about the corpse on the stairs? They phone tapped? Hadn't Manse been very careful to speak vague, though? He could remember he didn't say a body but 'another aspect', when he called Chandor. He named the suit and the shoes, but you could not do an identity from them. Did someone get in here and look – someone being Harpur or Iles or Harpur *and* Iles? There'd been that sign of a break-in, hadn't there? Maybe this really was an ordinary missing person inquiry, even though it took an ACC and a Detective Chief Super. And, then again, perhaps it pointed to something else. Things usually did point to something else, something more than the obvious, when this pair got interested.

Sybil looked at the picture and shook her head. 'Did you think Manse would know him?'

'We're getting around a lot of people,' Iles said.

'Did you think Manse would know him?' Sybil replied.

Harpur picked up the photograph and put it back in his pocket.

In the evening, Shale sat alone again at the big desk in his den-study, working through some more figures. Ralph Ember was due to arrive for one of their private meetings at about 10 p.m. The children would be in bed by then. Sybil had gone back to Wales. Manse wondered what she felt now. Obviously, that rough intrusion by Harpur and Iles had upset Syb and maybe made her think this showed what life in the rectory would be like if she lived here – special near-climaxes jinxed in front of the Hughes, followed by sudden inquiries about someone missing shoved at Manse like he was a suspect. Perhaps Ivor and Wales seemed more comfortable, after all. Iles and Harpur had left before her. 'Did you know him, Manse?' she'd asked.

'Who?'

'Photograph man.'

'I said no.'

'I know you said no. That was to Iles and Harpur. Did you know him?' Sybil replied.

'You got to be careful with them two. They can make a three weeks' trial plus the verdict they want from what I might say about a photo on the table.'

'You knew him, did you?'

'I think you really hit it when you said, How come people so high in the police was on ordinary missing person duty? They could really wrap anyone up if he said yes to a photograph like that.'

'Like what?'

'Like coming from Harpur's inside pocket.'

'Who is he, the man in the photo?'

Obviously, the rug love would be no good now, not a

rerun. He could not start all that up again, with the slow stripping and so on. The atmosphere was gone. If you had Iles strutting about this room and commenting on the pictures, and Harpur in that hobo suit, it would seem mad straight after to try for a screw situation and expect Syb to re-wet up. In the love aspect, there was moments, and there was moments that could never be moments, such as these, current. When he went to wave her off from the drive it seemed just like waving anyone off. He could not tell whether she would ever come back to the rectory to see the new wallpaper and carpet, that special, sincere gesture especially for her, as he truly hoped she believed. All this did make him miserable for a while. Probably no major police walked into that place in Wales like they had an invitation and flashed a pre-death picture of a murdered man in front of them.

Ember and Manse organized these private meetings every so often to deal with the way the firms had been doing lately. Although they was not partners, they had an arrangement, an association, and split the main trade between them in peaceful conditions. At this kind of rectory meeting they could discuss things as they factually and actually was and do their planning. They put on other meetings now and then at the Agincourt Hotel for all employees of both outfits – street pushers, managers, heavies, blenders, couriers and so on – with a worthwhile free dinner and wines and non-pay bar. Manse or Ralphy would give a statement on recent business and the future, but this statement had to be a careful job, not with any awkward confidential figures included, obviously. It would be stupid to hire a big hotel dining room to give yourself problems. For instance, you could not tell people at the Agincourt that Manse and Ralphy took home over half a million each year from the profits. That could of made some folk dissatisfied with what *they* was getting theirselves and might interfere with the way staff worked and sold. Most likely people could *guess* Manse and Ralph took more than half a big one each year, but guessing stayed guessing and did not add up to undoubted reality.

The one-to-one meetings usually happened in Manse's den-study because Ember would not allow that kind of trade discussion at his sacred dump club, the Monty, and, of course, definitely not in Low Pastures, the brilliant bloody manor house where he lived – big chimneys, lead on the windows, stables, a paddock, or paddocks. His family and his fucking club had to be so white, didn't they, the holy prick? Aloof. That was it, the word. Ralph wanted the dirty trade, but he also wanted to stay aloof as far as that club and his home was concerned.

Manse decided it would be best not to tell Ralphy about the carry-on with the pictures and the corpse on the rectory stairs. It might seem like Hilaire Chandor had started a business campaign against the Shale-Ember alliance, and this would look to Ralphy like Chandor thought Manse was the dodgy one and could be cracked, could be frightened and pressured out, leaving space in the association for dear Hilaire. Ember would most probably have an armagnac giggle about that, and maybe help Chandor along, or pretend to. Anything that made Manse weaker would help dear Ralphy. If Chandor and Manse had to fight each other, Ralphy could sneak ahead while they was at it, and build more on to that half a big one plus. Ember wanted to buy his way up and up until he and his rathole club was dainty and eminent. Of course, it would never happen, but the idea kept Ralphy going and kept him scheming, the proud, pathetic twat.

This fine, wholesome friendship with Ember had lasted for quite a few years now. Ralph usually brought a bottle of Kressmann armagnac to the rectory meetings to make up for never allowing Manse into fucking Low Pastures or into the Monty to talk commerce. Of course, he'd get the armagnac cut price by bulk buying for the club. There was three or four topics that kept coming back in these sessions, and they talked about them again tonight.

1. A price slump worldwide in the commodities mainly because of over-production by greedy sods in South

America and other regions had made things difficult for a while, but also gave increased sales.

2. Then this new Chief Constable. The old one, Mr Mark Lane, could be a bit weak, and Iles had run things, really. Great. He didn't mess about with Ralph's and Manse's businesses as long as they kept things to no violence, or not too much. Iles thought drugs was here to stay, so fit the trade into the general law and order system. But this new Chief seemed tougher. He didn't like blindeyeing. Iles's power might start sinking any day now, though not yet.

3. Other outside firms fancied the rich and steady look of things here and wanted to edge in, trying to set up trade in untraditional districts away from Valencia Esplanade. Some was foreign, especially Albania. There'd been battles. Hilaire Wilfrid Chandor might be starting that kind of move, but like more subtle, the sod. The drugs laws had been made easier lately, and all sorts wanted a go at trading now. The good understanding with Iles didn't seem so necessary any longer.

4. Harpur. You could not tell about that one. Of course, you could not tell everything about Iles, either. But Harpur disagreed with Iles's wise policy towards Manse and Ralphy and would get troublesome sometimes. A boyfriend of one of Harpur's daughters might of been pulled into the street battles and that had affected how Harpur saw things.* This situation seemed to of sorted itself now, though.

Ember said: 'Workmen in, Manse?'

'I got like tired of how things looked on the stairs.'

'The stairs can set the whole mood and tone of a house, I always think,' Ember replied.

'Exactly, Ralph.'

'At Low Pastures many of the walls are simply the natural stone, you know.'

'That so?'

* See *Girls*.

'Oh, yes. I can save a couple of quid on wallpaper! And the stairs – just the original mahogany. No carpeting.'

'Sensational.' Shale wondered if this fucker had heard a whisper of what happened here on the stairs. Was he giving a bit of torment by talking about the papering and carpeting? It would be *so* like the scheming lout.

'There's a word around that Iles is getting on top again, despite this new Chief,' Ember said. 'Harpur, still a minor problem, yes, but Iles is Iles. Iles is the power.'

'I been looking at the accounts for last month, Ralph, and they're nice. All right, the prices are down, but that means bigger turnover. What it seems to me is the customer base have widened. We're making inroads.'

Ember had brought the Kressmann armagnac bottle and they done some sipping, no hurry. It was good stuff. Then for half an hour they really examined the accounts, not just last month's but a full quarter's, and plenty of detail – noting selling points up, selling points down, weekends against weekdays, talented personnel, dozy personnel, club discounts, supply costs, wholesalers. Things had really righted since their last conference.

'But we see off one lot of competition – more than one – yes, more than one – we see off a bucketful of competition and then there's another trying it on,' Ember said. 'This Chandor – Hilaire Wilfrid.'

'I've heard of that one.'

'He could be grave trouble,' Ember replied.

'That right, Ralph?'

'He's a thinker. He has his own ways of getting forward. Supposed to be property development, a perfect screen.'

'That right, Ralph?' And so Shale decided Chandor better be killed. This would be what they called on the international scene 'a pre-emptive strike'. Although Manse came to this conclusion so sudden, that did not make it easy or thoughtless. He would never be casual about murder. And this would be a murder that might lead Iles and Harpur to Manse if they knew about the body on the rectory stairs. But Chandor had to go. No, not an easy or thoughtless judgement, just unavoidable. Probably the first thing to do was find his home address. Manse knew Chandor's business headquarters – the property development outfit – was down on the new marina, and maybe some property deals did go on. If you started a mask firm the firm had to look like it operated, and marina property projects paid good most likely, anyway. Manse must try to work out where might be the most happy spot to do him, perhaps on a drive-by, perhaps something else. As soon as Ralph left tonight, Shale began some planning.

He believed in an entirely open mind, and in good preparation. He would work with an assistant. Most likely Chandor always had minders around. It would be stupid to take them on by himself – cocky, gung-ho. Good, considerable fire power was vital. Shale hadn't made up his mind yet who would suit as aide, although a lad called Eldon seemed the proper sort. Of course, if Denzil still worked for Shale, the choice would of been obvious. Or if Alfie Ivis hadn't died like that.* Denzil used to piss about now and then and refuse to wear a chauffeur's cap, the bolshy, chauffeuring prat, but he understood fire power, loved fire power. Didn't he have not just one but two gun barrels in his mouth when they found him dead? And then, Alfie. He shot Big Paul Legge in the 1980s. Alf was such a famed example of enterprise and vision.

Both out of things now, Denzil, Alfie. Never mind. Shale's firm had some very gifted people – Eldon and others – and it would be just a matter of selection. Manse considered himself intuitive on Personnel, one of his greatest flairs. Obviously, nobody could run a company without *some* of that flair, but Manse felt his own intuition and its extent had to be regarded as a marvel . . . a marvel because he could not say where this Personnel flair came from, only that he had it. There was no courses to go on for intuition, not that he ever heard of! Genes. Birthright. A natural interest in people as people, because that's who people was – people, though not everyone seemed able to grasp this.

* See *Pay Days.*

71

Manse put out an inquiry and discovered Chandor lived near his firm's offices on the marina. Shale used the Ford Focus, not the Jaguar – too noticeable, even if he changed the plates – yes, he chose the Focus and took a drift around the waterfront, again driving himself. He had a personal rage on against Chandor, but as well as this it would be business tactics to remove him. So, two reasons why Shale told himself it had become unavoidable. Part of Mansel's rage concerned the art. Of course. He hated to think of them Chandor creatures, and maybe Chandor himself, manhandling his pictures – manhandling them twice, once to take away, once to bring back. And then their total fucking carelessness about where the pictures hung. Manse had really worked at planning the right spots for them, gave that task true sensitivity, but them crude sods thought anywhere was as good as anywhere. No wonder Matilda felt so upset when she saw paintings in the wrong places. Clearly, this girl had absorbed some of Manse's taste and his touch at presentation.

He also blamed Chandor for defiling the rectory, and for causing Manse such humiliation and anguish – that abandoned love-making with Syb, and then Harpur and Iles tramping about in the house like they been invited, and Iles rapping the drawing-room door and talking insolent – the only way he knew how to talk. Somehow, them two guessed there'd been incidents at the rectory, and they'd come out to have a prod and a stare, causing in this way the break-off of a glorious, intelligent screw in a very favourable spot, and Syb's coolness afterwards.

Shale thought Chandor might try something evil again, to wear him down and get him out of the trade. This was what Manse meant by 'pre-emptive' and tactics. He would not just sit there and wait to be a target once more. He would flatten any threat, destroy it. Manse saw this reaction as very much in line with his personal character. He knew how to turn a situation around. People might try to make him a victim. He would show he was never that, could never be that, or he would not be Mansel Shale no longer. He needed to guard his true self. No other sod would for him. And there were the children to provide for, provide plenty for.

Chandor had a neat-looking town house in a side street near what had once been a dock, now transformed into a rectangular, ornamental lake used by ducks and swans. Someone took care of the bit of lawn in front and the curtains seemed clean enough. The talk said he had a woman partner and a son of six or seven. This woman might do something part-time in the firm. Chandor's offices occupied one floor in a former bonded warehouse, now converted, a few hundred yards away. If he walked from his house to the office every morning or home to lunch, this could be how and where to knock him over. There was a decent road to get clear on afterwards, probably not too chock-a-block even at rush hours.

Manse liked the idea of seeing him off near his business premises – cancel him just before he got there or just after leaving. There'd be a message in that. It would say, unambiguous, Kindly don't try to float higher in the commercial scene by struggling to push Manse Shale under because Manse Shale is not the sort who gets pushed under, he is the sort who pushes others under when required, such as doomed losers like you. That first name of Chandor – Hilaire – really gave Manse gut pains. Hilaire, bollocks!

Harpur and Iles might not mind seeing someone like Hilaire Wilfrid Chandor snuffed on their behalf. Iles aimed for clean, safe streets and he expected help in keeping them clean and safe – that is, safe for most people, not for H. W. Chandor. So, all right, if dear Hilaire got it and Harpur and Iles thought this must be Mansel at work, they'd feel grateful, especially Iles, who was the power. Ralphy had that correct. Ralph could be a big-talking prat, but he could also see things spot-on. Of course he could, or would Manse have a lasting trade pact with him?

Chapter 4

Naturally, Harpur asked the computer to say its piece on Trove and, also naturally, Iles had to be told the result because he knew about the photograph and knew about the body on the stairs, knew about the body on the stairs better than Harpur, most probably, or definitely. In fact, Iles always tended to know plenty, despite Harpur's eternal fight to keep him at least half out of things and so achieve basic sanity in running the patch.

The computer had nothing on Trove, just as it had nothing on Chandor. For both or either, this could mean innocence, or it could mean cleverness and/or luck and/or a shortage of talking witnesses. Harpur had begun to wonder about some kind of earlier London connection between Chandor and Trove, which had then been transferred to these parts. If Iles wondered the same, it would upset him badly. Iles loathed London and considered the capital produced only evil, except for the Queen and a barber in Holborn who understood his scalp. Perhaps the ACC had had some personal reversal up there, and this for ever darkened his view. Iles thought he'd brilliantly fashioned a kind of modified but tolerable Garden of Eden locally. He wanted to keep it isolated, manageable, sort of sanctified. Yes, sort of. In the ACC's view, London sent serpents, only serpents, their poison metropolitan, and therefore obscenely plentiful and fierce. Iles approved of a Tree of the Knowledge of Good and Evil, as long as he was it. The failure of the computer to come up with anything categorical against Trove and Chandor would not console Iles. It might trouble him even more. He was sure to sense mystery.

Some evenings he would call on Harpur at home in Arthur Street. He came less often lately, and didn't dress as sexily for the visits as before. There'd been a time when he seemed worryingly obsessed by Harpur's daughter, Hazel, still only fifteen, and wanted to be near her as frequently as he could, and to impress with his profile, slim-fit trousers, wit, quotations from Lord Tennyson, charm, varying hairstyles, power and shoes from a personal last. But then, a little while ago, Hazel's official seventeen-year-old boyfriend, Scott, had seemed likely to get pulled into drugs turf wars, and Iles skilfully, selflessly, helped bring him permanently clear and restored to her. Since all that nobility, Iles seemed unable to get back to embarrassing, panting paedophilia, thank God. He no longer turned up in the crimson scarf worn dangling or flung back over a shoulder, nor even in his fine brown bomber jacket. He treated Hazel as a very safe uncle might, even a castrated uncle – politely, considerately, distantly. Harpur was not certain Hazel liked this. *He* did. He loved it. Hazel read zoology books and outdoor survival manuals and once called Iles 'the feral loony'. But Harpur had seen it might please and even excite a fifteen-year-old to have an Assistant Chief Constable (Operations) demented about her.

Harpur's daughters were out when Iles arrived tonight. Previously, he would have regarded that as a slovenly miscalculation, but now he appeared indifferent. He said: 'Of course, I've been mulling over Manse and Sybil so very close in the rectory Pre-Raphaelite gallery. What do you make of that, Col?'

'He said they were working on some papers.'

'Manse and Sybil so very close in the rectory Pre-Raphaelite gallery. What do you make of that, Col? '

'She's still an attractive woman,' Harpur replied.

'Try to think for a moment beyond the animal aspect of things, the flesh aspect, would you?'

'Beyond how, sir?'

'That room is symbolic for Shale, you know. His core. His soul lives there. It's all of one piece, Harpur.'

'What?'

'Manse-Sybil giving it a go among the art, and the redecoration and recarpeting.'

'You can always draw elements together, sir.'

'At Staff College I was known as Desmond the Synthesizer. So, what have we got here, Col?'

'In what particular, sir?'

'These apparently separate factors – the Manse-Syb reconsummation on that genuine Afghan rug, and the home improvements.'

'I suppose it's –'

'He's been shaken, Col.'

'Manse? Well, yes, of course, if your intercept –'

'This is someone seeking the certainties, the stabilities, the comforts, of the past,' Iles replied. 'He trawls for these via Sybil, via the distinguished art from a former period, and via this cherished centre of a cherished, venerable building, the rectory.'

Iles had brought a bottle of Chiroubles. In the kitchen, Harpur discovered some reasonably recent pizza and cut a slice for each of them. They talked in the big sitting room. When Harpur's wife was alive this doubled as her library. Harpur had cleared out most of the books now. He used to find the sight of them depressing. They looked heavy on their shelves, and many titles seemed unhelpful: for instance, *U and I* and *The Rules and Exercises of Holy Dying*. But occasionally, when Iles did one of his vast mind leaps, such as this one about Shale and Sybil, Harpur would wish that some of these volumes were back and on full snooty show, to suggest he might have a brain as big as Iles's.

'Yes, Sybil and his marriage are the good, the grand, past,' Iles said. 'A spotless staircase is the past. Manse has a fierce need to convince Sybil that everything in the rectory is lovely because everything in the rectory *was* lovely in that past – its religious heritage, its art, its other-age furniture of solid mahogany, not veneer. What possibly infringes on that pleasant, indeed, elegant past, Harpur?'

'Well, I'd say –'

'Absolutely, Col – the continuation of Hilaire Wilfrid Chandor. Manse would see it as feeble to let that continuation . . . to let that continuation continue. Manse is one to face up. He can be strict with himself. Perhaps he wants Sybil back, and perhaps he doesn't. He's still entertaining those three, isn't he – Carmel, Lowri, Patricia – as and when, and never a plural, in his prim, economizing way? But he'll feel the humiliation of his ruined drawing-room conference with Syb – you and I disrupting like that in our autocratic style , and involving the decorator, because we'd learned somehow about Chandor's disrespect to the rectory and art and wanted a glimpse.'

'Yes, somehow.'

'Manse is a lad who craves dignity,' Iles said. 'That dignity has been damaged. He knows it might be damaged again. He'll act.'

'In what sense, sir?'

'Manse is not one to capitulate. So, Chandor has to go, hasn't he, Col?'

Harpur took a while with this. 'Manse will kill him?' he replied. 'Try to kill him?'

'Inevitable.'

'This is one theory.'

'Yes, it's *my* theory, Harpur.'

'Many people would wonder whether it was *only* theory, sir.'

'Which?'

'Which what?'

'Which people would wonder?'

'Many.'

'But many are not going to be fucking told, are they, Col?' Iles replied.

'It's quite a time since Manse had to handle a . . . what I mean is, Denzil Lake's gone, Alfie Ivis is gone. Shale's solo.'

'Think of that next child swap at Severalponds, Col,' Iles said. 'When Syb and Manse meet, what are their feelings? They look at each other and there is appalling shared shame at that aborted intimacy beneath Hughes. That is, shame unless –'

'You believe he'd tell her, "Oh, it's OK now, Sybil, we can re-romance utterly unjinxed in the drawing room next time because I've done Hilaire Wilfrid Chandor"?'

'He wouldn't have to say it, Harpur. It would be in his eyes, in his bearing, in his voice, although his voice would, on the face of it, be doing no more than ordering filled baguettes and Fantas at the service station. This would be the voice of a man who has come through.'

'Come through where?'

'It's a quotation, for God's sake. He has *won* through. He has triumphed. She would read it.'

'Read the quotation?'

'Read it in Manse's person,' Iles said.

'She's never heard of Hilaire Wilfrid Chandor. Or she might have heard of him if he's been killed and it makes the papers. But she'd see no link with Mansel and the rectory.'

'Jerk, she doesn't have to link it. What she has to know and feel through all her Being is that Manse is Manse again and has rid himself of a persecutor, a *cauchemar*. She will sense it and glory in it. He *knows* she will sense it and glory in it. *Cauchemar* is French for nightmare, Col.'

'They're probably worse in French.' Through the sitting-room window, Harpur watched Hazel and Jill come up the front path to the house. They let themselves in and soon appeared at the door of the sitting room together.

Iles smiled and said: 'Oh, hello, both.'

Harpur could see Hazel hated this – the gross equality of the greeting in 'both', the deadness of the word, the lack of particularity and throaty gasp aimed at her as her, not as one of an offspring pair. And the 'Oh'. So casual. Not Iles's previous 'Ah!' when he saw Hazel, a cry straight from the instant, uncontrollable burn in his entrails. Harpur would have liked to write a confidential, secretly passed note to Iles, 'Congratulations, ACC (Ops), you have come through!'

The girls moved into the room and sat down. 'We've been asking around, as a matter of fact,' Jill said.

'That right?' Iles replied.

'About Meryl's partner,' Jill said.

'This is the woman who brought the photographs of her boyfriend?' Iles said.

'From London,' Jill said. 'Meryl Goss.'

'Asking around where?' Harpur asked.

'You know, generally,' Jill said.

'Your friends?' Harpur said.

'Generally,' Jill said.

'Your select friends down at the bus station caff and so on?' Harpur said.

'Generally,' Jill said. 'Have you been able to do anything, Mr Iles?'

'It's a tricky one,' Iles said. 'This partner – an adult, he's entitled to roam where he likes. He doesn't have to tell anyone. His name's gone into the missing person machinery, but it's . . . it's a tricky one.' He poured Harpur and himself more Chiroubles and drank most of his glassful. 'But, look, Col, we've got burgundy, they've got nothing.'

'Cokes in the fridge,' Harpur said.

'I'll get them,' Iles replied. He went to the kitchen.

'Meryl's really scared,' Hazel said, 'like she suspects something.'

'Well, why she's come so far,' Jill said.

'He told her property development,' Hazel said.

'I heard "property development" is often just a code for something else,' Jill said.

'Heard where?' Harpur asked. 'Down the bus station caff?'

Iles came back. He'd opened the bottles. When he handed them to the girls Harpur saw no special antics for Hazel, no finger meshing or idolatry. Wonderful. She looked more chilled than the Coke.

'You know the old Woody Allen film that comes on the Film Channel?' Jill said.

'I don't mind them,' Iles replied.

'*Broadway Danny Rose*,' Jill said. 'Danny's at a party with some crooks but doesn't realize until one of them says his business is cement. Then Danny cottons. In the US everyone knows cement's often a cloak for villainy. Here, maybe it's not cement but property.'

'Probably you don't need us to tell you all this,' Hazel said.

'What?' Iles replied.

'Masks – these mask businesses, like fronts for something else,' Jill said. 'With Chandor, for the drugs trade.'

'There's that other film,' Hazel said. '*The Firm*. It pretends to be a lawyers' office but they're the Mafia, with Tom Cruise.'

'This film says lawyers and the Mafia are different?' Iles asked.

'Hilaire Wilfrid Chandor,' Jill said. 'That's the name the buzz comes up with. He's Property, or supposed to be.'

'Which buzz?' Harpur said. 'Insights from skateboarders and junkies down the bus station?'

'Some people deal with him, buy from him or his team – and not property,' Jill said. 'He's like starting up as a street firm, trying to.'

'Which people?' Harpur said.

'People,' Jill said.

'People down the bus station caff?' Harpur said.

'Property is what they call theirselves, but really it's the other stuff,' Jill said.

'*Them*selves,' Harpur said.

'And then the computer,' Hazel said. 'I mean, you know his name – Graham Trove from London. You could see if he's on it.'

'Nothing,' Harpur said.

'But you did try,' Jill said.

'Routine,' Harpur said.

'It shows you're worried,' Jill said.

'Routine,' Harpur said. 'Gossip around the bus station from pushers etcetera isn't what we'd call real information.'

'You know all the stuff we've heard and something extra, do you, Mr Iles?' Jill said.

'This is a very early stage,' Harpur replied.

'Of what?' Hazel said.

'A very early stage,' Harpur said. But does the buzz tell you Chandor took on someone new lately, with a London background possibly like his own? Harpur could not actually ask this, though, because he'd just dismissed bus station gossip and needed to keep it well dismissed for now.

'He's going to be big,' Jill said.

'Who?' Harpur said.

'Hilaire Wilfrid Chandor,' Jill said.

'Who says?' Harpur replied.

'This is the word around,' Jill said.

'Ah, not "the buzz", but "the word around".'

'He's moving in on one of the princes,' Hazel said. 'That's what we hear.'

'Princes of what?' Harpur said.

'The substances trade,' Jill said. 'So, it's either Mansel Shale or Ralphy Ember. Has to be. The ones Mr Iles uses to keep things peaceful.'

'All the world wants peace,' Iles said. 'I think of the United Nations.'

'I don't know which,' Jill said.

'Which what?' Harpur replied.

'Which one Chandor will try to push out,' Jill said.

'Doesn't the buzz say?' Harpur asked.

'I'd think Manse Shale,' Hazel said. 'Ralph Ember's got that club and the money from there on top of everything else. He's too strong. Letters in the paper about the environment. Ralph W. Ember has civic status.'

'And Manse Shale is single parenting,' Jill said. 'Difficult.'

'Your dad's an expert,' Iles said.

'But Manse Shale picks girls to live in and maybe help,' Hazel said. 'Like a rota. Most have heard about this.'

'Well, I suppose your dad has that kind of help, too,' Iles said.

'No, Mansel Shale's arrangement is not the same as dad's,' Jill said. She grew a bit agitated. 'All right, he's got

Denise from the uni, and she's here sometimes and sleeps over and does terrific breakfasts – fried bread, black pudding, everything – but she's the only one. Isn't she the only one you're interested in now, dad?' Both Harpur's daughters could be tough on morals – his. They feared everyone born in or near the liberated 1960s slept around by nature.

'You mustn't fret, Jill,' Iles said. 'I'm sure he's devoted to Denise, his sweet and loving local undergrad.'

Now and then, unpredictably, Iles could be helpful, considerate even.

'Denise is busy this time of the year working for exams,' Jill replied. 'So she stays at her Jonson Court room in the student residences, which is Jonson without an h, being named after *Ben* Jonson, who wrote many plays, and not *Samuel* Johnson, who did the first dictionary, and is *with* an h. She told me that. We like her.'

'Your dad's lucky,' Iles said.

'Well, he does need someone,' Jill said. 'Some*one*. She is the only one, isn't she, dad? She'll be missing just a few weeks. Denise is nineteen and very pretty but she doesn't mind dad's age or clothes or music, honestly. She knows French poetry and all sorts. We take them early morning cups of tea in bed, but then Denise gets up and does the terrific breakfasts with fried bread and –'

'The point is, this is the way of things in business,' Hazel said.

'Which?' Harpur said.

'We did it in Economics in school,' Hazel said.

'What?' Harpur replied.

'A business has to move forward all the time or it will get hit by something new and up-coming,' Hazel said. 'It can't rest. Known as "company stagnation". Remember how Rover and MG went under.'

'They say Shale and Ember are worried,' Jill said.

'Who does?' Harpur replied.

'This is the word around,' Jill said. 'And something funny at Shale's house.'

'The rectory?' Iles said.

'One girl I know – her dad's a locksmith. He had to change every lock, inside doors as well as out. He shouldn't of told her this, but he did because he was a bit puzzled, or even shocked. Marks of a break-in at a window. And a mess at the top of the stairs.'

'Shouldn't *have* told her,' Harpur said. 'Some think a locksmith should be like a priest or a solicitor – everything confidential.'

'Yes, well, she *is* his daughter,' Jill said. 'It's like private.'

'But she told *you*,' Harpur said.

'Yes, well, I'm her friend,' Jill said.

'And you told *us*,' Harpur said.

'You knew it all already, did you, dad?' Hazel replied. 'Has your informant been spouting?'

'I don't think we had any break-in reported from the rectory, did we, Col?' Iles asked.

'A mess?' Harpur said.

'Supposed to be he spilled some sauce,' Jill said.

'Spilled sauce can be a grave trouble,' Iles replied. 'Stains not easy to get out.'

'You do know all this already, don't you?' Hazel said.

Harpur said: 'When you were asking around did –'

'Did Meryl Goss come with us?' Jill said.

'Did Meryl Goss go with you down to the bus station and so on?' Harpur said.

'She gave us her address and mobile number in case we heard something,' Hazel said. 'She's staying at a Bed and Breakfast in Quith Place.'

'Yes. We'll have those at headquarters since she reported Trove missing,' Harpur said. 'Did she go with you?'

'We thought it was a good idea,' Jill said.

'She went with you?' Harpur replied.

'To give her something to do, not fret and that on her own in a Bed and Breakfast,' Jill said.

'And she heard the buzz?' Harpur said. 'The odd suggestions about Property not being Property, and the Chandor name?'

'That's all she's got, isn't it, the buzz?' Hazel said. 'Nothing else is happening. Nobody is told anything.'

'As always,' Jill said.

'And the girl reporter?' Harpur said.

'Kate?' Jill said.

'The *Evening Register*,' Harpur said.

'Yes, she came,' Jill said.

'I thought she would,' Harpur said. 'She's building a yarn.'

'But Meryl doesn't want her to write anything,' Hazel said. 'Not yet.'

'There isn't anything to write, is there?' Harpur said. 'Only the bus station buzz.'

'*So far* there's nothing to write,' Hazel said.

Next morning, Harpur took an old, unmarked car from the pool and drove to what had been dockland and was now the marina. He'd done a local check and found Chandor had his home and offices here. It was a useless kind of visit, he knew that. He hoped he might see Meryl Goss on her way to ask Chandor if, as a property dealer, developer, he had any knowledge of Graham Trove, who'd arrived in this area to join up with a property dealer, developer, but who'd disappeared. Possibly she suspected now, thanks to the buzz, that someone dubious in property might be the sort to know about Graham Trove. Perhaps she'd be with the journalist. They tended to stick, journalists. It didn't look as though Meryl knew of any London connection between Trove and Chandor or she'd have concentrated her search on him before this.

And if Harpur *did* see her or them, what came next? For the sake of Meryl Goss's continuing safety, should he try to stop her or them and explain that Graham Trove probably had his throat cut on an ex-rectory stairs, that his body had been subsequently carted away by a restoration party, and the spot tarted up with cleaning liquid and sauce while Iles watched? Harpur shelved this problem. Most likely he would not see her, them. Coming here and hanging about was a kind of conscience twitch, little more than that. The nagging by the children and their worries over someone like Meryl Goss could often get to him.

He parked and stayed in the car, watching the converted

bonded warehouse where Chandor rented a floor of office space. This would be less obvious than patrolling on foot. After a few minutes, though, he noticed the stubby shape of Mansel Shale who *was* patrolling on foot, taking the ozone, gazing about under that heap of dark hair with his gleaming, ferrety eyes, engaged on some serious sight-seeing. When he reached the car, Harpur lowered the window and said: 'Bracing here, I always feel, especially a.m., isn't it, Manse?'

Shale bent down to talk: 'Such an improvement, such an inspiration, Mr Harpur.'

'What?'

'The marina – when compared with the derelict old spot this used to be. Rebirth, very much so, enlightened, bold.'

'True indeed.'

'As you say, Mr Harpur, "bracing". A walk sets me up for the day.'

'Mr Iles is crestfallen,' Harpur replied.

'This saddens me, despite the bracing effect here.'

'For interrupting something so meaningful and conflu-ent with Syb in your gallery. He asked me to look you up and apologize. I knew you liked to greet the day at the marina. So, here I am.'

'One of my kids thinks that strutting fucker, Iles, was in her bedroom, Harpur, while we were away,' Shale replied. 'She had this feeling immediately she met him in the rectory after school. I could see it. Well, you've got children yourself, Mr Harpur. You know how they can be with instincts and that.'

'Mr Iles has promised he'll ring up in advance from now on if we're going to call, in case you're busy stoking a relationship at the time. Just say "Free" or "Not free", Manse – that's, obviously, if you can reach the phone, in the circumstances. No need to use a lot of breath.'

Chapter Five

One of the main points about Ralph Ember was his belief in duty. Although Ralph hated jargon and cliché, he thought his belief in duty probably deep enough to be called a mantra. All right, pretty soon he wanted to kick out most of the present ugly membership of his club in Shield Terrace, the Monty, so he could begin the admittedly quite tough process of raising it to the social level of, say, the Athenaeum, or at least the Garrick, in London. But, as to now, while the Monty's clientele remained its rubbishy self, he still recognized the obligation – yes, the duty – to behave as a host should behave and treat people who belonged to the club as if they definitely counted for something regardless. Often, he would get out from his spot behind the bar and do some true mingling with this prole crew, giving and receiving conversation, smiling appropriately, discussing undangerous topics. During one of these fraternizing sessions he heard about the staining at the top of Shale's stairs in the rectory, and the changing of locks throughout.

Almost at once, then, Ralph Ember decided he would invite Shale for dinner at Low Pastures, his own home. Of course, he recognized this as an immense shift in view. Normally, he would never have let Manse, or anybody even fractionally like Manse, into his manor house, entailing possible contact with the fabric and Ralph's family. Ember's older daughter, Venetia, still at school, could be very unchoosy about men and might not even notice the ferretiness of Shale's eyes. Ralph had sent her to a convent-type place in France for a while to see if nuns would damp her down, but she was back here now. Just the same, Ralph felt determined to ask Shale over. And, if he wanted to, Manse could bring one of those women he kept around his place from time to time, and *only* one, so there'd be a nicely balanced four at table, Ember and Margaret, Shale and the specially chosen squeeze. This should help keep Venetia off Manse. In any case, she and Ralph's other daughter would not be dining, having eaten earlier.

Ember intended to treat Shale's woman, never mind which, with total politeness. In fact, he'd go beyond that and show warmth, as long as she managed the civilities and maintained them, even after rich dishes, aperitifs, wine and liqueurs. He wanted no puke, no come-on drooling about Ralph's resemblance to the young Charlton Heston, no political, religious or underprivileged-state-of-women rants. Just as he would give any current member of the Monty full courtesy regardless of their absolute lack of class, so any guest at Low Pastures deserved proper treatment until his or her behaviour grew unforgivable. After all, invitations were rare and only those who on the face of it did deserve proper treatment got one, or came with someone who got one, such as Manse – for an evening. In fact, Ember felt nearly certain Manse wouldn't ever contemplate turning up with two or several women, if he still had several on his books. He could be fuddy-duddy. Apparently, Shale always restricted it to a solitary partner in the rectory at a time. This would be partly from dread of catfights on the premises causing shrillness and potential damage to the fucking art he gabbled about so much. Also he'd have consideration for his children, Matilda and Laurent – God, who hatched these names? Despite his indisputably authentic backwardness and crudity, Manse did follow some rules. Plus, he would experience vast awe from being asked to Low Pastures at last, and when meeting Margaret he'd want to seem something as close to polished as he could get, and sexually ungross. Ralph would have caterers in, people who knew the kind of excellence he required as a norm.

Staining and the locks – Ralph picked up this tale from

Felix Tullane, or Empathic Felix, as he was known. Ralph detested the nicknames of some club members. He realized certain people in the Athenaeum probably had nicknames, but these would be standard and rather British, to do with appearance or careers, such as Rusty if ginger-haired, or Sparks for someone who ran power stations – not mocking, and possibly the total opposite of someone's character. Ralph wondered whether Empathic actually had empathy for anyone bar himself. But Empathic did know a house-painter and decorator who gave him tips now and then on promising places to burglarize, and passed information about the rectory, where he'd been working. Empathic was not major enough or mad enough to consider doing a house owned by Mansel Shale, for God's sake, but he'd listened. Then one night in the club, when Ralph took on a kindly socializing stint with the Tullane family party and friends, Empathic mentioned that mess at the head of the stairs which looked like blood to his pal, although it had been attacked by scouring liquid, then disguised with sauce. And, apparently, while the redecoration was under way, a locksmith did a total refit. Ralph had seen the decorators at the rectory when he called on Manse but naturally lacked the vital background as to cause.

'My mate says it was like someone got it on the stairs,' Empathic said. 'I mean, got finality. Everyone knows stairs are a peril. You can be done from up top, you can be done from behind. Right, Ralph? Basic. Ever see off someone on stairs yourself?'

Obviously, the first thing Ralph thought about the staining was some roam-the-home boisterous sex game, such as 'Hail Veronica!' or 'The Brahms Mosaic', had gone badly excessive with one of those birds. The line between ecstatic pain and heart failure could blur. Manse looked the kind who'd like pervy stuff and give it some effort, perhaps too much effort – that snub, greedy face and his fat lips. Had he pushed the risks beyond? If so, Manse would do a temporary clear-up, dump the weighted body in the sea, with or without help, and afterwards order full renewal of paper and carpet for safety, and as high-minded tribute to the departed one.

But almost immediately Ralph realized his idea did not take account of the locksmith. If Manse accidentally killed the girl himself while sporting out of control with her he would not be worried about intruders. So, perhaps the blood around the stairs came from an outsider, not, say, an inadvertently haemorrhaging Manse mistress at all. To clarify this, he'd need to find out whether all the girls given interludes of hospitality by Manse were still alive. People in the club would be certain to know their names. Ralph could recall Shale once speaking admiringly of someone called Carmel and her terrific knowledge of porcelain and *Mein Kampf*. She might be a type willing to seek new frontiers during love frolics, but could come unstuck.

'Manse told them a stumble while running upstairs with sauce,' Empathic said. 'My mate agrees there *was* sauce, no question, but not *only* sauce – this is the point – and sauce put on as a final layer, over the original. In the house are two kids, and they keep on talking about the sauce so my mate thinks it definitely was not just sauce – the way those kids repeat and repeat it, as if needing to back up Manse, like hiding something, the same as how the sauce itself seemed to be smeared there to hide something. Kids in a blue and black school uniform when they get home. Private. Manse Shale has the money for that. Well, obviously, or he would not be doing redecorating just because of sauce or what's *under* the sauce.'

Empathic's mother, early seventies, in a beige suit, was among the big Tullane family group. She said: 'I can't understand how anyone would have a bottle of sauce, and an open bottle of sauce, going upstairs or coming down.'

Although Beatrice, her older sister, wearing denim skirt and jacket, might not know the games Ralph had thought of, she could add her own insights: 'There are some famous sex routines involving sauce or gravy, aren't there, Jane? But they get everywhere. It takes two or three goes in the washing machine to remove, and you can't send sheets streaked like that to the laundry, because of talk. Wasn't it the state of the bedding that helped them nobble Oscar Wilde?'

'I hate all these kinks,' Empathic's mother said. 'Nature should be nature, and no additives.' Many of the young male Monty members seemed to have very assertive older female relatives – mothers, aunts, even great aunts. Ralph thought of Dependable Jasper, bank robber – dead now – whose aunt and grandmother inherited all the loot.

'Why the locks, Empathic?' Ralph said.

'Some kind of break-in?' he said. 'Manse asked my mate to repaint one of the window frames where there'd been forcing. Who'd have the neck to break in at Manse's? Yes, odd. But maybe people from away who didn't realize the rectory was his.' Ralph knew club members felt mightily flattered when he spent time with them and they would talk all their secrets, trying to interest and hold him. Oh, yes, they'd launch a bit of cheek, also – such as asking if Ralph had ever annihilated anyone on stairs, but this happened only so they wouldn't seem too creepily grateful for Ralph's presence, which they were. Ember felt more or less sure he never *had* killed anyone on stairs, and certainly not on ex-rectory stairs, though stairs did offer grand chances, agreed.

'As long as it's OK for both I think anything's all right,' Beatrice said. 'Sometimes love can do with pepping up. Kinks and creativity – they'll overlap.'

'And then Manse is giving his actual wife one in the drawing room, door locked with a new lock, sort of testing it out on the job, you could say,' Empathic replied. 'She lives away but came back.'

'Was sauce or gravy involved in this?' his aunt said.

'My mate thinks on a rug from abroad and very special-looking. There's a lot of art in that room.'

'A rug might be ruined,' Beatrice said.

'Setting *can* be important,' Jane Tullane said.

'And in the middle of it all, who turns up?' Empathic replied. 'Guess who turns up?'

'Is this one of the in-fill girls, unexpectedly?' the aunt asked. 'Out of phase? There's screamed abuse and clawing between her and the wife? More blood, not sauce?'

'Iles and Harpur,' Empathic said, 'really working the door bell, then barging in. This is a famed building with a holy past, but they barge in just the same. My mate thinks Manse had to do *coitus interruptus*, not on account of birth control as in the old days, but because of Iles and Harpur with questions and conversation. They're not going to care about what point on his trajectory Manse had reached, are they? This is senior police. They think they have the right. So they're rapping on the gallery door, like a raid.'

'He'd get a pain in the testicles if he was close and had to cancel,' Empathic's aunt said. 'Semen all tensed up to shoot and then stoppered can turn baleful. Compare hounds trained for foxhunting but now prevented by law.'

'Iles and Harpur? What did *they* want?' Ralph replied.

'Just to get a look around. Nosing. That's how it seemed to my friend,' Empathic said.

'They'd had a tip of some sort?' Ralph said.

'About what?' Empathic said.

'The redecoration and so on,' Ralph said.

'Why would anybody tip them off about someone getting his house decorated?' Emphatic said.

'True,' Ralph said.

'Unless someone said it was blood not sauce,' Empathic said. 'That could be a police matter, couldn't it? Sauce would not be, no. You don't get an Assistant Chief and Detective Chief Superintendent out regarding a sauce spill, even on stairs. But blood. This could be of concern to higher ranks.'

'True,' Ralph said.

'Not all art would be helpful in an *amour* situation,' Empathic's mother said. 'There's a painting called *The Scream* that would put anyone off their oats, this terrible, staring face and the grimace, like a bayonet up his backside. Or no man's land pictures from the Great War. Paul Somebody. Anti-erotic entirely.'

'Mostly girls with long, auburn hair in clingy dresses,'

Empathic said. 'My mate could see inside from the drawing-room door. As a matter of fact, he thought it was called a drawing room because of the art. He's useful but dim.'

'Oh, now, pictures like that would be very positive in a rug collaboration,' Jane Tullane said.

'The wife's really going at it, asking Harpur and Iles what they want,' Empathic replied.

'And no answer?' Ralph said. 'Obviously, not from those two. They know how to ask, not the other way around.'

'My mate had to go back to work up the stairs,' Empathic said. 'But he thinks a photograph. He thinks Harpur had a photograph for them to look at.'

'Of what? Who?' Ember said.

'He's too far off by now, and moving towards the wall-scraping, anyway. But Manse stares at it and shakes his head,' Empathic said.

'Failure to recognize?' Ralph said. 'Or *acting* failure to recognize. Is that what your contact thought?'

'And then the children come in, ' Empathic replied. 'My pal's looking down into the hall from where he's working but he said the girl seemed to stare at Iles as if . . . well, "as if she thought he'd been into her life before but didn't know how." That's the way he put it – "as if she thought he'd been into her life before but didn't know how." Those words fixed themselves on me, so weird, and maybe not dim at all.'

'There's a flavour to Iles that scares people,' Ember said. 'You don't get made Assistant Chief without a vatful of it. The ability to start terror spasms in the populace is known as a "leadership quality". Mostly, people are born with leadership qualities, or not, but Police Staff College also puts on seminars where they're developed and plumped up. Folk will *imagine* they've met Iles before because of something evil glimpsed in a nightmare or horror movie and stored in the subconscious.' Of course, what really shook Ralph was the amount Manse Shale had not mentioned to him – the blood, the locks, the break-in, the Harpur and Iles reconnaissance, the photograph. All this

Manse had known about when Ralph visited him for their usual companies' meeting at the rectory, but no word. It meant something elaborate and wilfully obscured from Ralph was taking place and might ultimately encompass him, as well as Shale. Although no partnership existed between Ember and Manse, their working arrangement kept them close, or ought to.

Ember recalled Harpur's visit to the club, a visit unusually – maybe significantly – solo, and the questions about Manse – about Manse's 'problems'. What were they? Where would they lead? Ember felt left behind, excluded. He wondered whether if he let Shale fully into Low Pastures Manse would recognize the humaneness in this gesture and decide he must not soil such a happy friendship with miserable, scheming secrecy, the shady, mouth-shut sod. Ralph had always known that excluding Shale from Low Pastures must seem hurtful, even insulting. Until tonight at the Monty, Ralph never worried about that. After all, it was only Manse Shale. Now, though, Ember came to think this might be harsh and not sensible. Low Pastures had stood for hundreds of years and could hardly be damaged by the visit of Manse and a companion. She probably would not go on and on about Ralph's astonishing similarity to the young Charlton Heston, in, say, *Ben Hur*, for fear of making Mansel jealous. Nobody ever spoke of Manse as resembling a film idol. But if he did want to get in on references to *Ben Hur*, you could say he had a face like a chariot horse's arse.

Ralph moved on from Empathic's group. Chandor was in the club again with a few of his people. Tonight, they had a table over near the framed, splendidly cheerful, enlarged photograph of a Monty excursion setting out for Paris from Shield Terrace in a coach one summer, Bespoke Vincent and Caspar Nottage still unmarked and smiling joyfully at the camera before boarding. In Montmartre, Bespoke and Caspar kidnapped a tart for thirty-six hours and fractured at least one arm of the pimp who came searching for her. Caspar's neck and face were very badly torn by the tart's nails and Bespoke had his nose broken in the fight with the pimp. Ralph discouraged these trips since. A club like the Athenaeum probably did not have coach excursions abroad at all, and definitely not with repercussions. Ember took the picture down every couple of days to check for bugs behind, and could regard this table as one of the most secure in the club. Did Chandor somehow know that? 'We've been admiring the illustrations on the baffle board up there, Ralph,' he said. 'Sort of mythical.'

'Yes, a baffle board – to do with the mysteries of air currents, thermals and so on,' Ember said.

'I was explaining that to the boys here,' Chandor said. 'They thought a bullet-proof steel shield.' He had a chuckle at this, and Ralph joined in. Chandor said: 'What use a shield that gives protection only from one very restricted point? It makes me think of the Maginot Line in the Second World War – supposed to protect France but Jerry just nipped around the end of it.'

'Right,' Ember replied.

'Maurice says the illustrations are probably from a book by some poet,' Chandor said. 'He's a reader.'

'William Blake,' Maurice said.

'Right,' Ember replied.

'This club has a real ambience, and I don't mean only the baffle board illustrations,' Chandor said. 'It's an achievement, Ralph.'

'Thank you.'

'I don't think there can be many clubs outside London of this quality,' Chandor said.

'Kind. Which clubs do you belong to in London?' Ember said.

'A relaxed, civilized atmosphere and then the grand mahogany panelling and wonderful brass fittings,' Chandor replied. 'These speak quality.'

'A club is its membership, that's my belief.'

'But a membership takes its tone from somewhere. This has to be worked for. Yes, a notable achievement, Ralph, if I may say.'

'I regard it as reciprocal,' Ember replied. 'One does try to establish what you call a tone – rightly call a tone – but it is a tone that suits the membership, and is in fact part created by the membership as much as by me.' This fucker and his mates and his grease would be at the top of the Goodbye For Keeps list once Ralph began his transformation programme.

'And a club able to attract a Detective Chief Super,' Chandor said. 'Didn't I see Harpur talking to you the other night?'

'He drops in now and then.'

'Is he trouble?'

'Trouble? What trouble would that be?'

'He looks trouble,' Chandor said.

'Give him a glass of gin and cider mixed and everything's lovely.'

'And Iles?' Chandor said.

'Port and lemon for him,' Ralph said.

'And amenable anyway I hear,' Chandor said.

'He calls it "the old whore's drink",' Ember replied.

'At some stage, you and I must organize a general chat, Ralph,' Chandor said.

'In which respect?' Ember said. He knew in which respect. Chandor wanted to get in on the core trade. Hadn't Ralph mentioned him to Shale as a coming problem? It seemed like every week he and Manse had to destroy somehow or another attempts by new boys to get entry.

'Yes, general,' Chandor said. 'Maurice, here, he's not just a nose in a book. He advises me on business prospects. He thinks a general chat, you and I, would be constructive, Ralph.'

This infuriated Ember. Fuck off, Maurice. Maurice! Fuck off, Hilaire Chandor. Hilaire! It was not just the indelicacy of mentioning business concerns in the club, but the *way* they were mentioned – the offhandedness of it, the tacked-on nature of it. Chandor wanted a discussion, yet he had not approached Ember with a respectfully offered request, which might be acceptable. He had waited for Ralph to approach *him*, as if Chandor possessed the status and

Ralph should seek a hearing, like an audience with the Pope. Obviously, Chandor could not have known Ralph would come out into the bar and agree to talk to him tonight, but, because Ralph did, Chandor thought he'd take advantage by slipping in that proposal – a proposal which began, apparently, with this hanger-on, this all-rounder baggageman, this lover-of-literature, Maurice. Maurice! 'I've reached a consolidation point just now,' Ember said, 'am not in the market for new ventures. I'm like that, you know – cyclic. I aim to lie fallow for a while every few years, Hilaire.'

Chandor said: 'What Maurice and I have in mind is –'

'Yes, a consolidation point just now,' Ralph replied.

Chandor said: 'In our estimate, Mansel Shale isn't any longer up to running a –'

'Perhaps I'll be able to think of new ventures in eighteen months,' Ember said, 'but for the present I'm –'

'Pressures get to Manse, get to him badly. This can be proved by recent small incidents. We don't consider he'll be able to go on maximizing,' Chandor said. 'Look, I know he's a long-time friend of yours but isn't it time you –'

'A sabbatical. I feel due a sabbatical. That high-falutin? But industry, commerce and academe have come to recognize the value of the kind of break I award myself periodically,' Ember said. 'A refresher.'

'And such pressures on Shale are liable to mount,' Chandor said. 'He'll break.'

'Enabling one to come back and perhaps see things in a quite different and perhaps more fruitful way,' Ember replied.

'Director of Strategic Planning,' Chandor said. 'That's how I would describe Maurice's role.'

'Not that I can ever be totally idle,' Ember said, giving this a couple of wry grimaces. 'The Monty prevents it.'

'Manse running three women,' Chandor said. 'Not clever. One of them, two of them, might get jealous and angry and start blabbing to the tabloids for cash. Sex, drugs, big earnings – it's a story made for the *News of the World* or the *Mirror*.'

So fucking right. Ember said: 'I've noticed before that this table, near the excursion photo, feels maximum benefit from the baffle board. A pleasant current of air, Hilaire – gentle, invigorating, temperate.' It fucking rhymed – air Hilaire.

'After all, these women are not just pieces on the side with no claims,' Chandor said. 'They're installed – and then abruptly de-installed. This is bound to cause them –'

'Ah, there's Caspar, ' Ember replied. He spotted Nottage in a crowd at the snooker table and walked over to have a word with him. That skilled, unrestrained neck- and face-gouging on the Paris excursion caused a blood infection and for a time his right eye had been threatened. Even now, years later, Caspar still suffered occasional after-effects with his sight. Ralph went and checked how he was, not only because Ember worried about rips in the table baize if Caspar couldn't focus, but also to ditch Chandor and his damn overbearing truths. Personally, Ralph would be very watchful of nails if unpleasantness with a woman developed and she went for his face, tart or otherwise. He could not see that what might be under a tart's nails would be more poisonous than was under any woman's nails, unless tarts deliberately packed harmful stuff there to deter attackers. A French thing? Paris had a relaxed attitude to sex, yes, but did it also turn vindictive occasionally? Caspar would have to leave when the Monty began its change of character, but Ralph must be careful in case Nottage went to a tribunal and alleged discrimination because of his eye disability. Ralph could not defend himself against that kind of case by saying it was nothing to do with Caspar's eye, just his all-round slobbishness.

Ember considered Manse had dressed very nearly right for dinner at Low Pastures, even though Shale did not ask Ralph for advice. This was one of the things about Shale – he sometimes surprised by proving how sensitively he could measure a situation and react to it, despite the inveterate underclass looks. Obviously, no clothes existed that would ever make Manse appear radiant, but you could see he'd done what he could with himself and you felt moved by it, not tickled or contemptuous. Although Ember had seen Shale in excellent, very modish Paul Mixtor-Hythe oufits, he'd obviously decided he must choose something with a pedigree tonight, so as to tone with Low Pastures. He had on an old-style, dark, three-piece, pinstripe suit made of terrific wool and most likely bought from Oxfam or an Antiques Market barrow. You probably would never get this particular kind of tailoring these days – the beautifully gentle and rounded slope of the shoulders, and lapels doing grand honour to his chest in their width and sweep. Ember would calculate Manse had no holster under these lapels, or only something for a small, ladylike pistol.

Ralph could imagine suits like this at the funeral service of King George V in 1936, when values were still values and before everything went askew through Edward VIII and Mrs Simpson. Naturally, the suit showed some wear at the cuffs and elbows, but that only added to its aristocratic impact. People who wore outfits like this would despise an appearance of glossy newness. They wanted their garments to tie in with history and tradition. Ember felt sure there would be many suits of the type around major London clubs. And this one, plus the brilliantly polished black lace-ups, chimed perfectly with the historic materials and evident distinction of Low Pastures.

As if to moderate a little the formality of his main garb, Manse wore an open-necked mauve shirt, clearly silk, though, and with no necklace or medallion on show. A medallion glinting between lapels of that calibre would have been a sick let-down, like tinsel among diamonds. In Ralph's opinion, the only mistake Manse had made was in the mauveness of the mauve shirt. Although a less aggressive mauveness might have worked, his complexion seemed even worse when seen above and against this flashy colour. The suit jacket had enough length easily to cover weaponry in a waist holster, but on the whole

Ralph considered Manse would regard it as poor behaviour to come tooled up to a place like Low Pastures on a social evening.

Ember said: 'I've been thinking back, Mansel, and to my astonishment I believe this is the first time you've ever been to Low Pastures.'

'That so?' Sybil said.

'Yes, I'm more or less certain,' Ember said.

'Well, of course it is,' Sybil said. 'That's not what I meant.'

'Sorry?' Ember replied.

'I wondered if you were really astonished,' Sybil said. 'To me, Ralph, it always looked like your policy.'

'In what sense?' Ember said.

'To shut Manse out,' Sybil said. 'Sort of apartheid.'

The method of inviting Shale had given problems. Eventually, though, Ember decided a phone call would be all right, even if intercepts operated. This was only one businessman asking another friendly businessman and his companion to a meal at the first businessman's home. Iles on an intercept would not find much in that, surely. Of course, Iles might know Ralph usually barred Shale and would wonder about the alteration. But he could not do more than that, could he – wonder? Just the same, Ralph rang from the public call box at the Monty, hardly ever used since the mobiles revolution. This precaution probably wasn't one. If they had a tap on Manse the call would be heard, no matter where it came from, and Ralph's voice recognized.

A woman had answered when Ember phoned the rectory. He was ready in case this happened, and meant to be very guarded. Although he'd asked around and knew all three names of Shale's women now, Ralph must not give him heavy trouble by guessing and guessing wrong. And a mistake of that kind could lead to unpleasant tension at the Low Pastures dinner table ultimately. Neither he nor Margaret would like this. 'Hello, there!' he'd said. 'All well and so on? I wondered if Mansel's around?'

'Is that Ralphy Ember?'

Ember hated to be called Ralphy. He thought it made him sound half baked or juvenile. Which of those three short-contract consorts imagined she had the right to use that name? And which could identify him from a dozen words? He'd never spoken to any of them. 'Yes, Ralph Ember,' he said.

'Ralphy! I thought so.'

And then he thought *he* could identify from even less than a dozen words: 'Is that Sybil?'

'As ever was.'

'How good to hear you!' he cried. This really fucking threw him. Had she arrived on another day visit or returned as a permanency now? Was something intimate under way, like last time when Harpur and Iles called? He tried to remember the layout of the rectory drawing room. Did Sybil pick up the phone because she lay closer to it than Manse on the rug? 'It's been a while, Sybil,' Ember said.

'Yes, a while.'

'And quite a drive over.'

'Yes, quite a drive.'

Was she dressed? He thought Syb would look quite good stripped – unburly shoulders, breasts in proportion, non-sag behind so far, long legs. 'But perhaps you don't mind driving. Some don't.'

'Driving's *so* subjective.'

'I've always said that.'

'Manse isn't here now,' she replied.

'Ah.' He thought it must be a permanency, then. Shale wouldn't go out, would he, if Sybil were only on another visit? God, what kind of woman somehow got herself virtually clear of Manse and then decided to come back? So, not the rug, and she'd have her clothes on. He managed to hang on to the other image, just the same, for a minute more. 'Nothing crucial. I'll ring again,' he had said.

'Try his cell phone.'

'That's possible.'

'But insecure?' she said.

'I'll call later.'

'From a booth?'

He considered it would be stupid to talk on the phone about trying to counter phone intercepts, when a phone intercept might be taking place while he talked now.

'What's it to do with, the call?' she had asked.

Yes, that sounded like permanency. Yes, that sounded like wifedom. 'A certain topic or two,' Ember said.

'Well, yes, I'd guess this. Which?'

He realized he'd have to tell her. If he waited until he spoke to Manse before mentioning the invitation, and Manse then informed her, she'd know Ralph had been holding this back now, from uncertainty that she would be the one out of four Shale wanted to bring. 'Dinner with us at Low Pastures, if you can fit that in.'

'Really? *Really?* When?'

'When suits.'

'That'll be all right. I'll talk him into it if he's shy.'

And they'd come to Low Pastures, Manse in his splendid suit that one day might have been a duke's or topmost bookie's of pretty near Manse's measurements, Sybil wearing black trousers tucked into calf-high brown boots and a plum-coloured, round-necked cashmere jumper. Tonight he could add some items to his picture of her bare. She was about thirty-eight or -nine, small-nosed, dark-eyed, wide-faced, slim, the long legs, her hair fairish and seemingly without any grey yet. Ember had met Syb several times before, of course, during her and Manse's first spell together. He remembered Sybil for a strong tranquillity that always seemed about to drift into something else, though. To him, she appeared the sort of woman who'd leave a man as soon as she felt like it – leave her children, too – and return as soon as she felt like that, also. Syb would assume there'd still be a welcome for her. And maybe she assumed right. Manse was obviously content, even excited, to have her with him now.

Ralph wondered why someone as obviously confident and blunt as Sybil had not forbidden that fucking mauve shirt. Manse would be fine wearing it on holiday in Prestatyn, or checking around his pushers down the Valencia

Esplanade area. But that shirt did not chime with Low Pastures. Perhaps, though, she'd deliberately persuaded Manse to put it on, to demonstrate through its soaring naffness that they did not feel daunted by Low Pastures – the same kind of silly impudence as made her wear those high boots and tuck her trousers in, regardless of the occasion and setting.

She said: 'Ralph sounded *so* confused when I answered the phone at the rectory, poor old thing.'

'I wouldn't say confused,' Ember replied, 'but –'

'Utterly understandable,' Sybil said. 'If you were expecting a woman at all it would be one of those bed-warmers, Lowri, Carmel or Patricia. It was, "Hello, there, whoever you are and could I speak to Mansel, please?" They stand by each other, these laddies, don't they, Margaret? Ralph knew he mustn't drop Manse in it by getting the name wrong – faux pas of faux pas.'

'A marriage will shine through,' Shale said.

Like blood through sauce? Ralph did not say it.

'Yes, if a marriage has anything to it at all, it will shine through,' Shale said.

'That's a lovely, lovely idea, Mansel,' Margaret said.

Ralph wondered if she wanted him to think a bit about Manse's words, though she didn't look Ember's way. He nodded twice, however, good, firm nods covering a tidy distance, chin towards chest.

'Those other women at the rectory – I've always known they were only temps,' Sybil said. 'If one of them became pushy and proprietorial, she'd be banished. Well, one of them *did* become pushy and proprietorial, didn't she, Manse, and so he had every rectory lock changed to keep her out, including internal doors. This was decisiveness.'

'It seemed the simplest thing,' Shale said. 'A safeguard.'

'He won't specify which woman,' Sybil said, 'but that's all right. They're all very ex now, Carmel, Lowri, Patricia.' She gave the names big contempt, especially the i sound at the end of Lowri, which Syb turned into a high squeak, and the hissing soft c in Patricia.

'Ex, yes, just like it got to be,' Manse said.

It amazed Ember that someone in that shirt could get away with talking so much virtue. 'I expect you had the internals done as well, Manse, in case she – whoever, as they say – in case she got in somehow – for example, through a window – and defaced the art for revenge. I imagine the drawing room's new lock is there above all to make sure the paintings remain untroubled, though the lock could have other uses, obviously.'

'My thinking was along them lines, yes, you've hit it, Ralph. I feel like a custodian of the paintings, not just their owner, like caring for them on behalf of Art itself. What we all know, don't we, is a woman who thinks she been rejected can get so outright uncomradely and dwell on things.'

'Those famous lines – "a woman scorned",' Margaret said.

'They *think* they been scorned when they have not be scorned at all, only told they got to go. I don't call that scorning. I wouldn't say I'm a scorning sort of person. That's just telling them "Cheerio" plus proper, generous thanks.'

'I believe the cheap cows themselves should be scorned,' Sybil said.

'Quite a room this, in my opinion,' Shale replied. 'Just the kind of room I would imagine for Low Pastures.'

'Yes, and you *had* to imagine until now, didn't you, Manse?' Sybil said.

'The bare stones in the walls – it's such a thing to think of them going right back into old times,' Mansel said. 'When them stones was dug out and brought here for building a house it must of been by people who really wanted a house to last, not for theirselves, but going on and on. Like genuineness throughout. When they was choosing them stones they'd say, "This one, and this one, not that one," because it did not look like it would last the required centuries.'

'This house, plus the grounds, Ralph,' Sybil said, 'the whole spread – £2.5 million? Planning permission with any of the land?'

'A good family home,' Margaret said.

'When Britain ruled the waves and suchlike,' Shale replied. 'The country knew what it was then, was sure of itself. You can tell this from the stones. That's where a house like this goes back to. I got a rectory that goes right back, but this *really* goes back. We carry on something from that grand past, and we are proud to do it, the two families, I'm *so* sure of that. Like taking things over from that fine history, such as them stones for the walls, or my den room where many sermons was created – we take them over, these properties, with true respect and look after their changed life in the twenty-first century. A changed life, yes, and yet also linked to them previous days.'

'Manse had some redecorating done and new stair carpet, as well as the locks,' Sybil said.

'Perhaps a kind of touching welcome home to you, Sybil,' Margaret said.

'This is what I mean, the twenty-first century, but still keeping the properties connected to them historical periods,' Manse replied. 'When I think of our families in these properties I think of that idea of the way Man – signifying also women and children these days, of course – I think of the way Man didn't go under, despite like the Ice Age and disease and wolves and food so scarce – berries and that's all, unless you killed something and ate it.'

'Survival of the fittest,' Margaret said. 'Darwin's *Origin of Species*.'

'Right,' Shale said. 'I like that. *We* are the species who look after these good old homes because we are the fittest. We've proved it over and over. We are the fittest through our good businesses and the way our families are. These homes are in good hands.'

'When I'm in bed now I sometimes wonder which one of those three was last lying where I'm lying,' Sybil replied. 'I sniff at the pillow, though everything's been washed, naturally. But I'd like full fumigation. Would you fancy having your head on a pillow where some fly-by-night called Carmel slept, Margaret? Toenail clippings. Oh, yes. In one of the bathrooms. They're not mine or Manse's or the children's – I've checked them against their feet. If I ever meet Carmel or Patricia or Lowri, I'll say to her in a completely considerate fashion, woman-to-woman, "Did you leave anything behind at St James' rectory, following your last residential turn, blossom?" She'll get all flustered and jumpy in case it's something intimate and I'll bring out a little box lined with purple velveteen, the kind for earrings, and take the lid off suddenly and shove the open box up to her fucking eyes so she can see parings.'

'And we gladly spend cash on these residences,' Manse replied, '– modern here-and-now cash – preserving them, sort of nursing them, because we got the funds to do it through being fittest, so our houses can get that survival. New stair carpet, new wallpaper, they might seem only about the *look* of the house inside, but the look is important because it shows we will take care of the rest, also. It's a pointer. The locks – that's really looking after the place, isn't it? This is security. All right, it was brought on by *one* bit of trouble, but them locks will be good against all sorts. This is also about survival.'

'Mansel likes to put things into a wide context, ' Sybil said. 'I missed that when I was away temporarily.'

'Well, you would,' Margaret said.

The room they had pre-dinner drinks in was called in some of the older plans of the house the Round Room. Ralph liked this and they kept the name. The caterers sent two waitresses as well as the cook and her assistant, but Ralph handed out the aperitifs himself. He thought this would destroy any feelings in Sybil and Manse that Ember might have been lordly, arrogant, refusing to ask them to Low Pastures. He'd do his penance bit as a fucking waiter.

The Round Room was not totally round but had two curved walls, two straight. Margaret chose the furniture, mostly large, old pieces bought at auction. Ralph considered they suited well – a late nineteenth-century chiffonier, a heavy four-leaf table, also Victorian, some big

Edwardian armchairs, and a chesterfield that she'd had re-upholstered in patterned moquette. Ember thought that in his crude but earnest way, Manse had it right about how these old places – the rectory and Low Pastures – were now looked after and esteemed by people who could afford properly to preserve and improve them.

Ralph had mixed bloody Marys earlier and served them from large jugs. He'd read somewhere that, when it came to aperitifs and table wines, the proper thing was for the host to choose, not ask people's preferences. With liqueurs, options could be offered, though generally Ralph noticed guests went for his own favourite, Kressmann armagnac from its interesting black-labelled bottle.

As a matter of fact, they were on to the liqueurs in the dining room after their meal, and the caterers and waitresses had left when Ralph heard a car approach on the drive and pull up. Someone rang the front door bell. Shale put down his glass and seemed to grow anxious. He glanced towards Ember as if to ask whether he expected callers, and as if to say, 'What the fuck goes on, Ralph?' Manse's hand did not get in under those sweet lapels nor into a jacket pocket, so Ralph's guess that he had come unarmed, owing to the glory of the occasion, might be correct. Perhaps quality drinks made Shale jumpy.

Sybil said: 'What is it, Manse?'

'What?' he replied.

'What is it?' Ember said.

'What?' Shale said.

Sybil leaned across the table towards him and, dripping evil, said: 'Mansel, is this one of those hot-arsed, possessive birds? You told the children we were coming here.'

'Well, in case they needed to get in touch,' Shale said.

'She's called at the rectory looking for you and been sent on by them,' Sybil said.

'That's crazy,' Shale said.

Sybil sat back and turned now towards Margaret Ember: 'What I have to take into account is that those women could have built all kinds of understandings with my children – with *my* children,' Sybil said. 'Matilda, Laurent, they'd think it all right to tell any of them where Mansel might be.' She switched back to him. 'They've witnessed you in closenesses to them, haven't they? Haven't they?' Ember thought she might weep. So, perhaps it had been an error to bring Manse and her into Low Pastures after all. Demonstrations at the dining table he always found very off key. At least Sybil kept her voice reasonably down, yet it was damn vehement. She said: 'By turn, these women became part of the day-in, day-out, night-in, night-out nature of my children's lives. They actually feel they have a loyalty to them. Isn't it appalling? Isn't it, isn't it?'

'But you could be betting . . . I mean be getting all this . . . this all wrong, Syb,' Manse said. It was no big statement, but Manse stumbled. You could believe he might also stumble with a bottle of sauce on stairs. Occasionally, Ember spotted hints in Shale of that breakdown Chandor spoke of lately. This made Ralph feel strong. Who should be called 'Panicking' now, then?

Ember's daughters, Venetia and her sister, Fay, were in one of the other downstairs room watching television and Ember heard them go out to the hall and look at the closed circuit monitors showing the front porch. Then, Venetia opened the dining-room door, no knock, and said: 'Two women, dad.'

'Two?' Sybil said. 'My God, this is intolerable. Isn't it intolerable, Margaret?'

'Youngish,' Venetia said. 'One is, anyway.'

'At this time of night and on someone else's property, valuable property. I apologize for him, Ralph. I absolutely voluntarily return to Mansel, and is this the kind of behaviour I should have to meet? Is it? Is it?'

'Shall I let them in?' Venetia said.

'This is Venetia,' Ember said, 'and Fay in the background. Mr and Mrs Mansel Shale from the old St James' rectory. They are long-established friends, oh, yes.'

'Hello,' Sybil said.

'Hello,' Manse said.

'But I comprehensively *worship* the shirt, Mr Shale,' Venetia replied. 'In fact, the whole panoply. *So* on song!'

'I'll deal with the front door, shall I?' Ember said.

'Don't let them in,' Sybil said. 'Tell them it's over. Tell them it's no good coming here in an alliance. That's only evidence of how unmeaningful each of those relationships was.'

'What's over?' Venetia said. 'Are these scrubbers? They want to be awkward?' She pointed one finger: 'A shirt like that, Mr Shale, seems to cosset and yet project the wearer's neck while at the same time declaring its wearer so much a part of the today world.'

'I'll be reasonable but quite firm,' Ember said.

'*Quite* firm won't do with them,' Sybil said. 'They'll persist like wasps. You've got to squash them.'

'Who are they?' Venetia said, but lost concentration on that. 'And, God, the waistcoat, Mr Shale! This is really sublime. Look at the sublime waistcoat, Fay! This is history unleashed! That waistcoat plus the shirt – well, *really* intemperate. Mr Shale, give dad some lessons in modes, will you?'

The bell rang again, tentative but persistent, yes, a bit like wasps. Ember went out into the hall and glanced at the monitor. One would be about thirty – maybe a year or two more – the other around twenty-three. They both looked much too good for Manse, but Ralph thought this must be true of any even marginally presentable woman. Think of Manse's nostrils. Ember would almost never have a firearm on him in his own home, for heaven's sake, and he felt these two were probably alone and harmless, though maybe emotional and bitter on account of Sybil's return to the rectory, if they'd heard of it. He opened the door and stood square in the space so they could not rush past and get through to the dining room and inconvenience Sybil or Manse or the two. Ralph considered this kind of protection another of those inescapable duties of a host. If you invited them you looked after them, no matter how dubious they might be. The front door was wide, as used to be the case for all front doors of gentlemen's homes in earlier periods to give a castle-like feel, and Ember knew he could not entirely block any attempt at entry. He also knew he must be nicely framed in the space if these women had brought someone on contract with a gun to back them up and do their revenge. Just the same, Ember stayed there. When it came to matters of guarding his home or his club he hardly ever fell into one of his terrible panics. Territory backboned him. This would be so, even if Shale hadn't apparently taken over the panics.

'Mr Ember?' the younger, taller one said. 'Yes, it's Mr Ember, isn't it?'

'Ralph W. Ember,' he said. 'Can I help you?'

'We went to the Monty.'

'Yes?' Christ, who *were* these two? They wanted *him*, not Syb or Manse?

'People said, "Try the Monty," when we asked around. And, naturally, I knew of the club and said, "Yes, good idea."'

'In which respect?' Ember replied. 'Asked around about what?'

'People there know a lot, don't they? The buzz. Your membership is very . . . well, very various, isn't it?'

'We aim for an interesting cross section,' Ember said. 'Important for a club's dynamics. Just consider, would you, the many types at the Garrick or, even more so, the Groucho?'

'We're looking for someone. We showed a picture at the club, but no luck. A member said you'd probably be at home at Low Pastures – in case you, personally, might know the man we're searching for. I'm from the *Evening Register*. Kate Mead. This is Meryl Goss, a Londoner. She has to go back soon. She's a little desperate.'

'I've got the photo here,' Goss said. 'If you could look, please. What is it with this city?'

'In which respect?' Ember said.

'Indifference,' Goss said. She wore jeans, desert boots and a navy jacket. Her fair-to-mousy hair had been done in small spikes. Although he regarded this as a ludicrous error, to Ralph she looked a warmer prospect than Kate Mead. God, he must be getting old.

'Is everything all right, Ralph?' Margaret said. She had followed him to the door.

'Someone missing, apparently,' he said.

'Oh, dear,' Margaret said.

'We thought Mr Ember knows so many people and might recognize him from the photograph,' Kate Mead said.

Margaret must have realized then that these were not women who'd lived on shift with Manse. 'I think they should come in so we can see properly under the lights, don't you, Ralph? Stop standing there obstructing, like the Rock of Gibraltar.'

'Yes,' Venetia said. 'This sounds *really* important if she's come all the way from London looking.'

'Right,' Ember said. 'We have guests, you know.'

'Get an eyeful of the mauve shirt,' Venetia said.

'Our friends might be able to help,' Margaret said. 'Mansel Shale also meets a lot of people.'

'Oh, yes, with so much style he *must* get around or it would be wasted,' Venetia said. 'Stupendous clothes-sense like that deserves a bigger audience than he'll get at Low Pastures. Who wrote the poem about a flower blushing unseen and wasting sweetness "on the desert air"?'

Ember led them into the dining room and made introductions. 'These ladies have lost someone,' Margaret said.

'No, *Meryl* has lost someone,' Kate said. 'I'm a journalist tagging along.'

'Is this for the Press?' Shale asked.

God, he did sound shaky.

'The police have been told, but Meryl's not sure they'll really help,' Kate said.

Meryl put the photograph of a man aged about thirty-five, dark-haired, strong-featured, on the table alongside Sybil's liqueur glass. Ember did not recognize him. Shale gave the picture a long stare and shook his head. 'No.'

'No, nor me,' Margaret said.

'No, but a dish, if I may say, Meryl,' Venetia replied. 'Fay, come and look. Know him?'

'No,' Fay said.

'I reckon that's a Paul Mixtor-Hythe suit,' Venetia said. 'More modern than Mr Shale's but still a classic.'

Sybil looked and said: 'No, afraid I can't help.'

'Is there some background?' Ember said.

Kate said: 'He's Graham Trove and came here to meet contacts in property development.'

'Property development?' Ember replied.

'Property development,' Kate said.

'No names?' Ember said.

'Difficult, very difficult,' Shale said.

'Just arrived and disappeared?' Venetia said. 'Bizarre.'

'Of course Meryl has already tried many property firms for information, but no go,' Kate said. 'We had a list from the Chamber of Commerce. The buzz says it might have been someone called Hilaire Chandor. We've been there, but a blank. We need some more factual stuff before we approach him again.'

''Can we offer you something?' Ember said. 'Wine? Armagnac? I'm sorry we're a disappointment after your trek out here.'

'It's a lovely old house,' Kate said. 'Such a sweep to the drive. I adore bare stone.'

'A feature, yes,' Ember said.

'A sort of . . . well, genuineness,' Kate said.

'That has to be the word,' Shale replied.

'Well, thanks, anyway,' Meryl said.

'We'll keep on the alert for him, I promise,' Ember said.

'Absolutely,' Venetia said.

'We can always reach Kate at the *Register*,' Margaret said.

Ember brought a couple more balloon glasses from the sideboard and gave Meryl and Kate some armagnac although they hadn't replied to his offer.

'You know, you're incredibly like Charlton Heston when younger,' Meryl said. 'When *he* was younger, that is.'

'Charlton Heston! Good Lord! He's the *El Cid* one, isn't he?' Ralph replied. He found it a damn pity she might be going back to London. Desert boots could do a lot for legs, as long as they were good to start with. He liked to think of the man-made soles striding out over broiling sand, with the heat getting up the inside of her thighs, until the boots eventually reached an air-conditioned hotel with plashy fountains and garden tables under sunshades, where he'd be waiting wearing something cool and well-ironed in khaki or jungle green.

'Chuck Heston – big in the American gun lobby,' Venetia said. '"Every home should have one."'

'Yes. I've heard that about Mr Ember before, a Heston look-alike,' Kate said.

'Dad loves it when people mention the resemblance,' Venetia said. 'When *women* mention it, but always pretends he's amazed. It's called modesty – or as near as he gets.'

After the two women had left and the children were back watching TV, Shale, Sybil, Margaret and Ralph sat for a while in the drawing room with their drinks. Sybil asked: 'Would they really expect you or Manse to say if you'd seen the man in the photograph, Ralph? Don't they understand about you two – and one a local reporter, supposed to be au fait with local matters? Bare stone walls cost money and where do they think the money comes from? Yes, you'd imagine she'd know the scene, wouldn't you? You'd imagine she'd realize that whether you knew him or not you'd say you didn't because saying you did could lead almost anywhere and lads like you don't care for uncharted ground.'

'It's always best to be civil to such people,' Ember replied. 'They're entitled to do their search.'

'Civil but uncommunicative,' Sybil said.

'I *couldn't* be communicative because I have nothing to communicate,' Ember said.

'And likewise,' Shale said.

'This is two invasions tonight from the bad world beyond,' Sybil said. 'Manse and I first, then these two.'

'Oh, really, we don't think of you in that way at all,' Margaret said. 'Always welcome.'

'Indeed, yes,' Ralph said. Sybil hadn't gone into actual tears, so he more or less meant this.

'What's that bitch going to put in the fucking paper?' Shale replied.

'Only that someone's missing and Ralph Ember and Mansel Shale don't know anything about it,' Sybil said. 'Or their wives, or the Ember daughters. Can that matter? If she puts anything at all in the paper. People go missing every day. Routine, not man-bites-dog stuff or even dog-bites-man.'

'The Press – you got to watch them,' Manse said. 'Continuous. They can do bad bloody damage. They don't care, as long as it gives them a big headline.'

'Damage how?' Sybil said.

'All sorts of ways,' Manse replied. 'I believe there should be a law of privacy.'

'But in this instance,' Sybil said. 'It's a nil response, isn't it? What harm?'

'You got to watch them, that's all I say. Think of them two reporters that done Nixon in a film on TV sometimes.'

Margaret took Sybil to freshen up. Ember said: 'That's a very nice gesture, Manse – the redecoration and locks and so on, if they're to welcome Syb back. Yet typical of you.'

'I thought I got to do something to sweeten things. I mean, Ralph, them other females who been giving me companionship and so on – that's not pleasant for a wife to think about.'

'But *she'd* left *you*, Mansel.'

'Even so, I felt the repapering etcetera, like a compliment. In any case, I had a little stumble carrying a bottle of sauce on the stairs and so some staining. I saw I could put that right and at the same time do a what you call for Syb.'

'A gesture.'

'Right, a gesture for Syb.'

Ralph remained quiet for a couple of minutes in case Shale decided to cancel the bullshit and say what had really happened on the rectory stairs, as described by Empathic's decorator pal. The great thing about ferrety eyes was they never changed from being ferrety, so you couldn't read much there. Their eternal message – ferretiness. Manse picked up his glass and said: 'Here's to what's been a great fucking evening – lamb, wine, Kressmann's – on your magnificent property, Ralph.'

Ember raised his own glass in response and drank. Then he said with a thorough smile: 'And here's to a grand future for you at the rectory, Manse. Between us, we have given this region marvellous, sustained peace.'

'I don't suppose we'll get the sodding Nobel Prize for it, though,' Shale said.

'I believe we are appreciated by those with a proper regard for this city,' Ralph replied. They drank again. When Margaret and Sybil returned, Ralph topped up all round and Manse mobiled his driver and told him to bring the Jaguar in half an hour. Of course, Denzil Lake was a goner now. Manse must have taken on a successor. When the car arrived, Ralph went out to have a look. The replacement looked pretty solid and weathered. Ember knew Denzil used to defy Manse sometimes and refuse to wear the chauffeur's cap supplied, because Lake thought it made him look like the dogsbody he was. This driver had that kind of shiny peaked cap on and didn't seem to mind. He jumped out of the car to open the rear door for Sybil and Manse. 'Thank you, Eldon,' Manse said. Eldon's jacket tightened as he bent swiftly to the Jaguar door handle and Ralph thought he saw the outline of something sizeable in a shoulder holster.

Chapter Six

Harpur took another trip alone down to the marina and the region of Hilaire Wilfrid Chandor's offices and home. He recognized this as no more logical than his last visit, but he went, just the same. Harpur still worried that Meryl Goss, trawling for property contacts, collecting gossip at the bus station caff with his children, and elsewhere, would have heard Chandor's name and come here calling and questioning. Probably dangerous, if all his suppositions were right. And they would be.

It troubled Harpur that a police failure to find her man – a police failure even to look for her man – could push Meryl into risk. Harpur knew his daughters would feel a mix of rage and shame if he let things go bad for her. Although they'd accept that an adult like Graham Trove had a right to disappear or not as he fancied, the girls would expect something extra from Harpur, because Goss actually came to Arthur Street looking for support. They'd regard this personal contact as giving them and Harpur a definite guardianship role. In his daughters' opinion, if people called at the house they became sort of dependants, wards. This could be a right nuisance, but Harpur feared his daughters' contempt. Oh, hang on, he'd put it a lot higher than that. Harpur longed for their esteem, struggled to earn and keep the girls' admiration. As a single parent he lived for their approval. He could tell that the plight of this beautiful, sad, committed woman, Meryl Goss, searching in strange territory for her lover, would grab their feelings. In fact, her plight reached his own feelings, especially as Harpur more or less knew the search to be hopeless, and Meryl's lover dead. He could not tell the children that, nor even hint at it, and couldn't tell her, either.

Harpur saw only one way to help. He must make sure she did not drift into peril herself now by taking repeated inquiries to the wrong place, meaning the right place – Hilaire Wilfrid Chandor. What Harpur had to contemplate was the terrible possibility that not just Graham Trove's but Meryl Goss's body might one day turn up on this ground. Harpur's daughters would regard that as a disgusting, cruel blunder by him. And he'd see it like this himself. Then there would be Iles.

Apart from Goss, Harpur worried that Manse Shale should have been doing his little survey here, the medicinal morning stroll, obviously casing the area. Why? He planned retaliation? Had he built a big hate against Chandor – saw him as an insult and threat? That's how it had seemed on the Iles illegal transcript, hadn't it? Shale would be inclined to fight – to hit before he was hit again. He'd grown used to success and peace, and might want to remove anyone who jeopardized these. No, not *might*. Manse *would*. Perhaps removal of Chandor could be treated as a boon by Harpur – by the police generally. But bullets loosed off among ordinary, uninvolved people in an ordinary street could not be.

This time, Harpur parked a distance from the handsome old converted bonded warehouse that housed Chandor's offices and walked. Although much of the marina layout was cluttered tat, a few Victorian and Edwardian dockside buildings had been magnificently adapted to new roles. Manse enthused about the marina and, yes, parts of it did look good.

Harpur felt a need to be on his feet, he felt a need to be clearly seen, a reckonable presence. He thought he might have to intervene, not just observe. Now and then he got these feverish, white knight impulses. He felt he had to save Meryl Goss, already stalked by tragedy, though she couldn't know that yet in full. It was lunchtime. If Goss wanted to reach Chandor she would possibly attempt to confront him in the street at some predictable moment, like arrival, lunch, or working day's end. And the same tactics could appeal to Manse Shale. Perhaps Manse had discovered during reconnaissance that Chandor left the offices at, say around 1 p.m., maybe going home, maybe on his way to a restaurant. This wide marina highway could be turned into drive-by land – a big volley through the open window, windows, of a stolen, moving car and fast exit. It might appear fairly simple to Manse. Traffic here was usually light. Shots should not get blocked by other vehicles, getaway not hindered by jams. One essential: the ambush must happen close to the office building, for fear Chandor came out and jumped into a car. Shale might have thought of all this. He'd moved currently into a rich, sedate, rectory-blessed existence, but he wouldn't forget basic urban foray wipe-out tactics – the same kind of urban foray wipe-out tactics which . . . yes, the same kind of urban foray wipe-out tactics that most likely helped land him this current rich, sedate, rectory-blessed existence. He'd blasted his way to tranquillity, hadn't he?

As Harpur approached the bonded warehouse just before 1 p.m., feeling pretty relevant and saintly, he saw Chandor, plus a couple of other men, emerge from the front of the building, Chandor between the two looking fully Nordic. Protection? Well, naturally protection. Harpur thought he recognized the pair from the Monty. Chandor had on jeans and a short denim jacket. The two companions wore dark suits, white shirts, broad tie, flunkey garb, the suits loosish, perhaps to shroud weapons. Harpur walked a bit faster. In fact, the three did not get into a car but came towards him on foot, which should mean Chandor was making for his house, in a side street near where Harpur had parked. He got some amiable chat ready.

When Harpur and the three were a few metres from one another he saw a car, a blue Renault Laguna, coming at a brisk but unostentatious rate from behind the Chandor group. One man drove and Harpur believed there might be another in the back on the near side, but bent low. A thicket of Shale-type dark hair? It looked as though the driver had a scarf arranged around the bottom part of his face – nothing as telltale as a mask, yet doing a good concealment job, just the same. Who wore a scarf in June? He seemed a burly, athletic type. Yes, someone with a dark thatch still crouched on the rear seat. As Harpur reached Chandor and friends, the car was alongside and Harpur, in that public service style of his, stepped to the left and put himself between it and them, between it and them and other pedestrians.

And the Laguna passed, passed harmlessly, still at a sane, unnotable speed. The man in the back now seemed to have gone even lower and become hidden altogether from Harpur. The near-side rear window and front passenger window were down, as Harpur would have expected them to be down in preparation for a barrage, and he wanted to yell merrily: 'Mansel, dear! Did I fuck it all up for you? But we can't have blood all over the sacred marina, can we?'

The scarf fluttered slightly in the slipstream, possibly silk, untasselled, dark blue with a red and silver motif. Manse – and it had to be Manse – must have found this an appallingly tricky abort decision. After all, if he'd catered for three deads plus any collaterals, why not four plus any collaterals? But the fourth could have been Harpur – would certainly have been Harpur because of his martyr position on the pavement. And, because of that martyr position on the pavement, Harpur might have been the *only* one hit, a more effective shield than Ralph Ember's at the Monty. Shale probably realized in the second or two he had for thinking as the Laguna approached that you could not shoot a British Detective Chief Superintendent and then expect your life and your trade to proceed as heretofore, comfortably, sweetly, not even in this new, gun-spread millennium. And there wouldn't be time for marksmanship – pick off three, fire around the fourth. No, a broadside operation. It could even be that Manse felt a regard for Harpur formed over years and chickened out of riddling him. This idea gave Harpur a small glow.

He didn't get the Laguna number. What use? The car would have been stolen. And, besides, nothing happened, not even speeding. The hefty driver must be Shale's new chauffeur and general aide-de-camp after that problematic double-barrelled destruction of Denzil Lake. Perhaps his replacement liked Lagunas and knew how to annul their prize-winning anti-theft fittings. He did not have a chauffeur cap on for this jaunt. Possibly, he would have pulled up momentarily and joined in the salvo, through the front passenger window. There must have been some very urgent countermanding orders from Shale once he saw how Harpur had arranged himself. Would Manse be astonished, expecting Harpur to feel very all right about one outlaw knocking over three others in a cleansing spree? But probably even Iles would draw the line at that – heavy gunfire in daylight on a domesticated road busy with walkers in a prestige development like the marina.

'Mr Harpur, isn't it?' Chandor said with a happy smile. 'You were at Ralph Ember's club? Hilaire Chandor.'

'You have your base here, do you? Lucky. Beautiful setting.'

'One of the factors that brought us to the city.'

'I love a walk in the marina,' Harpur replied. 'Calm yet invigorating.'

'You should call in. I'd like to show you the view of the lake and so on.'

'Well, indeed, I might.'

'I brought some staff from our previous home, you know, and we all agree the move has been a wonderful success. Isn't that so, lads? Oh, this is Maurice, my Director of Strategic Planning, and Rufus, Personnel. Mr Harpur.'

'Grand here,' Rufus said.

'Grand,' Maurice said.

'The move from?' Harpur said.

'Eltham. London.'

'Quite a change,' Harpur said.

'We've integrated rapidly,' Chandor said. 'The Monty – a great entry to social things here.'

'Ralph Ember's a city stalwart,' Harpur replied.

'I doubt if there's another club of that quality outside London,' Chandor said.

'Do you belong to a London club?' Harpur said.

'And that collage on the baffle board. I'd guess not even the Carlton up there has anything to match it,' Chandor said. 'As I see things, Mr Harpur, we're quick these days to acknowledge creativity in the visual arts, literature, the media, but doesn't the kind of creativity displayed by Ralph Ember deserve similar acknowledgement? Maurice loves a collage.'

Harpur kept alert in case the Laguna gunship did a loop and returned. Its crew might hope he had gone, leaving the blast path open. But after a couple more minutes he thought that unlikely. He could end the chatter. 'Ralph's what I would call an all-rounder,' he said. 'Often he discusses environmental topics in letters to the Press. As Ralph W. Ember. Pigeon shit on monuments. That kind of thing.'

'We'll watch for those,' Chandor said. 'The environment is a real issue in this day and age.'

'True.'

Mid-afternoon, Iles called Harpur up to the Assistant Chief's suite at headquarters for a one-to-one. The ACC looked rotten. 'I worry, Col.'

'*I* worry.'

'This woman who gave you the missing picture of her man – could she be in some peril?'

'It's possible. You know some parts of this situation better than I do.'

'Is that right?'

'Of course it is. You get into Mansel's place and –'

'So, I worry,' Iles said. And it would be true. Of course, he had the standard excesses and lunacies of his rank, but he could become genuinely emotional about someone he thought at risk on his ground – *his*, as he would term it. Nobody would argue, except possibly the Chief and police committee, and 'Who gives a twopenny fuck for them?' Iles might ask, often *did* ask. Responsibility as well as malice, self-pity and general egomania inhabited the ACC. He could care, but you had to stick around and stay watchful to catch him at it. Harpur occasionally caught him at it. The caring did not necessarily involve lust. No, not necessarily. He had never seen Meryl Goss, for instance, and Harpur had not described her looks to him. Harpur thought that if Meryl Goss had been a man on the same kind of quest, but for a woman, the ACC would still have wanted to involve himself. This was how it could be sometimes: Harpur would see they were joined by common anxieties, dreads, intents. The double-act sparring and spite and abuse might conceal this shared purpose, but it lay there, always present, strong and mysterious. It was policing.

This certainly did not make the enmity from Iles to Harpur only a show, or negligible. Iles had great reserves of fury, continuously ready for mobilization like the National Guard. He could still grow frenzied about Harpur's affair with Sarah Iles, and the fact that Harpur got her, though you saw better dressed men in soup kitchen queues. This resentment was on eternal stand-by. Elsewhere in Iles, though, and in Harpur as well, the concern for some cause or for some person could more or less exactly coincide. That factor linked them unbreakably. Naturally, it was not to be spoken about and defined. Iles would have thrown up.

'Col, tell me this,' he said, 'is it right for us to allow this woman who's searching for Trove . . . is it humane, ethical, for us to let her go on trying to find him, go on *hoping* to find him, when we know he's dead?'

'It's bad. But *I* don't know he's dead, sir. I've not seen his body.'

'Almost a kind of cruelty.'

'And you can't disclose *you've* seen it because you shouldn't have been there, in Manse's rectory and Matilda's bedroom,' Harpur replied. 'You're an ACC, for God's sake! You can't even admit it to me, let alone to Meryl Goss.'

'There's a play called *Inadmissible Evidence*, Col. Rather seminal.'

'That right?'

'Oh, yes.'

'A pity. You could have used the title for your autobiography,' Harpur said. 'We've got a ton of it. And what might have happened if they'd found you spying? Did they bring *two* body bags with them?'

'So many shifts in the pattern of things, Harpur,' Iles said. 'I have to ask myself and ask myself again, do I still understand this domain?'

'What answer do you get?'

'For instance, Shale and Sybil went for dinner at Low Pastures, Col,' Iles replied.

'How do you –'

'Now, naturally, in your inquiring way, you'll ask me what I read into this.'

Harpur said: 'Well, no, sir, I don't think I'd –'

'Seismic, Col.'

'It's an evening out, that's all.'

'"That's all."' Iles smiled, but with some sadness. He did not give the 'That's all' an exclamation mark or turn it into a mocking question. He spoke the words flat, as though their absurdity didn't need pointers. 'No wonder you're stuck at that fucking rank, Harpur,' he said. The Assistant Chief was shirt-sleeved and wearing a turquoise tie striped with silver, probably some rugby club's colours. Iles refereed occasionally. God. He sat behind his desk. Harpur had an armchair across the room opposite.

He said: 'Look, sir, a couple of businessmen and their wives meet in pleasant social circumstances at the country house of –'

Iles held up one hand, like a benediction or traffic stopper. 'I don't know if you've ever come across the word "vision" at all, Harpur,' he said. 'It's fairly run-of-the-mill.'

'Well, yes, it's to do with –'

'Exactly right, Col. This is a quality I think of as among my prime gifts. One of the main differences between me and you. *One* of.'

'I should think you were known as Visionary Iles at Staff College.'

'And then, as well as the shock of Ralphy's invitation to Shale and Sybil, Manse's daughter came to see me earlier, of course,' Iles replied. 'Matilda.'

'What the fuck does that mean?'

'What?' Iles said.

'"Of course."'

'It means of course. A kid of that type.'

'Which?' Harpur said.

'Convinced by their own imaginings. It's commonplace. Known to be worse in girls.'

'Which imaginings?'

'They mistake them for second-sight.'

'Second-sight of what?'

'Arrived on her own by bus in the school lunch hour. A determined lass. I had them send up a chop and two veg from the canteen, though, plus bread and butter pudding and a ginger beer.'

'But here for what?'

'As to vision, Col, the Bible says, "Where there is no vision the people become diabolically stressed,"' Iles replied.

'Yes, actually it's, "Where there is no vision the people perish." Proverbs.'

'Ah, you did the King James version at your back street Sunday school, Col. "Diabolically stressed" is the Revised Prozak Edition. I think of Ralphy Ember – that terrible turmoil of his mind leading finally to an invitation for Manse to Low Pastures. Shale and those teeth in Low Pastures, Harpur! The implications for social class. Seismic, yes, Col. Emblematic. This is 1917.'

'1917? On your digital watch? The time Manse and his wife set out for Low Pastures? You always get things very exact. Vision, but also precision, if I may say.'

'1917 – the Bolshevik revolution, twat. Upending all settled ways for ever.'

'How did you find out Shale and his wife went to Low Pastures?' Harpur replied.

'What does this change of Ralphy's attitude to Shale *mean*?'

'*Mean*?'

Iles stood, took his jacket from off the back of a straight chair and put it on. 'Now, I think we should go and see Hilaire Wilfrid Chandor,' he said. 'I've got addresses.'

'See him with what purpose?'

'Simply drop in on him at his offices,' Iles said.

'Why? '

'I've got to look after that London woman. Well, we.'

'Thank you, sir.''

The ACC smoothed down his jacket. '*You* might be able to afford a suit like this one day, Col.'

In the lift, Harpur said: 'I ran across Chandor at lunchtime.'

'In what sense?'

'In what sense what, sir?'

'"Ran across."'

'Yes, ran across,' Harpur replied.

'You are not someone who runs across people, Harpur. You scheme. This was schemed?'

'He likes it here.'

'Why?'

'The ambience,' Harpur said.

'Yes, plenty of that around. This is the thing about ambience. It's ambient. You fret in case the Goss woman makes herself a target?'

'Of course.'

'Why you ran across him? Yes, it could be grim, Col. She sounds wonderful. Devoted.'

'I think so.'

They took an anonymous car from the pool. Harpur drove. Iles said: 'I wonder if anyone would come looking for me if I disappeared, Col? I wonder. I wonder.'

Harpur felt that to his credit the ACC fought off sobs. 'Are you thinking of going, sir? People would definitely notice.'

'Which?'

'Which what, sir?'

'Which people would notice I'd gone?'

'Oh, many.'

'Can you name them?'

'Many, sir. I'd probably need both hands off the wheel to finger count.'

'Why do I need this constant reassurance, Harpur?'

'A foolish yet becoming modesty, sir.'

'Yes, it could be that.'

'A selling of yourself short.'

'Yes.'

'Many have noticed this.'

'Who?'

'Many.'

'Think of Ralph dialling that number, the rectory number,' Iles replied. 'He's going to ditch – yes, actually going to *reverse* – all his former notions about Mansel as too deep-dyed coarse and non-grammatical for admission to a *gentilhommière* like Low Pastures. This was a brave act. Indomitably, Ralph picks up the instrument and phones. He has become the great ring-giver, like that guy in *Beowulf*.'

'You've had another illegal intercept done?' Harpur asked. 'Listen, the verse from Proverbs says in full, "Where there is no vision the people perish, but he that keepeth the law, happy is he." Do you ever think about keeping the law, sir? I'm sure it's crossed your mind.'

'I don't believe in happiness, Col.'

'Do you believe in the law?'

'In deciding on that phone call Ralphy had agreed to stoop, Harpur. Why?' the ACC said.

'Perhaps he wanted to put on a special friend-to-friend event, marking Sybil's return to Manse.'

'Except he didn't know Sybil *had* returned, arsehole. He rings. A woman answers. She says, "Is that Ralphy Ember?" You know what Ralphy's like about being called Ralphy – thinks it's a coddle name for some slow developer who's still peeing his pants at going on twenty-three. For a couple of moments he's wondering which of those sleepovers at the rectory would have the gall to cheapen his name like that. He'd known a woman might answer, but not a woman who'd call him Ralphy, for God's sake. In his courageous way, he's willing to risk talking to someone he can't identify yet is still bewildered when it's Sybil.'

'You get bewilderment on the transcript?' Harpur said.

'Ralph is anxious about something and suddenly wants this total fighting unity with Manse to resist a threat, or clarify a threat, a shadow, that he senses but can't actually pinpoint. He aims to deepen their relationship, freshen the alliance. Answer: invite him home. Not just business mates now, but mates per se, regardless of Shale's plebiness, teeth and complexion.'

'What threat?'

'I felt a need to *see* this crucial Ralph-Manse development, to witness it,' Iles replied.

'You watched him and Syb leave for Low Pastures? Why you have the time so spot-on, 1917? '

'I hope I'm not someone who merely sits in a poncy office reading damn transcripts, Col.'

'No, you break into people's homes and look about while they're at Severalponds, sir.'

'I thought I'd just watch Manse and Syb set out from the rectory. He wears a superb suit. Possibly aristocratic. At least boardroom. I'd say fashioned late 1920s and for someone not totally unlike Manse physically, only a few inches taller.'

'How did you get close enough to see?'

'There are bushes in the rectory grounds.'

'You'd noted that when you did the break-in, had you?'

'Plus a mauve shirt, open collar, to represent the nowness of now, the vivid informality, as against that bold antiquity of the suit,' Iles said. 'You see the significance of this suit, do you?'

They had come to the beginnings of the marina. Iles stared contemptuously at the cement brick, Lego-land architecture, as Harpur had earlier in the day. Iles, expounding, said, 'Shale saw the mighty implications of his welcome to Low Pastures. He knew there were overtones and dressed like overtones. I was present at history-making, Harpur.'

'Three-piece?'

'Would any marquis or rusk tycoon of that Imperial period wear anything less than a three-piece, Harpur? This suit, this visit, this return of a wife, speak of brilliant social stability – the kind I work and work for, and the kind we are charged to maintain. This Chandor might menace all that. Possibly has already menaced all that and given a warning more might follow.'

'Others have tried to destroy that harmonious social pattern here, sir. You've seen them off.'

'Yes, I have. We have.'

'Thank you, sir.'

'Park now,' Iles said. 'We'll walk the rest.' They were near where Harpur had left his car at lunchtime. 'Our dear, fuckwit former Chief, Mr Lane, could temporarily restore his optimism and belief in life by a gaze at this sprucing of the run-down docks, the "thrilling, forward-looking marina concept", as he smoochily called it. I keep trying for the same uplift. I do. I will now. I will.' They left the car. 'Manse would feel not only angry but humiliated by what occurred at the rectory, Harpur. That's a hazardous mix – anger, mortification. He'd think Chandor has selected him as the one to pressurize because he's the weaker. I bet Manse hasn't told Ember about the stairs and pictures. He's scared Ralph would accept Chandor's view and perhaps start thinking it's time to switch colleagues. But Manse, a proud man, is determined to resist. That suit, Col – a proud man's suit, probably with a long, proud history for at least one other proud man, possibly several proud men before it reached the Nearly New shop. Plus, Shale's wife home again. He wouldn't want to seem weak or victimized in her eyes. Life isn't only about banging her on the Afghan rug in the Pre-Raphaelite room. He has to show he's still a tearaway business force.'

Then, Harpur did consider informing Iles about Manse in the back of the Laguna. However, it might not have been Manse in the back of the Laguna. And the Laguna could be thoroughly innocent, its driver scarved up on account of neuralgia. In any case, Harpur had a sort of automatic cut-off mechanism that prevented him telling Iles more than he needed or deserved to know. This, also, was policing – at the highest levels. Harpur preferred asking the ACC troublesome but valid questions. 'The child – Shale's child, Matilda. Why did she come to you?'

'A woman officer sat with her in my room throughout, Harpur,' Iles replied at once. 'Absolutely throughout. This can be verified.'

'Of course. But why did Matilda have to see you?'

'Didn't I say – imaginings? She has some strange, childish, totally inexplicable conviction that I'd been in her bedroom at the rectory.'

They strolled alongside the former dock, now the rectangular lake, towards the old bonded warehouse building. 'This is a hell of a perceptive youngster,' Harpur said. 'She must have had a flash of intuition on first sight that you were the sort who *would* get into girl-kids' bedrooms and exude detectable thrill-sweat. She'd have sniffed traces around her wardrobe and dressing table. At least thrill-sweat.'

'She says she knows it was blood at the top of the rectory stairs,' Iles replied. 'Oh, the two children go along with the sauce tale because they can tell it's important to Manse, but they're both sure that's a ruse, Col. If you've been brought up by Manse Shale you're bound to have cottoned that wise, repeated lying will be vital now and then. I think Matilda is scared her father might have slaughtered one of the women he had in from time to time on rota.'

'She said that?'

'Of course she fucking didn't. My deduction. My *feeling*.'

'Oh, right.'

'She wonders, maybe a fight over Sybil's promised return, and an auxiliary lady refusing to go. Matilda's fond of Sybil, yes, naturally, but she's also fond of Lowri, Patricia, Carmel – kind of surrogate mothers, you see – and had to come from school at a rush and ask me whether I'd seen a body on the stairs if – according to Matty's mad, mad theory – I watched things from her bedroom. And, if so, whose body?'

'And you said, "Yes, Matilda, I did happen to be in your bedroom at the appropriate time, as might so easily occur, and can tell you that, in fact, the body was a man's." Trove's.'

'I said I'd find all three women for her and prove they're OK, Col.'

'Because you know they are.'

'We can do this, can't we?'

'I expect so. They'll be in Shale's dossier.'

'Get one of our photographers to do pictures of each on film with a date-time caption. Clandestine if possible. We don't want them scared. But I owe it to the worried child, after she made such a trek.'

Iles could be like this – another of those sudden, astonishing streaks of consideration, even tenderness. Harpur said: 'She won't want her father to know she's been putting that kind of hellish, murderous notion into your deductions mill. How will you fix for her to see the pictures?'

'My promise to find the women – find them alive – seemed to stem her worries, poor dear,' Iles replied. 'I had them take Matty back to school – in a plain car, of course. I called her Matty to relax her – help the child open up – open up in the sense of talking easily, that is.'

'If she came by bus in her lunch hour she must have already been keen to open up as to talk, mustn't she?'

'A woman officer present throughout.'

'You've said that.'

'I can give you her name. It seemed to me very necessary for her to be there, Harpur. This was a girl in school uniform. The blazer a really rich blue trimmed with black, Col. Tasteful and yet striking. You know how that kind of garb can get to some men – the numerous skirt pleats nuzzling one another busily, and spotless little white socks.' The ACC's voice grew phlegmy and his eyes misted. His breathing tightened up and for a couple of seconds he had trouble speaking the word 'socks', had to dredge for the cks sound. Harpur wished he'd brought some bottled water, not to throw over him but to loosen the ACC's severely hormonalled larynx. 'She sat where you usually do in my room, Col. Distance seemed important.'

'Yes, I like to keep a good gap between you and me.'

'The canteen meal and ginger beer on a tray on her little lap, Col. She ate willingly, yet without champing.'

'Will it get around via the woman officer that some schoolgirl with a nuzzly skirt thinks you slipped into her bedroom and emanated?'

'Matty said clearly in the officer's hearing that she was not present at the time – during her fantasy, I mean.'

'And she wasn't. You'd left them at Severalponds.' They could see Chandor's offices. Harpur again watched for the Laguna on a rerun.

'Ah, Severalponds! Changes since then, yes, Col? Why I say a shift in patterns. Syb back and Manse *persona grata* at Low Pastures. An immense turnaround. But maybe not altogether good, Harpur. Maybe totally bad, Harpur. It tells us that the settled state of things here is vulnerable, is possibly threatened. You've heard of the circle of wagons meant to repel attacks out West, Col. That's Ralphy bringing Shale to Low Pastures. And if Ember's worried to this degree, so are we, aren't we, Harpur? The peace I've – we've – built here begins to shake and topple. I said, seismic. I can't accept it. These strangenesses at the rectory, the missing Londoner, the collapse of Ralph's rigid standards for Low Pastures – indicators, Col. It's this fucker, Chandor, yes? Disruptive somehow? Why I want to see him, Col, and get him at least terrorized and possibly persuaded to up sticks altogether and bugger off back to Metroland.'

'If he won't?'

'I'd like him gone.'

'If he refuses?'

'He shouldn't do that, Harpur.'

'But he might.'

'This could be dangerous for him.'

'In what sense, sir?'

'Oh, yes, dangerous.'

'Danger from where?'

'Oh, yes. For instance, does he realize the peril he could be in from, say, Manse Shale?

'Or?' Harpur replied.

'Will we get gunfire on our streets?'

'Will we?'

'A bevy of possibilities, Col.'

'Manse has become more settled lately.'

'Did he seem settled on that fucking transcript, Harpur? If some sod leaves a body on your stairs would *you* feel settled? I think you'd want to get back at him,' Iles said.

'Which body is that? Which stairs? Is all this related to what the child, Matilda, Matty, so comically fantasized?'

'And the lad who's missing – Trove. A link to Chandor? A London link?'

'Nothing on the computer.'

'When you *ran across him*, did you ask yourself whether this might be a lad liable to cut a man's throat, and perhaps cut the throat of someone who came asking too persistently about that man?'

'He was with friends,' Harpur said.

'And did *they* look to be in that sort of line?'

'One was Director of Strategic Planning. The other, Personnel.'

'They *did* look to be in that sort of butchery line, did they?'

'Maurice. Rufus.'

'Their mothers and fathers will have thought considerably before giving them names like that, Col. These lads went out to their careers buoyed by the good hopes of such parents. Maurice. Rufus. Assertion there. Resonances there.'

In Chandor's big, third floor office overlooking the dock/lake, Iles said resonantly: 'What we're doing, Mr Chandor, is maintaining a practice – a fine practice in my opinion, not to mention Harpur's – yes, what we're doing is maintaining a practice established by the previous Chief here, Mr Mark Lane, now justly lifted to the Inspectorate of Constabulary, but gratefully remembered by all of us, indeed esteemed. It was Mr Lane's view that the marina development emblemized a kind of rebirth for this city, and, as such, those who came to set up their businesses in it should be given a proper, hearty, though informal, welcome. In his day, he offered that welcome in person. He would visit all newcomers and wish them well. Sometimes I accompanied him and, as a result, learned the importance he gave to such courtesies. I resolved that, should Mr Lane leave us – as seemed likely, owing to his multitudinous and massive talents – yes, resolved that if he went I would carry on this delightful tradition, as well as I could, pick up the, as it were, baton.

'And I decided also that when possible I would bring Harpur along with me so that he, in his turn, might learn the form and intricacies of the little unceremonious ceremonies. I believe he will respond. He has the right instincts, though they might not be immediately apparent in his demeanour and tailoring. It was Harpur who reminded me, after, I gather, running across you earlier today, Mr Chandor, that I had yet to bring you greetings, although you have been in place here now some little while. I knew I must correct that omission immediately, and so here we are.'

'This is a considerable honour you do myself and the company,' Chandor said.

'I have to apologize for the delay,' Iles said.

'I mentioned the view to Mr Harpur,' Chandor said. He walked to the big window and gestured towards the water and new buildings beyond. 'This seems to give us an, as it were, context – a context established by city effort before our arrival, yes, but a context into which we can happily fit.'

'I think I'd prefer you fucking didn't,' Iles replied, 'either happily or not.'

'Obviously, I wondered what was the significance of all that bullshit,' Chandor said.

'Which?' Iles said.

'The opening spiel,' Chandor said. 'The general verbiage. I'm told you considered Lane a total twerp and drove him mental.'

'Dim prick, I needed some rubbish tale to get things going, didn't I?' Iles said.

'You've been asking your data bank about me, us, I suppose,' Chandor said. 'But nil return. My condolences.'

'I've heard you described as "of Nordic appearance",' Iles said.

'Folk say that of you, too, sir,' Harpur said.

'Which folk?' Iles said.

'Many. I should think at Staff College you were known as Desmond of the Fjords,' Harpur said.

'I expected something cleaner cut, and with less off-putting skin,' the ACC said.

'This is a bully call, yes, Iles?' Chandor said. 'You bring the frighteners?'

'You'll remember, I was invited,' Harpur said.

'Where are the other two derelicts, Maurice and Rufus?' Iles said.

'They would have nothing to say to you,' Chandor replied.

'This I believe,' Iles said.

'We also picked up a tale you look after people, Iles,' Chandor said.

'Well, I hope so. What else are police officers for?' the ACC said.

'That you look after some people more than others,' Chandor said.

'"Look after" in what sense?' Iles said.

'Look after,' Chandor replied.

'It's true that some people I wouldn't want to look after at all or ever,' Iles said, 'though I might do them the honour of getting to their funeral if they died early.' He stood and walked to the big window, standing companionably alongside Chandor. 'Yes, a magnificent setting. Emblematic.'

'I have to admit, Mr Iles, I'm proud when showing it off,' Chandor replied. 'But perhaps forgivably proud.'

'Oh, entirely,' Iles said. 'You really mustn't blame yourself.'

'I'm so pleased you could visit, and I'm sure Maurice and Rufus will be, also, when I tell them.'

'Would I had been able to meet the two,' Iles said. 'Mr Lane liked to get what he termed "the full flavour" of a new company, and I follow him in that.'

Chapter Seven

Now and then, Manse Shale wondered about that psychiatrist woman with great legs in *The Sopranos* on TV. Shale
could think of a lot of private things he would like to
discuss with someone who had her kind of training re
minds, and who did not go spreading what she heard.
People in that job made a famous oath to keep their
mouth shut about patients. Of course, her patient in the TV
show, Tony Soprano, was just a total, savage fucking
gangster and thug. All the same, Mansel did see two
similarities with himself and his own position lately, especially lately.

First, certain troubles had begun to do his head in a bit,
including a phone call from the school, and the mess-up of
the Laguna project. Second, the troubles had to stay confidential – or as confidential as they could be. If he had a
psychiatrist like that, flashing thigh at him in what would
be known as 'an advisory capacity', he would not try
anything on, regardless of how suitable the consulting
room was with upholstered settees, but he would just
explain his problems to her and listen quietly to whatever
she said back. And he would pay the fees – probably big,
it didn't matter – he would pay the fees straight off out of
his Medical Fund (Personal) without expecting anything
more than these conversations. As Manse saw matters, a
woman psychiatrist could have good legs or ordinary, but
they was not the chief aspect of the meetings, which concerned conditions inside the brain. That's what psychiatrist
meant – someone who knew about minds.

Tony Soprano, out strolling one day, thought ugly dead

fish on a shop slab turned into men he knew and spoke to him, so anyone could see he needed a psychiatrist. Nothing of this sort at all happened to Manse, and, in fact, he never went near a fishmonger's, but he felt confused and would of been glad of advice. That call from the school certainly upset him, plus how Harpur snuggled up to Chandor and his charmers on the marina pavement that failed Laguna day, like true mates. Some deal there?

Shale did not like the way the headmistress suggested it would be better not to use the phone for what she had to say, but could he come to see her? This made it sound like she believed Manse was the kind who would have a police tap on his line. He found it a damn slur, coming from a teacher. There might be smirks and winks in the staff room if someone mentioned his name, like for Al Capone or Tony Soprano or Frank Sinatra. How could that school head know anything about the commercial scene that Manse glittered in and collected in?

But he did not argue with her. Perhaps she'd get difficult about letting the children stay on at Bracken Collegiate if he turned roughish. And, of course, cleverest not to chatter too much because there *could* be a police tap on his line. Why did Iles and Harpur turn up at the rectory like that otherwise, staring at the redecoration? Fucking telepathy? But Manse did not want some snobby, interfering headmistress from the private sector to behave like there would obviously be a police tap on his line, even if there was. This he considered a smear and very hurtful in view of the fees he had to pay.

And then women as women – another aspect that confused him. Always Manse had tried to treat them decent. He truly believed you should do what you could to give equality and some gentleness. Often this would cost you nothing. He definitely considered quite a few women deserved proper regard. There many a type of woman. But think of the one who arrived so unexpected at Ralphy Ember's place with the picture of that nearly decapitated lad who Manse naturally recognized right off

135

from his staircase. He could not tell her this, could he? Didn't that whole incident have to stay secret?

It seemed hard, though, to say he didn't know nothing about him and let her go on searching and hoping, taking holiday time from work. She obviously loved that lad or she wouldn't be so sorrowful and keen to find him. But then, look at it different. Would it of been kindness to answer, 'Oh, yes, as a matter of fact I seen this one not long ago with his throat cut in my place, the day the pictures went from the walls?' All right, Manse could agree it might of been done more gradual and tender than this, but at the end it came out the same, didn't it? If he had said to Meryl Goss, like slowing it down and softening it: 'Ah, yes, I believe he *does* remind me of somebody I saw not so long ago, as a matter of fact,' she would grow excited and ask, 'Oh, are you sure? Please say you're sure.' His reply: 'Yes, pretty sure.' Goss: 'But where? Was he all right, Mr Shale?'

Then he could not dodge no further and must reply: 'In the rectory. On my staircase, first floor.' She would cry out in amazement, maybe with a little puzzled laugh, 'On your rectory staircase?' Ralphy and Margaret and Sybil would also probably of cried out the same, 'On your rectory staircase, Mansel?' By then they'd have the idea that something must of been wrong with him, to be on a staircase – not moving on a staircase , up or down, just *on*. And this would mean Meryl Goss felt prepared a bit better for what had to come next. She might ask again, 'Did he seem all right?' Manse would have to say, 'I regret I got to tell you, Meryl, no.' 'Oh!' Margaret would say, or Sybil, or both. Goss might sense things and ask, 'Dead?' And perhaps Margaret or Sybil or both would whisper sadly, 'Oh, don't say that, please don't say that,' but knowing it must be right.

Ralphy might ask, 'Dead how?' because he was one for details and into tactics and action replays. Manse would still hold back and say, 'Dead.' 'But how?' Ralph would say, keeping on and being dogged. 'Dead,' Manse might reply again. Eventually, though, she would of had to be told, 'I'm afraid with his throat cut causing bad stains to the stair carpet and wallpaper, though please don't feel guilty about that, in the awful circumstances, Meryl.' Even if he could spin it out like this, as far as eventually, she would still get a rotten shock. He could not decide now whether it was more tender or less tender to say the way he did say at Low Pastures after dinner that he never seen the lad in the picture before, and shaking his head to pile on the no-ness of the 'No.' This was the kind of thing he meant by confusion. This was why if he went to a psychiatrist he would want her to keep all of it very tight under her bonnet.

For instance, he would not like the psychiatrist to visit some chum for what would be called 'a second opinion', about whether Manse must try to find Meryl Goss and admit he lied, and now frankly inform her of the staircase. They done a lot of that, medics and psychiatrists – getting second opinions. It was their way of making work for one another. But this was how dangerous facts got around uncontrolled. When two people knew something it could be a trillion times more than one knowing it. Cummerbund Spilsby gave him this guidance very early on Manse's career path. Naturally, that unusual word 'trillion' stuck in Shale's memory. This could be why Cummerbund picked it. He had a lot of wisdom and a lot of experience, in jail and out.

It was about Matilda. Shale didn't discover more than this from the headmistress on the telephone because of her buttoned lip. Extra confusion? He had certainly worried about Matilda lately. She did not seem the same after she said at breakfast it was blood under the sauce on the stairs. Some kids would most probably be all right in a while if they discovered blood under sauce on the stairs. Laurent seemed all right. Matilda, no. This blood under the sauce really registered with her. Maybe it was just a boy-girl thing, boys being able to think, if life had to be like that it had to be like that, such as that Golden Oldies number, 'Che Sara Sara', meaning what will be will be, though women sang that as well as men.

Shale went out to the school. He did not speak to Sybil

about the call, not at this juncture. It would take her time to get used to being a mother again, and he must not shove a crisis on to Syb yet. She might rebunk to Ivor in Wales if pressures started. Women sometimes seemed weak. That's why they needed plenty of care and politeness and should only be told items simple to handle, such as social matters and holiday ideas. Syb was a mixture. She could be a fighter, but, also, there would come days when she didn't want to bother.

Manse wondered whether Ember schemed it for that woman, Goss, to come to Low Pastures as a way of getting at him, like setting up a great dinner and good feeling and politeness, then suddenly smash it for the sake of giving a shock. But Ralphy could not of known about her, could he, nor about the man on the stairs and his photograph? Could he? Ember picked up all sorts of information some-how, mostly from the club. And it was the kind of ploy the sod might pull. That sudden invitation to Low Pastures – perhaps Ralph only offered it to bring Manse up there and get him troubled. Why, though? Manse failed to sort it out, but Ember had all sorts of smart tricks to get his firm ahead. He was not just them fucking wool letters he wrote to the papers about topics, nor he wasn't just the mad jerk who thought he'd make that tip, the Monty, clean and blessed and chic any century now. No human being could be made up of only them sides of him or he would be just a laugh. Ralphy knew how to push people under and hold them under, especially people you would of thought was his friends, such as Manse.

He regretted now putting his status suit on and spend-ing so much time choosing the mauve shirt. Ember obviously did not respect that kind of effort at all. Manse felt slighted, or what the young called 'dissed' – that is, given disrespect. He considered he might of taken such care with his garments just to step into a trap. This hurt. Respect had become important lately. A political party called itself that, and the government also thought more people should get respect and more people should show it. Shale felt he deserved some, and not only because of the suit and shirt, which could be regarded as nothing more than surface, obviously.

'Stressed, Mr Shale,' the head teacher said. 'Yes, we feel Matilda has been unusually stressed of late.'

'Children have their own private anxieties which might seem slight to me and you, but to them they are really real,' Shale said. He had practised a bit of a purr for talking to this headmistress of a very pricey school. You never knew what kind of gossip about him someone like this had picked up, so he wanted to make sure he sounded the refined and thoughtful sort, not some fucking rough hick trying to bulldoze everyone.

'And I thought it only right to discuss matters with you, Mr Shale, in case there are factors in Matilda's life we should, perhaps, know about, and possibly could help deal with. May I ask, have you, yourself, or your . . . or anyone adult in your household . . . noticed unusual tension in your daughter recently?'

'My wife, you mean?' He felt a real victory with that. Clearly, she didn't know Syb had returned. Of course, she would of heard on the rumour circuit that Syb went, and maybe about Lowri or Carmel or Patricia, and this was why she stopped herself saying 'wife', and picked instead that bit about adults in his household, meaning women. There might have been gossip, although he had made damn sure that none of them, not Carmel nor Lowri nor Patricia, ever went near the school to his knowledge. He would definitely not take one of them to a parents' meeting.

'Well, yes, your wife,' she said.

'Tension?' Manse replied.

'As if abstracted.'

'Abstracted?'

'Her mind elsewhere.'

'I –'

'Why I asked whether there might be factors, special, new factors, affecting her. Family? Domestic? Health? Anything.'

'Matilda's always been a sensitive one,' Shale said. 'I remember when she was only a baby that –'

'When I say "special", in part I mean special to Matilda. Her brother seems quite as ever.'

'Chalk and cheese. It's what I had in mind about sensitive,' Shale said. 'Perhaps it's girls. So, I didn't mention to anyone that I was coming here today. I thought Matilda might grow anxious – on account of being sensitive if she heard.'

'She's wholly unwilling to discuss some matters.'

Well, I should fucking hope so – or just ladle out lies. But what Shale said was: 'Like I mentioned, they have their private anxieties. Youngsters will seem relaxed and carefree and noisy as a zoo, but underneath they –'

'We keep a very careful check on children who take lunch on the school premises,' she replied.

'Wise.'

'We don't allow them to wander off, especially the girls – girls of their age.'

So, what the hell was this to do with? 'I'd agree with that, oh, definite in this country as it is now.'

'The other day Matilda disappeared throughout.'

'Throughout?'

'She ate no meal here and could not be found. Her brother said he didn't know where she was.'

You let her fucking slope off somewhere alone for ninety minutes, you idle, casual, money-grubbing, slack cow? However, Manse reshaped this thought: 'A few days ago? Disappeared? Let me just send my mind back a bit.' He did a pause, then smiled, but not an easy smile, a smile that had built-in apology. 'Ah, I think her mother might of picked Matilda up for some shopping. They had lunch in a café, I expect. Yes, I do remember now, they mentioned that. Matilda must of forgotten to notify the school in advance. Wrong of her. I'll definitely have a word with Matilda re that kind of thing in future.' Another slice of guidance from Cummerbund Spilsby was, if a conversation looked dangerous and you couldn't tell which way it would go, shut it down, like rats would not go around the

S bend in drains, Cummerbund said, because they could not see ahead. Although such a conversation might turn out harmless or even helpful, don't risk it, stick the stopper on earliest.

'As a matter of fact, she did come back in a car with a woman driver,' the head said.

She fucking what? 'Yes, that would be it, I expect. My wife, Sybil.'

'We were concerned not just about Matilda's absence, but also whether she'd had something to eat. On that matter she consented to talk and assured us she ate a proper lunch, with pudding and ginger beer. But we could not discover where she went.'

'It was good of you to worry, but Sybil would be extremely particular about nourishment for her.'

'A teacher had gone out looking in case Matilda was outside school grounds but in the neighbourhood and saw her put down some distance away, apparently so the car wouldn't be spotted. Matilda walked from there.'

'And was back in time for afternoon lessons. That's a relief!' *So, what fucking car and who fucking drove?* 'You know how children can be. They don't like their friends to see parents fussing over them.'

'Because of our anxiety, the teacher noted the car's registration number. A silver Astra. We haven't done anything about it. I thought I'd speak to you first and get your opinion.' The headmistress passed Shale a piece of paper.

'Ah, Sybil's. Yes,' he said, glancing at it and nodding. 'But I'm sorry we've give you so much trouble.'

'At least it's good to solve that mystery,' she said.

Shale did not like the 'at least'. He could tell it meant there would be more poking about and curiosity, but he shifted in his chair as if to leave now the lunch-break problem was settled. But would she of asked him to see her just for that?

'We come back to Matilda's general state,' the head said. 'The signs of strain.'

'I don't think I've noticed any, I got to say,' Shale replied.

'High spirits, oh, yes, but that's natural to a growing girl, don't you think, even a good thing?'

'And your wife?'

And my wife? What did a question like that mean? The headmistress had adapted very quick, hadn't she? She spoke this word now just like it was natural. 'My wife?' he said.

'I wondered if *she'd* observed a change in Matilda.'

Sybil might notice if Matilda grew another ear or became suddenly see-through, but the state of the children was not never one of her *main* things. 'I'll certainly consult her about this,' Shale said, 'and refer to your concern.'

'I wondered, you see, if your wife had come here on impulse to give Matilda a special outing, having seen she was a bit down. That would explain the rather irregular way the absence occurred. And perhaps she wouldn't even tell Laurent.'

Ah! Bingo! 'Impulse. This could be it, indeed,' Shale said. 'Sybil does have impulses. Shrewd of you, if you don't mind me remarking.' Wasn't it a bloody impulse that took her to Ivor? And another bloody impulse brought her home. Syb would love people to think she ran on impulses – someone dashing and free. She and Manse spoke about impulses only a little while ago. 'You told me Matilda wouldn't talk about where she went. That's because she doesn't want to land her mother in any bother with the school, I should think.' He had a small laugh. 'Known as *omerta* in the Mafia, which I learned from TV dramas.' He could tell this sweetheart would like to ask how long Syb had been back at the rectory and if she would stay. 'Sybil's very quick to pick up on anything unusual in one of the children. Like radar? And Sybil will respond, immediate.'

'A fine quality in a mother.'

'Oh, yes.'

'I fear not all have it.'

'Really?' The headmistress's room looked out through big french windows on to a square courtyard. Her secretary had done cups of tea for both of them. Now and then kids in blue and black uniform crossed the yard on their way to classes, boys and girls, mostly girls. Manse tried to imagine what that steamed-up prick peddler, ACC Desmond Iles, would be like if he sat where Manse sat now, watching. Answer – trouser-tight, short of breath and twitchy.

The headmistress was about thirty-six, with a pretty good short nose, not one of them curlew jobs of some women teachers. Perhaps he'd been cruel to regard her as snobby. He thought her teeth looked like her own and no lines on her neck yet. Manse did not at all mind talking to her, as long as she kept off anything in depth. But, of course, in depth was just where she wanted to go. Most likely she got her job because she could do stuff in depth. Fine, as long as this stayed at study of the pyramids or pond life or the Psalms. He did not want crafty, round-about questions re other matters, such as the personal elements. But maybe some of her questions was to do with a genuine schoolmarmy fret over Matilda. 'And nothing exceptional in your daughter's life that might have unsettled her?' she asked.

'Not that I can think of right off, no.' Here was someone else who wanted to know about the staircase without knowing she wanted to know about the staircase. It would really puzzle her if he said most likely Matilda felt upset because of the blood, and unable to find out whose. But, naturally, he decided against that. 'I'm going to give it thought, and so will Sybil, I'm sure,' he replied. 'I know I speak for her also when I say I'm very grateful you took the trouble to raise this with us.'

'It's how the school relationship with parents and pupils should be, I feel,' the head said. She did not have no rings on. Her name was Ms D. Norvenne. 'This is very much a three-sided concordat.'

'True.' If Syb went again, it would obviously be impossible to have this headmistress in the rectory for spells, although being thirty-six did not by itself kill the idea. Manse hated ageism. Think of Charlotte Rampling. But the arrangement would be wrong for the children. They'd feel mixed up – this woman, chief of the school for the day, and then around the house in the evening and weekends, showering and out on the patio wearing flip-flop sandals with a coffee. And what would they call her? To them, Patricia was Patricia and Carmel Carmel and Lowri Lowri and Sybil mother or mum. They could not call their head-mistress Delphine or Daisy or Debbie. And they could not call a permitted, partnerly resident, Ms Norvenne. Now and then it could be vital to keep different facets of your life with a good gap between, although they all added up to the youness of you. Facets was what Manse believed a personality had plenty of.

'Some shock, for instance?' Ms Norvenne said.

'I don't think so. Or, let's say "Not to my knowledge."'

'A change in the pattern of things?'

'No, can't help, I'm afraid. Days are much of a muchness, as my mother used to say.'

'A loss?'

'Again, not to my knowledge.'

'And any serious loss *would* be to your knowledge, of course, wouldn't it, Mr Shale?'

'I would certainly expect so.' He would have liked to use her name, but didn't fancy saying 'Ms Norvenne'.

'They form bonds, you know.'

'Who?' Shale replied.

'Children. The breaking of something like that may cause great distress, even a kind of disorientation.'

Manse had come across this word before almost for definite, and he loved the way Ms Norvenne got her tongue around it, no hesitation or spitting. He spotted the tongue tip for a moment between her top and bottom teeth, which still looked to him like her own, all of them. This tongue tip seemed to Manse of the educated but friendly kind and not frantically pink. He had a chair a little distance off, but could tell her breath would be a treat. The desk looked untidy. This pleased him. He hated show. It was a cool, light square room with framed pictures of buildings here and there, probably the college she went to, really impressive, with big wooden gates like a castle or jail, open in these photos, but which used to get shut and severely locked to keep women students in in the old days, so they couldn't wander at night looking for experience before the pill.

He thought how strange and out of order it would be now in this schooly room if he said to Ms Norvenne, 'I had a great, tit-for-tat drive-by massacre lined up which would stop any more violence from a certain, new pushy villain, causing pressure to Matilda, but some holy cop called Harpur put his fucking self smack in the way, I'm not sure whether deliberate.' Facets. Everyone did contain a bunch of facets. They all counted in making a total person – this meeting counted, and the Laguna project counted. Probably she knew Manse must be the sort who'd have things like a drive-by execution and the substances game in one part of his mind, and that would be why she made a fuss about Matilda. Perhaps she felt scared Matilda got dragged into this side of his life somehow and became what the teacher called 'stressed', which, in a way, could certainly be true – as with the staircase blood. Oh, yes, Matilda did seem upset over that when she mentioned it at breakfast and would not believe the sauce tale.

'And imagination as well as being sensitive,' he said. 'Matilda – so strong on imagination. Usually this is a great thing, such as for artists and writers. They wouldn't be nothing without it. Well, I don't need to tell *you* this! The Pre-Raphaelites. They had models to copy from, yes, so you could say they did not need their imagination because they painted the real item in front of them, but it was their imagination that brought the special glow and turned them into the Pre-Raphaelites, I think you'll agree. However, imagination can go a bit far now and then. It unsettles people. On the whole, it's best to have *some* imagination, but, also, you got to watch it.' He thought she'd be quite surprised to hear him speak about the Pre-Raphaelites. This could be just because she'd heard a buzz to do with only one side of him. Although she might be a head teacher, he could give Ms Norvenne a lesson about people being very various within their actual selves and having facets.

'Well, imagination, yes,' she said. She started digging through some papers in the heaps on her desk.

'Many's the amusing tale Matilda makes up and tells us, coming from inside herself, not lifted out of books or films or anything like that,' Manse replied. The way the headmistress was on the search for something bothered him and he thought he better get ready a knock-down in case Matilda been talking around the school about difficult stuff from the rectory to do with staining, and Ms Norvenne had notes. If she found unnecessary items said by Matilda, such as blood under the sauce, Shale could try a laugh and reply, 'Oh, that's so like her – such an imagination!' He would make it sound a little bit fed up with Matilda for her far-fetched stories but also fond and understanding and full of wonder at what she could think of even so young. He didn't really believe Matilda would get too blabby, because he had brought her and Laurent up to be careful what they said. They surely must of learned that habit. But Manse always tried to prepare for what was known as 'the worst scenario' in case it came. Any executive, any leader of an organization, had to, known also as 'Plan B'.

'Her teacher asked Matilda's class to write a kind of very personal pen pal letter to a Third World child, describing their lives in Britain to someone ignorant of our ways,' Ms Norvenne said. 'Ah, this is Matilda's.' She held up a couple of A4 sheets.

'It sounds *so* interesting, ' Manse said at once. *Oh, what the fuck!*

'We have to teach them how to write a formal letter, because the skill is disappearing, owing to e-mail. And the art of description is called for when the letter cannot assume the recipient knows anything at all of the writer's circumstances and setting. So, it's a doubly useful exercise, you see.'

'Very, very true.' Although Manse felt scared, it delighted him to hear that things got planned here, not just catch-as-catch-can. When you read *Daily Mail* reports about ordinary comp. schools, in what people called 'the state system', you saw how teachers and heads used most of their time making sure kids didn't strangle or rape one another or the staff, or spend all the French lesson screening porn on mobile phones under the desk. But if you paid out lavish for your children in a school like this one, Bracken Collegiate, you expected plenty of good schemes to do with true education, such as this Third World idea. Although he thought they might of stolen it from a movie called *About Schmidt*, where Jack Nicholson writes to a lad in Africa, telling him about America, Manse would not say this to Ms Norvenne because he liked her confidence and the way she got words, big and small, to line up for her without no trouble, like an army drill squad.

He still thought it must be awkward to bring her into a stay at the rectory for a while, but, if he did, he could tell she would be great for conversations when he felt like it on many subjects. To reach Bracken Collegiate from the rectory was simple – just go left out of the drive, on to the Spoor roundabout, third exit and then more or less a direct bit of country road. This would be a plus if he did ask her.

'We supplied each of them a name to call their pen pal by, so as to make it seem vivid, you see. A one-to-oneness, the essence of good letters. I don't know whether you've come across the letters of the poet, John Keats, for instance, Mr Shale.'

'You don't get more one-to-one than him.'

'Matilda's pen pal we named Dauda.'

'I wouldn't be surprised at all if there are people called that over there.'

'Well, yes, there are. We took names from government lists in Whitaker's Almanack.'

'This makes it seem truly real,' Shale said.

'That was the idea. Verisimilitude.'

'Yes.' Manse enjoyed all this, watching her enthusiasm and the playful way she fingered a proper, fully nibbed fountain pen, not a Biro, on her desk. But, also, Manse did worry about the real real, instead of someone from this fucking Whitsun Almanack. Where did Matilda go in the lunch hour? It was not to see Third World Dauda, and

Dauda didn't bring her back and drop her where it would be secret. He had the car number and make, but the lad who used to sell info from the police computer had been picked for an accelerated promotion course. The replacement officer seemed short of talent, and was scared of Harpur and Iles, so would not play. 'I see this Dauda idea as really exciting,' he said. It all showed Manse again that people had different aspects, and these could be present at the same time. One part of him felt thrilled to think of Matilda writing to somebody cooked up, with a genuine foreign name. But another part of him wanted a good long sight of that genuine woman driving the Astra and, of course, not Syb. He must decide whether he could ask Matilda about this. He did not like the idea of making her uncover things in her life if she wanted them private. That was the wrong way for a father to treat a daughter.

Manse had thought Ms Norvenne would give him the letter, but, no, she read it to him. He liked her voice. Some voices did not suit the faces they came out of but her voice did. This was a voice he wouldn't mind listening to now and then or even oftener. It didn't have that sickening boominess and clatter some women's voices did. It was just a voice that told you things, like serving up a fair meal on a warmed plate. She said: 'Here goes, then: "Dear Dauda, I'm going to let you know first about my house, which was once upon a time a rectory. That's where a clergyman used to live but my father bought it although he is not really a clergyman at all at this moment in time."'

At this moment in time. Did she think Manse would want to become a clergyman one day, so it would be more suitable for him to live in the rectory? Or, probably, she'd just heard that saying, 'at this moment in time', and liked sticking it in. 'It's clever to tell Dauda about the house, because it could be absolutely different from where he lives, such as a mud hut in one of them villages,' Shale said.

'"There are a lot of pictures on the walls in the rectory. Many people have pictures on their walls because of the colour and scenery. The other day when I wasn't there my father changed them all round. It was terrible, Dauda. I came home and had a bad shock. It made the house seem like somebody else's house. I don't know why he did that. I became upset. I felt like lost."'

'Sensitive, you see,' Shale said.

'"Then, when I went to my bedroom I could tell someone had been in there, a stranger. I don't know how I could tell but I could tell. Also, my father tripped up on the stairs and spilled sauce. When I say stairs I mean for going up from the hall to where the bedrooms are."'

'She got to show what stairs are, because a mud hut wouldn't have no upstairs,' Shale said.

'"We soon removed that sauce by ordering new wallpaper and a new stair carpet. My dad put the pictures back right. I began to feel better then. But a man came to the house and I knew he was the one who had been in my bedroom. I don't know how I knew this but I did. I'm telling you this, Dauda, so you will see the kind of person I am. I know some things but I don't know how I know. Is it the same for you? I think you might have magic and witch doctors where you live and I think this might be magic for me, also. My name is Matilda. Well, that's all for now, Dauda. I hope it is not too hot for you in your country. It is raining here. My dad doesn't usually carry sauce when he is going upstairs or coming down but he did this day, honestly. He doesn't usually move the pictures about either, but he did this day. Perhaps everyone has days that are not usual, not just about pictures and sauce but all sorts. I don't know if you have heard of a conservatory, but we have one. It is like a glass room on the end of the house in the garden. It has eight sides. Many flies and insects get in there because of the warmth. In your country I expect there are flies and insects, anyway, without a conservatory, because of the sun. With many best respects, Matilda Shale."'

'I should think conservatories over there would get really steamy,' Manse said, 'what with the Equator.'

'I wonder how this letter – supposed letter – strikes you, Mr Shale.'

'Them pictures – she *was* upset.'

'That's why I asked about special factors, you see. Her teacher and I both detect in this piece of writing an almost overwhelming sense of insecurity, of sudden rootlessness. Matilda thinks the house has become like someone else's house, because you'd moved the pictures around. That might appear an extreme reaction. I suggest it is possibly symptomatic of something wider – Matilda's general sense of bewilderment, of alienation. She believes the privacy of her bedroom has been abused and even believes she can identify the invader, and now, according to her, this invader has returned to the house. She feels terribly menaced. Her home, which should offer protection and safety, can no longer do that. She is battered by the loss. Her mind cavorts: she ends the letter with "that's all for now" but then has to get back to the matter of the sauce and pictures and, finally, the conservatory tacked on to the letter, as, indeed, a conservatory is tacked on to a house, the conservatory colonized by flies and insects. She feels she does not *belong* anywhere, you see, Mr Shale. The house is not *her* house because switching the pictures means it looks different. Her bedroom and the conservatory have been taken over. Whereas the flies and insects might be natural in Dauda's country, they are incursors here. All these factors amass to bring her abnormal stress. I see in Matilda's work a *cri de coeur*. She seeks support. I said they were asked to do a personal letter with some background about the British scene, but Matilda's is exceptionally revealing, exceptionally autobiographical.'

Manse really loved all this heavy chatter, including French. Most likely you would never get talk of such quality from the head of a comp. Some of the words twinkled in his memory – 'rootlessness', 'alienation', 'cavorts', 'amass', 'incursors'. This woman must be almost worth half the cruel Bracken Collegiate fees on her own. She could truly jaw. And yet she went careful, also. He knew what she really wanted to say. What she really wanted to say was that the uncertainties about Sybil had begun to get at Matilda and confuse her. Did the children's mother belong at the rectory or not? Would she remain now or skedaddle again when the itch came? Perhaps Ms Norvenne knew this itch herself, personally. This was why Manse thought she might like a season at the rectory.

But although Ms Norvenne sounded off brilliant about many matters, she knew she must not try to elbow her way into certain areas, for instance, Syb. Of course, Manse had that uncertainty, too. He could not be sure whether Sybil wanted to come back for good to the rectory. And he had another uncertainty on top of that. He did not know whether he *wanted* her to come back for good, although it might be best for the children. If your wife been over in Wales living with someone called Ivor who was a bus driver or charity shop manager or that kind of thing, you could not think of her as exactly like she used to be. Sorry, impossible.

The children said Ivor was really dull and ordinary. But for a while, anyway, Syb liked being with him better than she liked being with Manse. He felt injured by that. He did not think Carmel or Patricia or Lowri would go off with someone dull and ordinary in Wales, even though Lowri had a Welsh name. 'Maybe I should of thought it out a bit more careful when I decided to move them pictures around just like willy-nilly,' Shale said.

'You were probably hoping to give the children a harmless, even amusing, surprise. You might have wondered – and quite reasonably wondered – if they were fed up with the way the paintings had been arranged for so long.'

'Well, perhaps I did. All the same, I feel guilty. I ought to of remembered how sensitive she is.'

'You were alone in the house, were you, when you did the swap around? Everyone away for a while, perhaps?'

'Paintings can get to be like friends,' Manse replied. 'And you expect to meet your friends in familiar places. Otherwise, it's as you remarked, "rootlessness". Possibly one day you'll visit the rectory and give us your view on whether the paintings are in the right spots on certain walls. That would be a treat. I don't know if you might of come across the work of Arthur Hughes and Edward

151

Prentis. The Pre-Raphaelites had what is known as "a Brotherhood", which always seems to me just right for art.'

Ms Norvenne stood. 'I agree with you,' she said, 'that it would be wisest if Matilda doesn't hear about our meeting today, for fear of distressing her. But, of course, she or Laurent might have seen your car outside and wonder.'

He'd come in the Jaguar, with Eldon driving and wearing the cap, no fucking rebel arguments at all, the way there used to be from Denzil Lake. Although Manse did detest show, he thought that at Bracken Collegiate a quality motor and chauffeur would be normal for many parents. He felt he should keep up this standard, for the sake of Laurent and Matilda, known as 'image'. A duty, really. Eldon was waiting outside in the playground with the car. He seemed more or less settled in the job, although he could not understand why they had to chuck the Laguna operation just because it would of been four not three. It truly irritated him. That might sound like simple, crude, blast-off thinking, but now and then Manse wondered if Eldon had things right.

After all, what was happening? As Shale saw it, this lout Chandor wanted a way into the business. He knew it would be hard going, so he starts by showing what he can do – lifting the pictures, dumping a body, the idea being to get Manse jittery, even scared, before Chandor makes the approach, like dropping them two atom bombs in 1945 and saying 'Talk, or Tokyo's next.' The body could be a total unknown male as far as Manse was concerned. Chandor might even regard that as an extra bit of pressure. It showed he could do what looked like a random, meaningless killing, if this helped his case along. *Oh, dear, a corpse on your stairs, Manse. Sorry about that slip-up. I wonder who'll be next.* And then he considerately removes the body, puts the pictures back – although any old how – offers compensation, to show he also has that kind of reasonable power and flair. Didn't it all mean that pretty soon there would be either another bit of terrorism, or a formal approach to Manse by Chandor, asking for a slice of the trade? *Talk, or Tokyo's next.* Oh, yes, the suggestion would be there that, if Manse refused him a share, the terrorism would restart.

So, perhaps Eldon's ideas made the best sense, even if they would of involved knocking over a Detective Chief Superintendent. Or maybe *especially* if they involved knocking over a Detective Chief Superintendent, if the Detective Chief Superintendent had been taken aboard by Chandor as part of his operation. Harpur – supposed to be more or less straight despite his rank, but was that right? It could be that Eldon saw a situation not just simple, or too simple, but beautifully clear. It could be that Eldon brought Manse real possibilities. Not all chauffeur-bodyguards had to be as thick as Denzil. Manse remembered a great lad who worked that role for him a while ago, Neville Greenage, black and with a terrific brain. But he'd gone off to start his own commercial organization in Yorkshire or Austria or somewhere like that. Eldon might turn out to be in this class.

Manse thought Ms Norvenne's point about the kids maybe seeing the Jaguar was sharp. 'An idea. We'll say I came to pay next term's fees, if they ask, shall we?' he replied. He made his voice cosy now, like adults getting together to fool a couple of kids, but in a nice way, such as telling them about Father Christmas. Manse had a couple of pocketfuls of used twenties and tens from trade around Valencia Esplanade the last two nights. They was not in rolls or rubber-banded but loose. He did not want to look like some fucking on-course bookie, did he? He counted out a stack of twenties on to her desk. 'The story is, I was passing and my tailoring had got plumped out of shape by this build-up of business funds, as can happen so easy, can't it? And so I think to myself suddenly, "Why, Mansel, here I am, near Bracken Collegiate, so I'll just pop in, see whether the head's around, and, if so, offload. She'll do me and my jacket a good turn, I'm sure, and take it."'

'In notes? This is *very* unusual, Mr Shale.'

He believed she would really prefer to call him Mansel, but her high post as head stopped this for now. Perhaps next time, or definitely if she ever came to stay at the rectory. He could tell the grubby heap excited her – not the amount, which would be the same if he'd written a cheque, but how he could produce a couple of thousand plus in raw spendables, sort of casual from his coat, as though just everyday cash flow for him. Shale felt sure about the word she would stick on him after this in a fond way – *swashbuckling*.

She'd be familiar with that word from tales of knights and squires when they used to get out and about doing gallantries. Manse didn't mind it. From films he'd seen on TV he would say George C. Scott as General Patton was swashbuckling, and Tyrone Power when Zorro. Probably anyone called Tyrone would be bound to have a swashbuckling side. In the staff room with the teachers, on her way to the bank, the head would probably let them see the money in her briefcase and remark: 'That Mr Shale, would you believe it, simply arrived at my room and, in his cheerful, swashbuckling style, flung this lot at me, not even asking for a receipt.'

She stopped playing with the fountain pen and instead put out her hand and touched the money, pressing it down from the top, making the column of paper tighter. Then she took her hand away so the pile slackened upwards again and grew higher. She did that three times. Some would think she didn't believe the loot was real and had to check by touch. Manse saw it different. He reckoned she knew this must be grubby, street money but money just the same, and it thrilled her to get it against the skin of her finger. It gave her closeness to a world separate from her usual world of original-style fountain pens and kids' letters to the Third World. Manse liked watching and stayed quiet. He thought of it as a kind of ritual, such as in church. He said: 'The house itself is interesting, and the conservatory not just insects and flies, believe me! Some lovely plants and flowers, many from abroad. I think you'd enjoy a visit.' She wrote him a receipt saying, 'Prepayment fees, received with thanks.'

It always pleased Shale to know that some of the turnover from trade went into education here, like positive. This idea felt at its strongest today, because of the living currency. It made things more head-on, direct. Ralphy Ember's children went to a school on the other side of the town, also private, naturally. Just like Manse, Ralph wanted to make sure his two stayed out of that comp. jungle. Shale wondered whether Ralphy had ever flung a wedge of money across the head's desk there. Ralphy liked to think he was refined, so maybe not.

Not far from the Spoor roundabout, in a 40 mph limit length of road on their way back to the rectory, an old brown and beige VW camper van overtook the Jaguar, cut in hard ahead and suddenly slowed, a real tactic, making Eldon brake. 'What the fuck?' he said and took one hand off the wheel. He reached under his jacket, chest height.

'It's all right,' Shale said. He was in the back.

'No, it fucking well –'

'It's all right.' The van signalled left and turned into a lay-by. 'Follow her,' Shale said.

'What?' The point was, Eldon stayed jumpy and confused after that mess-up with the Laguna. He thought if you went out on a shoot mission you shot. Well, perhaps. He did have a case. But there could also be some subtle facets to life that you had to take care of. Knowing such things and being aware of facets was probably the difference between a leader and a fucking chauffeur in a fucking comical cap, but correct.

They parked behind the VW. Eldon kept a hand under his jacket. Carmel left the van and walked fast to the Jaguar. She had on lightweight cream trousers and a man's striped shirt, not tucked in at the waist. Manse thought she looked good, though, of course, still a bit too heavy, and very upset. Well, the way she drove her clapped-out tin box would of showed that, anyway. Women did wrangle. You had to put up with it. Often they had something to wrangle about, and not just weight. 'It's a friend, from before your time, Eldon,' Mansel said. 'A very considerate lady who keeps in touch with her parents regardless.' He opened the rear door and she climbed in with him.

'I thought I recognized you, Carm, just from the back of your head.' Her hair was dark, worn straight to her shoulders. Eldon half turned in the driver's seat, watching her, no sex in his eyes, just watching.

'I've been hanging about, driving about, sauntering about, hoping I'd spot you on the way home from somewhere,' Carmel said. 'Obviously, I couldn't call or phone, could I? Your wife's there now, isn't she, re-rectorified?' A snarl arrived with this. Carmel could do snarls, although she said her name came from a mountain with prophets on in the Bible.

The Jaguar had that glass partition between the front and rear seats which Manse hardly ever closed, because he loathed snootiness. Good man management said you should not make employees feel they was low grade, and this helped you manage them – that is, keep them low grade. Yes, even when Denzil drove, Manse generally left the partition open and allowed conversation, if you could call what Denz said conversation. 'I like the camper, Carmel,' he said. 'Vintage, almost.'

'For God's sake, what's happening, Manse?' she said.

'Yes, what *is*? Eldon was scared we'd been ambushed, weren't you, Eldon? He's into stress and tension these days.' Manse could borrow a couple of excellent terms from Ms Norvenne.

'You might have got shot, Carmel,' Eldon said. 'Carmel? That your name?'

'Have you sent someone, Manse?' she replied.

'Sent someone where?' Shale said.

'Does she want to see what I look like, then?' Carmel said.

'Who?' Shale said.

'Your damn wife,' Carmel said. 'Dearest reinstalled Sybil. She has to know how jealous she should be, does she, and also who she should watch out for in case I try to come back? Well, I won't. She should relax. I've got someone really true and good now.'

'Is it his van?' Eldon asked. 'This looks like a van of somebody really true and good.'

'That kind of thing could spoil it all for me,' she said.

'What kind of thing?' Shale said.

'He's as angry as I am,' Carmel replied.

'Who?' Shale said.

'Phil, of course,' she said. 'He's bound to wonder. It could turn him off.'

'He's the van man?' Eldon said.

'What happened?' Shale said.

'Oh, you bloody well know what happened, don't you?' Carmel said.

'What happened?' Manse replied.

'Yes, what happened?' Eldon said. 'I can assure you, Mansel is genuinely puzzled and I personally can't offer help, not knowing the situation.'

'Who's he, Manse?' she said.

'Eldon looks after various aspects,' Shale said. 'More than just a chauffeur. The cap's not the full story.'

'Like a Denz figure?' she said. 'Another caddy?'

'Not really, no,' Shale said.

'Have you told him about the two-course pistol feast in Denz's gob?'

'What is it that troubles you?' Shale replied.

'You've had the tale, Manse, haven't you?' she said.

'Which tale?' he said.

'Yes, which tale?' Eldon said.

Carmel said: 'I come out of the flat with Phil –'

'So, Phil *is* the van man, is he?' Shale asked.

'– and nearly straight away I spot some sod taking photographs of us. Squat guy, forties, boozer's heavy red cheeks. He's trying to be secret about it, using a parked car for cover, but, hell, Manse, he's so obvious. I don't know what you're paying him, but I'll tell you he's not worth it.'

'Photographs of you and Phil?' Eldon said.

'Both. But it's me he wants. Phil being there – just an accident.'

'Wants you why?' Manse said.

'*You* tell *me*.'

'He's focusing on you, is he?' Eldon said.

157

'Close-ups of my face.'

'Good taste. Maybe you been discovered, Carmel,' Shale said. 'About time.'

'Don't fuck about, Manse,' she said. 'This is a predicament, and you made it. You've got the pictures, have you? Do you look at them together, you telling her how much more beautiful she is?'

'Who?' Manse said.

'Sybil, your damn wife,' she said.

'There used to be a lot of street photographers around, doing snaps on spec. They back in fashion?' Eldon said.

'You know the street. I sent a change of address card, Manse.'

Shale said: 'Well yes, of course, I know the street, but that don't mean –'

'Just because he received a change of address card doesn't signify Manse sent anyone,' Eldon said.

'Fuck off, spokesperson, will you?' Carmel replied. 'This is between Manse and me as previous items. Do you want to know what he said to me?'

'Who?' Shale said.

'This really riled Phil. We're supposed to be going on a trip to Italy,' Carmel said.

'In the van?' Eldon said. He didn't seem bothered by the swearing. Probably he'd had a lot of it in his career – someone so pushy. This could be a useful lad in a minor post.

Carmel said: 'I shout at the photographer guy, "What's it about, then? Who are you?" He keeps on clicking away, even while he's talking. Brazen.'

'He answered?' Eldon replied.

'He said: "You're Carmel Arlington, once of St James' rectory, yes? I've got it right? And I'd say you're definitely alive in all particulars, wouldn't you?"'

'What's that mean?' Eldon said.

'He's got my biog, hasn't he?' Carmel replied. 'Who could give him that – who could give him the name, St James' rectory? That's why I say, what's it about, Manse? What you trying to do? Is that supposed to scare me?'

'What?' Shale said.

'This guy's answer – "I'd say you're definitely alive, in all particulars, wouldn't you?" If somebody tells you you're alive in all particulars – like *so* bloody obvious I'm alive, isn't it? – if someone says that, what does it mean? Does it mean they're thinking that because I'm alive I could be killed?'

'Have you got enemies, Carm?' Shale said.

'I don't know. Have I?'

'This photographer is taking pictures to prove to someone you're alive, right?' Eldon said.

'Does that make sense?' Carmel said. 'Manse knows I'm alive. He'd have heard if I wasn't.'

'It might not be for Manse,' Eldon said.

'Of course it's not,' Shale said.

'Who then?' Carmel said.

'I don't think we can answer yet,' Eldon said.

Actually, Manse didn't mind this too much, not too much – the way Eldon took over, like replying for both of them. No, Manse didn't mind that too much. Not too much, because he saw maybe he, himself, *could* answer. This would be a point where you spotted another difference between a chauffeur and him. Manse possessed special insights. Hadn't Laurent and Matilda, both, thought that the mess on the stairs must be due to a bad fight, a fatal fight, with Lowri or Patricia or Carmel while the children was over with Sybil and Ivor in Wales? Laurent might have give up worrying about that, but possibly Matilda couldn't, and so the edginess Ms Norvenne had noted, and which Manse himself, as a good father, had noted. Matilda would not tell the school or the Third World what *really* upset her, but suppose she told someone else, and someone else decided that the way to soothe her, reassure her, was to produce pictures of Lowri, Patricia and Carmel obviously still OK. Suppose, suppose. Who'd do that?

When Manse tried to answer this, he had another thought – another thought Eldon couldn't equal or share, being just a fucking chauffeur. It had looked to Manse pretty evident that Matilda in that weird, mysterious, maybe fantasy way of hers suspected ACC Iles went into her bedroom sometime while she was away, as she'd half mentioned to Dauda – but no name for the ACC there. Perhaps she thought Iles *saw* who'd been on the stairs and could say whether it was one of the women.

And, perhaps – another, lousy, frightening perhaps – perhaps she had gone to call on Iles during that mitched lunch hour to ask if he knew anything about the rectory stairs, because she worried and wanted to get some peace through the right answers from Iles. He could be a bullying lout – usually was. But he had his amazing moments of decency and kindness. Manse had never seen any, but people did speak of them now and then, and he half believed it. Iles might pity Matilda and admire her for making the journey. Did he send the photographer? Fat, boozer's face and the insolence – it sounded right for a cop with a camera. And Iles would probably arrange for some police vehicle to take her back to school. The idea of his daughter possibly meeting up with police in a cooperative style dazed Manse, of course, and especially with that famed drool-at-schoolgirls yob, Iles. But Manse knew he had to consider it. The idea made him even more angry with Chandor. Had he caused this terrible move by Matilda? He'd destroy a family if not stopped.

Of course, Shale carried in his wallet with the Monty membership and organ donation cards, French claret by-the-year vintages guide, and other usual stuff, a typed help sheet containing registration numbers, makes and colours of unmarked police cars identified by him and his people around the Valencia and elsewhere. Because of the sort of arrangement with Iles for the sake of peace, these patrols did not usually give no trouble, but you had to be ready in case all that changed one day. Plan B. Ralph Ember and *his* people also contributed, and the list was continually updated and exchanged between the two firms, like the CIA and MI5 swapping insights. Once, during a sweet jokey mood, that fucker Ralphy had told him he shouldn't keep the organ donation card in a breast-pocket wallet because if he got shot by police marksmen trained to aim at the heart, not only would the heart itself get destroyed but also the authorization for the rest of him. Now he had the thought about Matilda and Iles, Manse took the piece of A4 out and unfolded it. Only three silver Astras figured. The third's registration matched the one Ms Norvenne had given him.

'What's that, Manse?' Carmel asked.

'We'll do some inquiries,' Shale replied, putting the paper back into his wallet. 'We might be able to trace the cameraman and find out what's what.'

'It'll be tough,' Eldon said.

'Are you kidding me now, Manse? It wasn't you who sent him?' Carmel said.

'Definitely not us, I can swear to it,' Eldon replied. 'Not at all how we operate, believe me, Carm.' Carmel went back to the VW. Eldon called out: 'Enjoy Rome, do!' The van pulled away. Eldon said: 'Nice piece, Manse.'

'She can be difficult.'

'I could see that, right off. Oh, yes. But obviously devoted. Perhaps difficult *because* obviously devoted. How I'd read it. They can become a nuisance then.'

'Well, yes.'

'But considerately sends a change of address card in case you want to –'

'That's what I mean – difficult. An open card like that. The postman has a giggle, most probably,' Shale said. 'Tells mates. A general joke. *Carmel Arlington is now living at such-and-such, don't you fucking know?*'

'Yes, I guessed she could be awkward.'

'A gem, but she can be awkward.'

'Right,' Eldon replied. 'I wondered if you ordered photos so you can hand them out for identification and get her hit by someone. Is she really making things hard for you? They can be like that. And putting the kilos on? In one way, stupid of her to send the changed address card. Gives a location.'

'I didn't order no photos.'

'No need, as it happens, because I've seen her face to

face and close. I wouldn't depend on photos if you want something done. But she's going to be away in Italy.'

'I didn't order no photos.'

'No, right,' Eldon said. 'You didn't order pictures. Message received. I've got it.'

'I mean it.'

'I said I've got it, didn't I, Manse?'

Shale could tell Eldon didn't believe him. He was a lad who would see some things very clear and some things very clear and very wrong. That's why he was still only a fucking chauffeur and general heavy and would stay there. Eldon drove the Jaguar to his place, not far from where Detective Chief Superintendent Harpur lived in Arthur Street. When Denzil Lake was alive and doing the right-hand man stuff he occupied a small flat at the top of the rectory. But Eldon had a partner and a couple of small children and needed more room. Shale gave him and a few other members of the firm a bit of a subsidy to help with the mortgage as essential staff. You had to, owing to the bottom rung of the housing ladder being so hard to get on these days. In any case, Manse didn't like the notion of Eldon on the premises, with or without his family. Probably once he got in he'd start talking about 'our' rectory. Manse switched to the driver's seat and went home.

In the evening he took Sybil and the children to a performance of the *Messiah*, at St James' church. He felt that if you lived in what used to be the rectory for this church you ought to support any of its special activities by attending and coughing plenty to the funds for reroofing and missionary efforts. The church could not afford to run the rectory now, but, due to certain ventures, he luckily could. And he thought that brought a duty. He went in an ordinary suit, not the special outfit he wore to Ralph Ember's place. The important things here were the sacred music and singing, not how he looked, for fuck's sake. It would be bad to try to steal attention through fine tailoring.

This kind of music and singing, Manse could put up with pretty well. Naturally, the children wanted to dodge out of going, but he told them education should be more than just school, such as finding out about oratorios. This was what the leaflet from the church called the *Messiah*, written by Handel who did many, and all credit to him – at the start of his life German, but then turning English. Manse hoped the children would get familiar with all sorts in the arts. When she kicked up about having to go, he felt like saying to Matilda that that Dauda in the Third World would never have the chance to listen to an oratorio just around the corner even if he existed, an oratorio by a true oratorio expert. But Manse did not mention he'd been up the school and knew about Dauda, and neither of the children seemed to have seen the Jaguar or heard from other kids that a Jaguar was there.

He thought sections of this music might help soothe Matilda and get rid of some of her tension. There were quiet parts, not that blah-blah rowdiness and beat of rap. *Comfort ye, comfort ye, my people.* Great. And, big cheerfulness came, also – *His name shall be called, Wonderful,* really given a true blast by the choir. Manse wondered whether Matilda and Laurent could join this choir soon, as another good link between the rectory and the church. It might help to keep Matilda bucked up. He liked to think of a vicar at the church telling friends that although they'd been forced to let the rectory go, they still had a very pleasant connection with it through the children of Mr and Mrs Mansel Shale, now living there, if Sybil stayed. The end of that line about being called Wonderful said another name was Prince of Peace. Manse loved that idea – a *prince* of peace. Always he looked for peace.

At the end Manse congratulated the vicar on a great show because he liked to encourage this kind of person. Vicars didn't really have any idea what life was like now and how to make enough to run a rectory, but they knew about the past and music, and these was important in their little way. He took the family home and later picked out one of the Heckler and Koch automatic pistols from the wall safe behind his Arthur Hughes and did a tour of the Valencia Esplanade district where he had a lot of people

163

trading. Peace. He wanted to make sure things around the Valencia enjoyed this peace. Also, he would harvest. He had dished out plenty of cash today, on the school fees and in church collection boxes, and needed a refill wad. All right, the notes might give a bulge to his coat, as he said to the headmistress, but you had to have something in your pocket for various purchases.

Obviously, he tried not to use banks much. Banks recorded all their ins and outs and people like Iles could arrange a gaze at these figures – maybe legit, maybe otherwise – if he got suddenly nosy and hard, which he did, often. Or, in fact, which he almost always fucking did. This kind of visit to the Valencia was routine for Manse. He always went in the Jaguar, and almost always alone, say six nights out of the seven. Folk in his firm would not resent the Jaguar or a BMW or Merc because if things developed all right for them they knew these was the sorts of motors they'd buy theirselves. But a Rolls or Bentley they'd regard as showy and royal, with God knows how many layers of paint to stop scratch marks. And they wouldn't like it, either, if he came to the Valencia chauffeured, especially chauffeured by someone under a cap. In leadership you had to think of these things, known as 'employee relations'. Although Manse did fancy a Roller, some sacrifices seemed crucial for the sake of keeping the workforce unbolshy. It would be the same if he was offered a knighthood for his activities in the commercial scene. This would be the *open* commercial scene, of course – the haulage and scrap businesses – not his real money-making side of things relating to the commodities. He'd have to refuse a title, though with full politeness. He thought he would reply that the firm he led was a team and it would not be appropriate for him to accept a special award.

Of course, on the other fucking hand, suppose they asked Ralphy Ember to become a Sir or even a Corporal of the British Empire, that gent would have his 'Yes please, your majestic Majestical' letter on its way back to Buckingham Palace by return or sooner. Already some people called him 'Milord Monty'. If he ever made it to Sir Ralph it would be because he really did the magic on that dregs of dregs club, the Monty, and zoomed it up the social league. But, on the whole, Manse considered that probably neither of them would get picked for accolades by the narrow sods who decided these things in smart state rooms up there. They only dished out gongs to friends they knew from Eton College or Alcoholics Anonymous. This was called The System. Well, Manse had worked out his own system and a lot of it operated here, around Valencia Esplanade.

He parked in Dring Place and then went on foot along the Esplanade itself. Nobody would touch a car belonging to Mansel Shale and the Jaguar was all-round recognized. The Esplanade had tall old houses facing the sea. Probably it got called Valencia Esplanade because in them times you could watch freighters on their way to and from Spain carrying bauxite or lintels or oranges or that kind of thing. Someone had told Manse that the word 'esplanade' itself came from Spain, which could help explain half the name. It might of been Ralphy who mentioned this. Ralphy thought he knew every fucking thing because he went to college as a mature student for a while. Down there they probably had lectures on words such as 'esplanade'.

These houses used to be truly select on account of their size and the outlook – owned by merchants, ships' masters, custom house biggies – but then, when the port trade started to go down, so did the class of the houses. Landlords divided them up into rooms and flats, referred to as 'multi-occupied'. You'd see mattresses, armless teddy bears, old fridges and such in the front gardens, which was not gardens any more. This used to depress Manse, although the multiness meant there was more customers handy to buy stuff from his staff on the street. Now, though, people seemed to realize again these was great, solid houses in a great spot and they was getting done up and going back to one family living there, pretty shrubs or golden gravel out front. This had not knocked sales of the substances too bad here yet, but Manse and Ralph watched the accounts. They might have to get a discussion going on the topic soon, described as 'regentrification', Ralph said. He had a word for everything.

Making his way along the Esplanade, Shale had short chats with several of his pushers. He gave true praise for their work, as any sensible chief of a firm would, and picked up good funds in tens and twenties to rebuild his readies. Obviously, all his reps was totally banned from taking fifties, due to many fakes in circulation. Tens and twenties did cause that bulk, but it had to be and, as Manse said sometimes, it was better to have bulk than bugger all. He went on alone towards the end of the Esplanade, enjoying the breeze off of the bay and the sound of waves curling on to the beach, then pulling back over the pebbles with a grating roar. The sea was not one of Manse's favourite space fillers. He had an idea that one day it would get up over the Esplanade and other Esplanades worldwide and just drown everything – cities, out-of-town shopping centres, TV masts, soccer players' mansions, churches, snooker halls. This dread had been with him since long before the tsunami chaos in Indonesia. That only showed Shale how damn right he might be. He'd always realized Nature could be a total, ungovernable sod. It just went its own way, like that clever maniac, Iles. Cliffs and sea walls was supposed to keep back the great waters, and good luck to them, but any time he walked a coast path he had his fucking fingers crossed and his eyes as sharp as sharp in case he noticed too much forward briny creep. Tonight, though, he considered the sea sounded all right and like what would be termed by estate agents a 'feature' of the area, meaning a happy extra, such as a train station or bowling green. Esplanade houses given the treatment made more than half a million these days.

He saw Hilaire Wilfrid Chandor approaching, also alone and on foot, jeans, black open-necked shirt, black slip-ons of most probably decent quality. Shale would of passed him with maybe an RIP nod, nothing more. Obviously, Manse's main thought was Chandor ought to of been morgued after that Laguna outing, and this, plus the previous disgusting behaviour of his troupe, and maybe himself, at the rectory, might prevent ordinary conversation on an Esplanade stroll. It was not something you could go up to an acquaintance and say, *You should be fucking dead, mate, as dead as that character you debased my rectory stairs with*. But Chandor stopped in front of him: 'I knew you came here regularly, Mansel,' he said. 'I planned a one-on-one intercept. So, here we are. I thought it time we talked privately.'

This one-to-one was another that did not have nothing to do with that poet, John Cleats. 'Re what?'

'And talked where we knew there couldn't be that other kind of intercept.'

'If you're referring to phone taps, it's something I fortunately don't never have to worry about,' Mansel said. 'I believe it's only them seriously suspected of something by the police get that kind of intrusion. Is this why you're bothered?'

Chandor gazed into the darkness towards the sea. 'Do you know what this reminds me of?' he replied.

'What what reminds you of?'

'The breakers.'

'They come and go.'

'In the film, *Atlantic City USA*, a young crook and an aged crook, Burt Lancaster, make their way along the promenade, the old man full of tales – probably false – about his big-time past as a villain. The young crook says: "I'd never seen the Atlantic ocean until just now." Lancaster replies: "Ah, you should have seen the Atlantic ocean in those days."'

Manse guessed this might be meant as a kind of joke. But what Lancaster said seemed damned sensible to Manse, because in the old days the ocean had turned out to be more or less OK, and usually stayed on the proper side of the promenade, the ocean side. This was simple to prove. You couldn't tell it would do that for ever in the future, though, could you? Manse hated smartarse lines from films. 'I don't watch crime movies,' he said.

'When I say it's time we talked, what I have in mind among other matters is that episode with the Laguna recently.'

'Laguna?' Manse replied.

'Chauffeur up front, you in the back, and in a project

where you and he could have scatter-gunned and seen off not just myself and colleagues but that ugly cop, as well. I regard this as a magnificent act of mercy on your part and, yes, of statesmanship, Mansel. It's one to which I must respond. The chauffeur looked angered by the failure to clinch, which makes me certain this humane order came from you – probably as a second thought. Thank you. But a touch-and-go moment? I'm grateful yet also worried. That's why I'd like talks now, before any question of a repeat.'

'Laguna?' Manse replied.

'It's all right. I don't think Harpur noticed you.'

'Noticed me where?'

'This was a beautifully planned coup, I'll give you that.'

Some would regard that as a compliment but not Manse. What this jolly boy meant was Manse could handle all the scheming and backroom, blueprint stuff, like some clerk or field marshal, but failed when the moment came in the actual street, the way Panicking Ralphy so often did. Shale resented any sort of comparison with Ember.

'And perhaps after that rectory incident we deserved it, I'll give you that, too,' Chandor said.

A wooing time?

'But then, bent low in the Laguna, you get a sudden creative vision of what could be possible between you and me, Mansel – the positives. And you have the guts even so late to countermand execution of . . . countermand execution of the executions. A decisive word, up from the rear leg space to the driver. This was maturity. This was, indeed, statesmanship.'

A wooing time. 'You refer now to the dead one on my rectory stairs – I've never heard of a filthier trick than that,' Shale said. 'It might be all right for London, but this is a tidy town.'

'Excessive, undoubtedly.'

'In someone's extremely personal, cherished family home,' Shale replied.

'Trove. You mention London, Mansel – Trove did a slice of work there for me and really skimmed. I mean, really. We're talking up to a hundred grand in dribs and drabs.

He thought I hadn't noticed – like that secretary woman who milked her bosses' bank accounts of millions in the City of London. Well, me, I *did* notice, I notice just before he finds I've moved down here and comes looking for more work – and more skimming. So he had to go.'

'He didn't have to go on my fucking stairs. His partner's around, searching. There's sadness to this. And cruelty.'

'Meryl? I'm not sure whether she knew what sort he was, although she must have realized he brought in exceptionally big earnings, not shop assistant's pay. She came to us at my marina offices, yes. Of course she did. He'd told her he had property contacts, so she visits all the firms here that do property and she soon reaches us. Plus she's absorbed some sort of buzz locally, I'd guess. She's with a reporter and a couple of kids. I understand her concern.'

'What kids?'

'These are Harpur's kids. They're sort of looking after her. She's been to the police. They're not going to do much, are they? Britain has 200,000 people go missing every year. Trove's just another one. We treat Meryl and her little group absolutely right – with kindness and sympathy and promises to keep an eye and ask around. But, obviously, we can't help.'

'No, you can't tell them he was put dead on my stairs – the stairs of a fucking much-respected Church property dating right back.'

'I hope she'll return to London and try to forget all this. I've said before – I do regret that now, the body and lifting the pix. It wasn't necessary, Manse. We just wanted you to know we were in the neighbourhood as a permanency and serious about commerce. I'd told my people this was our aim – to give you some kind of unmistakable and perhaps mildly forceful message, a cautionary shock, and left the detail to them. We see someone beautifully established like you and your firm, and we know that an ordinary approach and request in search of an entrée to the trade scene will get rejected. I wanted a little out-of-the-blue pressure – something to make you receptive, Mansel, amenable. A sign. Or known as semiotics. But my people overdid things. Luckily we were able to put matters more or less to rights for you following your highly justified phone call.' He sighed: 'Yes, Graham Trove. Ask anywhere around Eltham and they'll tell you, a skimmer. And then the cheek of wanting to go on further operations with us. I can see how this would inflame some of my people, but that doesn't excuse the brutishness of their behaviour. You're right – they've witnessed and taken part in a lot of very rough battling in London and, unfortunately, bring those standards here.'

More threats. Shale wanted an end to this meeting. It was not good to be seen talking to Chandor and gazing conjoint towards the environmental sea like buddies. 'I've got some other calls to make,' he said.

'Two things forced me to accelerate my programme, and got me down here solo to put a proposal, Mansel,' Chandor replied. 'One, obviously, the Laguna operation. This shows real possible peril for me – its flair and aptness. I can do without a further attempt, thanks, which I might not live through. But, then also its positive side, the cancellation. I take that as promising, Mansel.'

'Where is all this supposed to have happened, for fuck's sake, the "Laguna operation"?'

'In addition, I note the invite from Ralphy Ember to Low Pastures for you and your wife,' Chandor replied. 'My information is, this never happened before. I couldn't say why – snobbery? Ralph's disdain? – but apparently that's how it was. What does it show? I'd say it plainly reveals an increased closeness. This could make conditions even trickier for me, couldn't it? Your cartel with Ember, looked on permissively by Iles, getting stronger, more solid. And so, I decide I should get in at once, before these new conditions have properly settled and cemented.'

'Low Pastures?' Shale said.

'You and your missus, acceptable guests at the manor house – unprecedented as I hear.'

'I don't care what you fucking hear.'

'I put a tail on Trove's girl, Meryl Goss, after she called on us, naturally. She could be stirring some delicate material and I wanted her monitored. Harpur's kids go off – go home, I suppose – but a couple of my folk follow

Meryl and her pal, the girl reporter, to the Monty. They'd presumably be looking for Ralph Ember as a font of gossip. Rumour reaches him via club members, and perhaps more than rumour. He's apparently not there and they decide to go out to his home. My lads follow. They get their car out of sight and watch from behind cover inside the grounds – plenty of shrubs and trees. The house is lit up and there seems to be some kind of occasion going on. The women – Goss and the reporter – get invited in, just the same. Obviously, we can't know what they discovered, if anything. After a while they come out and drive away in the journalist's Renault. My contingent follow again.

'But Meryl Goss goes to a Bed and Breakfast in Quith Street and that seems to be the end of activities for the night. The journalist turns towards the middle of the city and is obviously also on her way to bed. Our lads decide they can restart the watch on Meryl Goss from the boarding house next morning but are curious about what goes on that night at Low Pastures – or they *make* themselves curious. They know I'm interested in Ember – am interested in *any* firm that seems to dominate. And, additionally, Mansel, these are two of the people I savaged recently for what they'd done at your rectory. Most likely they were scared of coming to me with nothing, scared of getting blamed for a second cock-up. So, they go back and put an eye on Ralphy's place again. Soon, they see the famous Jaguar arrive, chauffeur in place, cap on, and you and your wife come out from Low Pastures – you in a terrific suit, they said, and a great mauve shirt, aglint under an external security light. Ralph Ember also appears, to say goodbye. They feel they've got something to report now, don't they? And me, I'd agree. Significant. A suit like that.'

'A social outing. Routine.' Shale had listened for any accidental hint from Chandor that he personally was at the rectory for all those unforgivable events, and perhaps in the party who followed Meryl Goss, also. He heard no evidence for either, but believed it about both. Manse wanted to focus his hate on some*body*, not on some firm. It seemed obvious to him that when Chandor spoke of the suit and shirt this was mockery, not meant as a true compliment.

'That kind of tarted-up mateyness with Ralph is in some ways a difficulty for me, as I've mentioned,' Chandor said. 'But in some ways a plus, Mansel. I like to look for advantages in even the most dire events – seemingly dire. That's how I've progressed. It means Ember listens to you, respects your views. Well, certainly. It's probably always been so. I gather there are conferences between you and him at your house, as well as the regular beanfeasts for your respective mobs at the Agincourt Hotel. But this elevation to treasured guest level at Ralph's manor house emphasizes his recognition of your status and wisdom. As I see it, Mansel, you could talk to him about possible advantages in opening up your alliance to a third member – a third member with a store of very dynamic, very workable, very tested ideas, believe me. This wouldn't take anything from you, from either of you. It's expansion, not division. I've put in a lot of thought on potential development of the substances commerce here.

'Yes, *you* speak to Ralph. It would be no good coming from me. He'd see it as a try at levering, as menaces, even. And if, despite your recommendation, Ember is unhelpful – well, I admit, that's possible. He's panicky but he can also turn stubborn, I expect. I've had a thorough look at the Monty layout, though, you know. All right, there's a poetic shield. And it's very . . . very . . . well, poetic – just a bit of decor, no protection except from some hasty amateur chancer who pops in at the door, is afraid to go further, and tries a shot or two. And this only if Ralph happens to be where he's supposed to be behind the bar. That's not how Ember would be done in a properly man-aged ploy if he remained obstructive. I suggest, Mansel, that what we have to ask about someone who believes a shield of that kind can possibly provide real protection, is whether he's capable of leading a major firm. Have his wits and judgement begun to go? Has the famous inclina-tion towards panic become dominant in him? Can you afford association with such a one, and dependence, to a degree, on such a one?'

172

Chapter Eight

Harpur could tell his daughters wanted a major discussion. These sessions usually made him very uneasy, and he would have liked to dodge out, but the girls came suddenly and together into the sitting room at 126 Arthur Street and sat opposite him, in that planned way they had, undemure, dogged, foolable, of course, but not *easily* foolable. 'Chandor,' Jill said.

'This is a property firm on the marina, dad,' Hazel said.

'Right,' Harpur replied. 'You've spoken about it before. Featured in "the buzz", yes?'

'We went to see them,' Jill said.

'Who?' Harpur said.

'I told you – Chandor and his people,' Jill said. 'Chandor himself and Rufus Somebody and Maurice Somethingelse.'

'I meant, who went to see them?' Harpur said.

'That's Meryl and the reporter girl, Kate, who's hoping for a story one day, and us,' Jill said.

'Why were you with them?' Harpur said.

'Oh, yes, we went along,' Jill replied.

'Why?' Harpur said.

'Oh, yes, we went along,' Jill replied.

'Meryl had a list of property companies and she's called on quite a lot, showing the picture of Graham Trove and so on,' Hazel said. 'She wanted the research to be thorough. We went to some with her. Plus, as you said, dad, she'd heard some talk about Chandor. So now she thinks it's Chandor for sure. She was going to give up and return to London, her holiday time being over. Instead of that, though, she'll stay and do more inquiries about Chandor. She told her boss in London.'

'She wonders if they'll keep her job for her, but she doesn't care, because of Chandor,' Jill said. 'This is truly a mission. This is a matter of love for Graham Trove.'

'She's nearly certain,' Hazel said.

'Of what?' Harpur replied.

'That this company, Chandor, was the one Graham came to – what he called his "contact" here,' Jill said. 'The question is, what happened? Obviously, we'll try to help her.'

'Help her what?' Harpur said.

'Dig,' Jill said.

'Dig?' Harpur said.

'Dig into this Chandor, to find what's what,' Jill said. 'Yes, he's the one I had the buzz about at school and down the bus station – drugs and that. Property only a mask. Maybe Meryl's partner, Graham, isn't too clean, either, or why does he go to Chandor? But she doesn't seem to know anything about this. We haven't asked her if Graham could be crooked. That would seem cruel.'

'Chandor's name's Hilaire, would you believe?' Hazel said. 'Like some writer.'

'He seemed all right, and the people with him, but you can't tell, can you?' Jill said. 'I mean, if they've got rid of someone, and if the property side is just a cover, they might put on a sweet face to fool us – *And would the children like a fizzy drink?* – that kind of eyewash to Meryl and Kate.'

'I don't want you to talk like that,' Harpur replied.

'Like what?' Jill said. '"Eyewash"? That's what it was, most probably.'

'"Got rid of someone." "Just a cover." They're accusations based on nothing. And I don't think you should be involved, anyway,' Harpur said.

'No, not based on nothing,' Hazel said.

That made Harpur worried – more worried. Hazel could sound very factual, very grave.

'Don't think we should be involved in what, dad?' Jill said.

'In what you call "digging" into the Chandor company,' Harpur said.

'Do you think it's dangerous, dad?' Hazel said.

Yes, dangerous, dangerous. This was a firm that advertised how dangerous it might turn out to be by leaving bodies on stairs. 'I just don't believe it's sensible,' Harpur said.

'Why not? Because it's dangerous?' Jill said.

'Because it's not your role,' Harpur said.

'Whose role *is* it?' Jill said. 'Yours? But you're not doing anything, are you?'

'At this point, there isn't anything *to* do,' Harpur said.

'At which point?' Jill replied.

'Now,' Harpur said. 'I've nothing to go on.'

'Is that right?' Jill said.

More or less. He had Iles's intercepts and, possibly, Iles's view of things from Matilda Shale's bedroom and his obvious recognition of the man in Meryl Goss's photograph, which might mean Matilda's bedroom was more than possibly. None of this could be disclosed to his daughters, nor to anyone else. 'Of course it's right,' he said. 'We can't act without information.'

'Someone's missing,' Hazel said.

'That has been reported and the usual procedures are operating,' Harpur said.

'Which?' Jill said.

'Which what?' Harpur said.

'Which usual procedures?' Jill said.

'There are established, reliable procedures for tracing an adult missing person.'

'But they're no good, are they, and *not* reliable?' Jill said. 'He hasn't been found.'

'Early days,' Harpur replied.

'Meryl doesn't think so,' Jill said. 'She's scared. And she's sure Chandor's lot know something.'

'Why is she?' Harpur replied. 'It's only because you've been giving her the "buzz" stuff.'

'If you think it's dangerous, dad, doesn't that show there's something wrong about Chandor?' she said.

'I didn't say it was dangerous,' Harpur said. No, he had made sure he did not say it.

'But you think it is, don't you?' Jill said. 'I can tell. Your voice is rough and sharp.'

'Meryl believes Chandor had her followed,' Hazel said. 'Maybe even followed her himself.'

Hazel's ace.

'You see, dad? Why would he do that if there wasn't something dark going on?' Jill said.

'We don't know that he did. What makes her think Chandor had her followed?' Harpur said.

'She spotted someone,' Jill said. 'How else do you find out you're being followed?'

'Jill and I came home after that meeting with Chandor, but in the evening Meryl and Kate went to Ralph Ember's club, the Monty, because they'd heard he picks up a lot of gossip from his riff-raff customers,' Hazel said. 'He wasn't there, so they went to his house.'

'A dinner party going on there,' Jill said. 'Ralph Ember introduces them to Mansy Shale and his wife. Naturally, Kate recognized Shale, anyway – another drugs prince, isn't he? She's a local paper reporter – knows the scene. Meryl says he's done up in a crazy old suit that someone bigger most probably wore for the Armistice celebrations in 1918, and a mauve shirt. Like an important occasion.'

'But Meryl and Kate discover nothing,' Hazel said.

'Except Ralphy invited Mansy to a dinner party at Low Pastures,' Jill replied. 'Kate is surprised because the rumour around for ages was Ralph Ember would not let Mansy into the house, he being as crude as crude. She thinks something vital is happening. She believes she's on to what's called in the Press a "scoop".'

'Anyway, Meryl and Kate Mead leave,' Hazel said. 'They're in Kate's car and making for Quith Street, where Meryl's staying. In her mirror Kate suspects she spots the tail. A Toyota. It stays well back, so they couldn't get the reg, but Meryl thinks three men aboard.'

'It might be nothing at all,' Harpur said, 'just people going in the same direction.'

'Yes, it might, but it wasn't,' Jill said.

'The Toyota stays with them and parks at the top of Quith Street when Meryl and Kate pull in at the boarding house,' Hazel said.

'Meryl goes in. Her room's in the front and she takes a peep outside from around the edge of the curtains,' Jill said. 'She thinks there was a man on foot hanging about on the pavement – like that scene in *Casablanca* on Movie TV when Paul Henreid and Ingrid Bergman are being watched. He's in the shadows but Meryl believes he could be one of the people from Chandor's office.'

'"Suspects". "Thinks",' Harpur said. '"Believes".'

'Corl?' Hazel said. 'Maurice Corl? So, Meryl guesses that the Toyota had been with them since the Chandor interview, but they hadn't noticed earlier on their visits to the Monty and Low Pastures.'

'She looks up the street and the Toyota's gone. Maybe they had something else to do, and left one man to keep an eye on Meryl,' Jill said. 'And this man they left – he's got some big title.'

'Director of Strategic Planning,' Hazel said, 'if it was Corl.'

'Yes, "if",' Harpur replied.

'He's supposed to be Director of Strategic Planning, and yet he's doing a night watch shift in the street,' Jill said. 'What sort of a firm is that, dad? I mean, it's like Prince Philip on sentry go at Windsor. What's it mean, Director of Strategic Planning? Snoop?'

'I think Meryl Goss should go back to London now,' Harpur replied.

'That's what I mean,' Jill said.

'What?' Harpur said.

'Your voice rough and sharp,' Jill said. 'Anxious.'

'You're afraid for her?' Hazel said.

'Yes, it's foolish of Meryl to risk her job,' Harpur said.

'Is that the only risk?' Hazel asked.

'I think she needs protection in her quest,' Jill said. 'That's what it is – a quest. Me and Hazel must be near her

177

and ready whenever we can arrange it. The reporter's not always available. The paper puts her on other work.'

'"Hazel and I",' Harpur said.

'Oh, great! You'll help? So, it's Hazel and you and me,' Jill said.

'No, I meant you should say "Hazel and I" not "Me and Hazel",' Harpur said.

'Whatever,' Jill said. 'The important thing is, are you going to help Hazel and I look after her?'

'"Hazel and me",' Harpur replied. '"Help Hazel and me".'

'Oh, God,' Jill said.

'What does she mean when she says "dig"?' Harpur asked, knowing what she meant and unhappy with it.

'Oh, you know, dad – dig,' Jill said.

'How does she dig into the Chandor company and his activities?' Harpur said.

'Sort of . . . well, dig,' Jill replied.

'Focus on him and his outfit only,' Hazel said.

'He's what's called "in the frame",' Jill said.

'Yes, but how does she intend doing it?' Harpur said. He felt he was losing them. They had told him as much as they thought he should know. 'If she's going to ask questions all round about Chandor he'll hear of it.'

'Is that dangerous?' Jill said.

Yes, dangerous. 'He might resent it,' Harpur said. 'The implications.'

'Are they dangerous?' Jill replied.

'Meryl Goss thinks Graham's dead,' Hazel said.

'No,' Jill yelled.

'Has she told you that?' Harpur said.

'No, but I can see it in her face,' Hazel said.

'No, no, we must search,' Jill said.

'It's a hunt for the truth now, not a search for him,' Hazel replied.

'Stop saying that, Haze. Stop!' Jill said.

'Meryl believes he was killed,' Hazel said.

'This is double guesswork,' Harpur said. 'You're guessing that's what she thinks and, if she *does* believe that, she's guessing, too.'

But not bad guesswork.

'So why hasn't his body been found?' Jill said.

'These are smart people,' Hazel said.

Yes, they were smart people, and Harpur did not want his daughters running against them. He didn't want Meryl Goss running against them, either. But mostly he thought about his daughters. They were *his* focus.

'I hate thinking he might be dead,' Jill said. 'So sad for her.' She sniffed a little but did not weep.

'We all hate it. But he might be,' Hazel said.

Jill sat stiff, staring at nothing much, as far as Harpur could tell, perhaps in a bit of shock. After a while she said: 'If he's been killed and Meryl starts *really* poking about, digging, she might get . . . I mean, she might not be safe herself.'

'That's why I think she should stop now, go back to London,' Harpur said.

Jill turned the stare on to him. 'Signifying *you* think he's been killed, dad,' she said.

'Signifying I think she's better off out of it,' Harpur said.

'Can you arrange protection for her?' Hazel said.

'There aren't any grounds,' Harpur said.

'We've just given you enough grounds, dad, haven't we?' Jill replied.

'You mean, because she might have been tailed?' Harpur said.

'No might,' Jill said. 'It happened.' She had kept the stare on Harpur, an appraisal stare. 'It's like something holds you back, dad. It's like you've got information but can't use it, or won't.'

'And what information could I possibly –' The phone rang and Harpur felt glad he didn't need to complete this thought. He went into the hall to answer. Iles said: 'They've got a bit of an awkward situation at the service flats in Pendine Road North, Col. Linklater House, Number 22.'

'What awkward situation, sir?'

'This is Matilda's brother.'

'Laurent Shale?'

'I'm getting over there personally now,' Iles replied. 'I feel obliged.'

'Why?'

'Yes, I'm getting over there now, personally.'

'What is this address?' Harpur said. 'Whose?'

'You'd better get there, too.'

'I'd like to know what the –'

'It's part of things, Harpur.'

'Right. I'll come.'

'I'm sure you will,' Iles said.

'But what's it about?'

'Manse has been informed. He'll be there. Possibly Sybil and Matilda, also. It's not just the girl who's disturbed, you see. We make a mistake in thinking boys are unshakeable. For instance, Harpur, as a youngster I was remarkably sensitive. People spoke of it.'

'And are now, sir. I've often heard folk mention it.'

'Which folk? Have you got names?'

'Many. But what's Laurent Shale done?'

'Number 22, Linklater House, Pendine Road North is occupied by a Carmel Arlington,' Iles said. 'I have a captioned photograph of her outside it.'

'Manse's Carmel?'

'As was, perhaps. She has a partner there now, Philip Dell. Some of my photographs show both. I gather they're away in Italy. A camper van. The boy went looking for Carmel and became disturbed when he couldn't find her at Flat 22. If you ask me, Col, he's like his sister and thinks something bad-to-the-point-of-frightful happened to one of those women in the rectory while they were away. Perhaps he was especially fond of Carmel. Or perhaps hers is the only address he has of the three. He turns obsessive and goes there to check she's all right. He gets unhinged when he can't, kicking at the door and yelling. What I mean by sensitive. It can be a thing with the exceptionally sensitive, Col. They will become unhinged.'

'That right, sir?'

'What's that mean, you sly fucker?'

'What?'

'"That right, sir?" Are you hinting *I* grow unhinged sometimes because my sensitive side cannot bear the thought of you with my wife?' So as utterly to disprove unhingedness, the ACC kept his tone to only a moderate shriek, and very little surplus spit interfered with his consonants or seemed to clog the mouthpiece.

'First the girl comes to see you, now this,' Harpur replied.

'Possibly a troubled mind takes a little longer to show itself in a boy than a girl. But the troubles are there, just the same, deep inside. It takes only a minor setback to bring them out. His behaviour is such that neighbours ring us, alarmed. I can show him the photos, to ease his mind, poor kid. Carmel spotted the photographer, so the photos catch her irate and pugnacious, but obviously alive.'

'These are the photographs of all three women that you had done for Matilda?'

'If she comes with Manse she can see them, too. Fortunate. I couldn't work out how to get them to her without seeming to – seeming to show an improper interest in a young girl, Harpur.'

'That sort of thing doesn't usually bother you, sir.'

'Do I go to her parents or schoolteacher and say I've got some photographs to show her? I'm an ACC, for God's sake. I mentioned her multi-pleated skirt and the socks to you, did I? Very white socks.'

'I think so. Your larynx sort of seized up.'

'I'm an ACC, for God's sake.'

'It can be a burden.'

'Look, I don't like talking about this sort of thing on an open line, Col. There's a hell of a lot of illegal intercepts these days.'

Harpur went back into the sitting room. 'I have to go out,' he said.

'Is this to do with Graham Trove?' Jill asked.

It might be, in some roundabout fashion. As Iles had said, 'Part of things.' 'No, not at all,' he replied.

'But, obviously, an emergency,' Jill said.

'An incident of some kind,' Harpur said.

'Why can't Graham Trove be an emergency?' Hazel asked.

If his body turned up, he would be. 'That was Mr Iles on the phone,' Harpur replied.

'Did he ask about Hazel?'

'Quiet, mange,' Hazel said.

'He's gone cool since helping with Scott,' Jill said. 'No, not cool. He's gone decent. Amazing!'

'Keep out of it, earwig,' Hazel said.

When Harpur arrived at Linklater House, Pendine Road North, Sybil Shale said: 'Yet more brass?'

'There's no need for this – all you high officers here as well as the other cops because a lad goes a bit haywire,' Mansel said. 'That's all – a bit haywire.'

'King-pin Iles and now his sidekick turn up after a kid makes a small scene,' Sybil said. 'Crazy. Or do I miss something?'

'Laurent has been rather upset, Col,' Iles said. 'These kind neighbours – Mr and Mrs Parry looked after him.'

'He seemed so frantic, so desperate,' Mrs Parry said. 'Attacking the door.'

'A bit haywire,' Manse Shale said. 'Everyone knows it can happen with boys.'

Iles said: 'Laurent came here looking for someone and when he couldn't find her he became –'

'Became really beside himself,' Mr Parry said. 'Calling her name – "Carmel," "Carmel," "Carmel, where are you? Carmel, are you all right, tell me you're all right?"'

They were in the sitting room of the Parrys' flat, Number 24, next to 22. 'We told him Carmel had gone to Italy in the camper van with Phil. But he wouldn't believe it,' Mrs Parry said. 'He seemed to think something terrible had happened to her, not here but elsewhere. I mean, really terrible.'

Laurent said: 'The mess at the top of the stairs – it's only sauce, you know. Definitely. A little accident, that's all.' He was sitting with a glass of water in one hand on a long, loose-covered settee. He looked pale and restive, but he kept the glass upright and gave his statement perfectly, as though pre-recorded. The loose covers had a dark red Regency-type stripe on a silver background. The wallpaper continued this Regency theme.

'He said this before,' Mrs Parry said, 'about the sauce. I don't understand.'

'Definitely only sauce,' Matilda said. She had on a navy track suit, not the pleated skirt, and trainers, with no socks, so Iles might be fairly all right.

'I asked him, "Which stairs?"' Mr Parry said. 'Did he mean the stairs to the flats? He said, "No." But he didn't say *which* stairs. There's something on his mind.'

'It's only sauce,' Laurent said.

'Definitely only sauce,' Matilda said.

'This would be an unfortunate incident at home, but all put right now,' Mansel said.

Mr Parry said: 'What we don't follow is how the accident with sauce . . . we don't follow how this accident with the sauce is connected with . . . well, why it would make Laurent come here looking for Carmel, and so urgent, so pressing.'

'I wanted to see her,' Laurent said. 'But she's not here. I know this is her address. She sent a card. Where is she? Where is she? That was only a little accident with sauce, but where is she?' His voice suddenly became a howl, almost like Iles in one of his sensitive fits.

'She's gone to Italy, son,' Mr Parry said.

'People say that,' Laurent answered, 'but where *is* she?'

'We decided we should all come over as a family,' Mansel said.

'It's a real damn palaver, isn't it, but isn't it?' Sybil said. 'I'm his damn mother but we're all here because he's bawling about some woman lodger who's at the rectory for . . . for what . . . weeks at a time, and with no real standing, none at all? So hurtful, so disgraceful. What will Mr and Mrs Parry think of our family, our household, Mansel? Did you ever consider the likely effect on the children of bringing these creatures into the property?'

'Luckily, I have some photographs,' Iles replied.

'Photographs of what?' Sybil said.

'Oh, yes, these will settle things down, I'm sure,' Iles said. 'All of them automatically date-captioned and wholly convincing proof that not just Carmel but other rectory guests are in bonny shape.' He had a briefcase near the armchair where he sat and picked this up now, opened it and spread about a dozen snaps of Carmel, Patricia and Lowri on the pink fitted carpet. In some of the Carmel shots, what must be Philip Dell also appeared.

'Yes, this is Carmel,' Mrs Parry said, 'taken in the road outside. And Phil. I don't know the others.'

'I should bloody well hope not,' Sybil replied.

'Why have you got these photos, Mr Iles?' Mansel said.

'As I understand it, all these dates are after the incident with the sauce at the rectory,' Iles replied. 'So, they're all right.'

'Again, I don't get this,' Mr Parry said.

Laurent smiled. 'Yes,' he said.

'Oh, yes,' Matilda said. 'Thank you, Mr Iles.'

'Yes, thank you, Mr Iles,' Laurent said.

'How would *you* like it, Mrs Parry?' Sybil said.

'What?' she said.

'I'm their mother, but these two seem more worried about three . . . three on-call part-time helpers with no blood connection whatsoever,' Sybil said.

'Not blood,' Laurent said, 'not at all, it was definitely sauce. Dad will tell you.'

Iles pointed down at the photographs: 'I don't claim you can see in Carmel and Phil's faces the certainty that they will soon be setting out on a trip to Italy, but they are clearly very close to each other in spirit as well as physically, and to me seem the kind who would love to take a camper van and go paired into Europe. This entirely explains her absence. I know Harpur feels the same.'

'I believe the Chief Constable will wish to send a personal letter of thanks to Mr and Mrs Parry for their prompt and caring response to today's challenging events,' Harpur replied.

'Why have you got these photos, Mr Iles?' Mansel said.

'Because they build dossiers on people like you,' Sybil said. 'They have to know it all, and document it all. I don't suppose there's a pic of *me* in their collection, though. I'm wife and mother but it's these marginals who get noticed. I don't know whether you've got children, Mrs Parry. If so, you'll recognize my feelings. Not everyone appreciates the holiness and force of family bonds, the sanctity of the family home, especially a former rectory.'

'Harpur wouldn't be too good on those bonds,' Iles said. His voice changed again, not to the thin, breathless squeak that came when he spoke of items such as Matilda's socks, but now more like the beginnings of a full Iles scream. 'Harpur is the sort who'd actually ask Mansel whether he wanted copies of these girl pix. Harpur's not one to show delicacy towards the marriage of others. I appreciate that there are children present, so I'll phrase this delicately. But, it's quite well known, for instance, that, having decided he wanted my wife, Harpur simply –'

'Camper vans have almost all the comforts of a caravan, I always think,' Harpur said, 'but escape the tricky driving problems that towing can often bring. A caravan will sometimes veer away from –'

Iles said: 'At times, oh, yes, this took place in the sanctity of my own home, Idylls, while I was away on courses. Harpur would be entirely indifferent to the degree of betrayal of a very senior colleague involved in –'

'I'll check whether Laurent has damaged the door of 22 in case it needs patching up on security grounds,' Harpur said.

'He can be like that,' Iles said.

'Which?' Sybil replied.

'Which what?' Iles said.

'Like abusing the sanctity of your home or fretting about the security of someone else's,' Sybil said.

Matilda said: 'In school, we did a pretend letter to someone in the Third World telling him what life here was like. Even if this had happened before I wrote the letter I don't think I'd put it in because someone in the Third World

185

would not understand why Laurent and I were so worried, but not now we've seen the pictures.'

'The Third World will soon catch up on all that kind of thing,' Iles said. He gathered the photos together and put them back in his briefcase with a finality shove, as if proclaiming the crisis over, the women utterly the past and their pictures of no concern to Manse. This was Iles in his Marriage Guidance mode.

He and Harpur went down with the Shales to the entrance of Linklater House. Manse's Jaguar must have been waiting in some parking spot from which the driver could see the doorway and it drew in now, the chauffeur wearing a cap. 'Ah, this is the new, skull-intact Denzil, is it?' Iles said. 'Eldon Dane.'

'Do you see what I mean about a dossier on you, Manse?' Sybil said.

When the Shales had gone, Harpur and Iles went into a nearby bar. It was a famous roughhouse. Iles wore civilian clothes today. He bought himself a port and lemonade mixed and Harpur a gin and cider mixed. They sat in a corner. 'We can defend this, Col,' Iles said.

'People in this sort of place might think port and lemon a quaint drink for a man.'

'Which people?'

'Well, customers generally.'

Iles stood and walked to a group of big men in dark suits sitting in another corner of the bar. The ACC looked small and slender against them. He carried his drink ahead of him in his right hand. 'Do any of you louts think I'm at all quaint because I ask for port and lemon?' he inquired.

'You're Iles, yes?' one of them said.

'Iles,' Iles said. 'Does that matter?'

'Drink whatever you like, Mr Iles,' another of them said. 'That's your right.'

'Thank you. What are you scheming here – a bullion heist, a kidnapping?' Iles replied.

'You drink what you like, Mr Iles. Your taste for port and lemon is known worldwide.'

Iles came back and sat with Harpur. 'Obviously, I'm concerned about Shale, Col. He's part of the fabric.'

'Which fabric is that, sir?'

'Syb won't stay. She wants tranquillity. Children's spiritual agonies bore her. That episode at Linklater House – a trial to her. Wales rebeckons. And if she goes, where does that leave dear Manse? Carmel's with Phil now, vanning. In the pix he looks as if he could be genial, though he's not actually genial as portrayed, because of Carmel's outrage. Phil had to harmonize, as a partner should.'

'That relationship might not last. Two people in a camper van for a while is a lot of proximity. Not all couples could survive it.'

'Many elderly US couples sell up their homes and follow the sun in camper vans. They regard it as liberation. I've thought of it for myself and Sarah when I retire.'

'But you're exceptionally mild and conciliatory in any domestic setting, I should think, sir.'

'Why should you think it?' Iles had his drink up top his mouth and began to shout across it now. 'Would this be something you discussed with her after one of your damn shag sessions in my fucking property or in some tenth rate hotel?'

Perhaps the landlord was on a relief stint here and did not know the city. He came from behind the bar and said to Iles: 'Kindly watch your language, mate, or I'll have to put you out.'

'You'll have to fucking *what*?' Iles replied.

'He'll be fine once the drink starts to soothe,' Harpur said. 'I can vouch for him more or less one hundred per cent. Or at least forty.' The landlord looked undecided but then nodded once and went back to serving. 'And there are Manse's other two, anyway, sir. Patricia, Lowri,' Harpur said.

'Perhaps. Will they resent being dropped for Sybil, though? Girls like that, kicked out of a rectory because of someone's wife – they'll bear a grudge. I thought they looked as though they bore grudges in the photos, didn't

187

you? Carmel, obviously because she rumbled the camera-man. But Patricia and Lowri, also. In-built grudges.'

'They've been chucked out before and come back,' Harpur said.

'Cumulatively, Col. Look at it cumulatively. And, any-way, Manse has other pressures.'

'Laurent and his mental turmoil? But you've dealt with that, sir. The photographs were a brilliant answer for him and the girl. They're lucky to run across someone of your humanity and perception.'

'These are instinctive with me, Harpur – humanity and perception.'

'Anyone can see those in your face, sir.'

'I do notice people in here staring at me, perhaps read-ing those qualities.'

'No, that's because most of them recognize and hate us, sir.'

'Equally?'

'You more, because of rank,' Harpur said.

Iles smiled, gratified. 'But undercurrents, Col.'

'Which?'

'Manse and Chandor.'

'In what sense?' Harpur replied.

'I happened to see them in concentrated discussion late the other night at the Valencia. I believe the sea was one of their themes, but beyond that, also.'

'You were down there with Honorée on waste ground again?'

'I'm not close enough to hear what they're talking about, but this seemed a long, serious communing, and they're both gazing out in heartfelt fashion towards the briny, like Spencer Tracy and Freddie Bartholomew in *Captains Courageous*. Yes, communing.'

'Did they notice you?'

'An anon hire car,' Iles said.

'Clothes off? No glint off your shoulders or arse skin under street lights?'

'Is Manse being pulled towards Chandor and away from Ralphy, Col? This would be a massive shift in the commercial landscape. Yes, seismic. I don't think I'd like that. I'd seek to prevent it. Has Manse caved in to Chandor because of threats to his paintings, and the body on the stairs?'

'Which body would this be then, sir?'

A few days afterwards, Jack Lamb phoned to arrange another meeting and they went to the foreshore blockhouse, Number 3 on their rendevous list, and perhaps Jack's favourite. This concrete box, never called on to do what it was built for and throw back Adolf, could just the same reach deeply into Lamb's being. 'Manse Shale was in touch, Col. And his chauffeur, Eldon. Why I needed to see you.'

'Shale's buying more pix?'

'Well, he is, he is, but for a very particular and, in some ways, touching purpose,' Lamb said.

'There's an emotional side to Manse.'

'He's worried about his children. They've been suffering, it seems – mentally. But perhaps you know.'

'His children? This would be Matilda and Laurent, yes?' Harpur said. It paid to act dumb with Jack. He grew demoralized if he thought he was bringing old stuff.

'They've had some big shock, both of them.'

'That right?'

'You know this, do you?'

'Manse came out to Darien to see some art, did he?' Harpur replied.

'With the new chauffeur – even more pushy than Denzil.'

'That right?'

'And then I gather Manse's wife has gone again. Done one of her flits. Returned to Wales. This is the tale around. But you probably know that.'

Jack wore his 1930s Italian army officer's gear decked with two rows of distinguished service ribbons, some possibly for the smart use of poison gas in Mussolini's Abyssinia campaign. At his country house, Darien, outside the city, he must have a couple of wardrobes of international services uniforms. He liked impartiality. His trousers were tucked into calf-high black boots, possibly cavalry issue, and he carried a black leather-covered cane.

189

He swiped his right boot now with this, the kind of thing he might have seen in a *Gunga Din* type film on the movie channel. 'Manse is suddenly feeling the father role as a very tricky one. His kids are upset, possibly something to do with that business at the rectory, whatever it was, and now they've lost Sybil again.'

'So he buys paintings. Manse is a complex object, despite how he sounds. Art must be a comfort thing for him – the way some people eat, or buy shoes, to ease their angsts.'

'These will be works for the children, one each,' Lamb said. 'He has the idea that if Matilda and Laurent see a beautiful, joyous, genuine painting on the wall of their rooms it will give them a feeling of . . . of, well, rightness, stability. It's the kind of feeling he gets from his own pix collection – the Pre-Raphaelites and so on, quite a few of which are authentic. This is what I meant when I described Manse's scheme as touching. He's a one-parent family – as you, yourself, are, of course, Col, so you'll sympathize, especially as his children appear to have had bad trauma. The girl thinks there's been an intruder haunting her bedroom and can't rid herself of this fantasy. I told Manse to give her a different room – the rectory has enough – but, no, he wants to meet the problem squarely, sort of exorcise it finally, and will do it, so he thinks, by purifying the room with art. I'm going to make sure both these pictures are impeccably genuine, Col. That's the least I can do for him and the kids.'

'People do rally round for Manse. Mr Iles is the same.'

'Manse is part of the . . . of the . . .'

'Fabric?' Harpur replied.

'That's it, the fabric. And then, Eldon Dane.'

'The chauffeur?'

'We spoke briefly while Manse was upstairs in the gallery selecting his pix. Look, Col, I promised myself that if he chose anything phoney I'd dissuade him, and point him to something honest.'

'He'd appreciate that.'

Lamb paced a bit, a huge, vague outline in the darkness. His boots crunched magnificently on nearly seventy years of very various additions to the cement floor. 'Eldon Dane has the idea that Hilaire Wilfrid Chandor is the one who's brought all the pain to Manse and the children, Col. Manse knows this and tried to what Eldon called "deal with it", but backed out.' Lamb struck the boot again with his cane. This time it was a call for full attention. 'And listen to this, Col – backed out because suddenly Manse concluded Chandor might have an understanding with you . . . with *you*. I don't know what "deal with it" means – he wouldn't specify – but I'd say this boy Eldon carries something. Now, you'll see why I had to contact you again. Eldon talks as though Manse has been knocked so hard by his troubles that he – Eldon – had a holy summons to act for him. Or maybe to act jointly with Manse. It's like a duty that comes with the chauffeur's cap. He says, "We still have to deal with this." It's "we" all the time. Manse's troubles are his and, if Manse can't handle them, Eldon will.' Lamb came close, vast and Italianate, the chest ribbons near Harpur's eyes and almost gaudy, despite the shadows. 'Perhaps *you* have to be "dealt with", Colin. I told Eldon Iles might have an arrangement with Chandor, but you wouldn't. Never your style. I don't know if he believed me.'

'Thanks, Jack.'

'Obviously, you're not going to tell me if there's an understanding between you and Chandor.'

'I've spoken to him and his people in their offices and on the street.'

'And?'

'I was on my own when I spoke to them in the street.'

'And?'

'It might have looked like friendship, like an understanding.'

'Eldon saw you? How?' Lamb said.

'A Laguna passed. I wondered about it. They might have been on a hit trip, but aborted.'

'There could be another trip, Col. Eldon seemed to think the failure is affecting Manse's mind and should be "dealt with". I had the impression Eldon might act solo or get Manse to help, as a kind of cure.'

'If there's another trip, Chandor will be the target.'

'Only?'

'Perhaps his pals.'

'What about yourself?' Lamb said.

'No. You gave me a testimonial, Jack. The chauffeur will accept it, I'm certain. He'll see that Mansel relies on your total trustworthiness in the art game and Eldon will deduce from this that you are credible, impeccable, all through. Which is, of course, correct.'

'Oh, I couldn't let Shale buy forgeries for his afflicted son and daughter, could I?' Because of the lack of light it was hard to be sure, but Harpur thought Jack made a movement with one hand so that his knuckles brushed the medal ribbons. It would be meant to signify that someone with that kind of glorious record would never pass off dud daubs on kids.

Chapter Nine

One of the things about Ralph Ember was he could never be certain when a woman came to see him, apparently on business matters, whether she'd really come for another reason – to be blunt, an appetite reason. Generally, he did not *mind* women noticing his similarity to the young Charlton Heston, but, occasionally, this kind of confusion might result. He felt such uncertainties now with Meryl Goss. She arrived alone today, not with the *Register* reporter, and, obviously, that possibly indicated her scheme. When those two called at Low Pastures during the kindly dinner given for Manse and Sybil, Goss actually mentioned the Heston resemblance and dwelt on it with a degree of rapture, though Margaret had been present and listening. Ralph knew from other encounters that his looks would provoke women into such brazenness and compulsive hunger. At times, Ralph unquestionably felt his beauty a drawback, though there could also be pluses.

Also unquestionably, this piece, Goss, had quite a few pluses herself – a neat, lively front frame, worldly arse, teeth very white and not too big, smooth neck. The spiked hair nauseated him – Ralph used to speak of the style as 'the new barberism', hoping folk would get the pun – but at least the hair seemed her natural fair colour. And, on top of this very inviting appearance, she would probably be grateful for affection now her boyfriend seemed eternally gone. Ralph did not object to giving some women consolation if they had the body and face and were preferably not over thirty-five. He thought Meryl to be about thirty-two, a useful age, when women could still act young but also had the experience to see what a trophy Ralph Ember might be.

Today, she came not to Low Pastures but to the Monty. It was just after 10 a.m., and normally he wouldn't have been there. The staff reported at 11.30, to clear up from the night before and prepare for opening at noon. Ralph had arrived early to make an uninterrupted, unobserved, unhurried survey of the possible hazards to himself, as described by Hilaire Wilfrid Chandor recently when discussing the high shield. Although Ralph recognized that most of what Chandor said were gross, mouthy threats, he also recognized they were workable gross, mouthy threats. For long spells he contemplated something pre-emptive against Chandor – blast him first. But perhaps the threats had been meant to push him that way and into a trap. He still had cleansing elimination for him in mind, though.

As a less risky notion, he wondered whether the shelf-desk behind the bar where he often sat might have a capsule of bullet-proof glass around it, so he could watch club activities and remain totally, 360 degrees, sheltered. This should be easy to fix and totally effective. The glass must be guaranteed big impact-proof because, featured in a transparent shell like that, he would be declaring himself prey. But such glass, he knew, did exist.

Yet Ralph disliked this notion of a special cabin. He saw it as a cave in to, to long-term panic. He knew that some people already called him Panicking Ralph or even – disgraceful, this – Panicking Ralphy. He would acknowledge that sometimes, under abnormal stress, a panic *could* take over, virtually disabling him, mind and body. Ember almost always fought it with maximum force and often achieved a kind of victory – that is, the panic did not last more than, say, seven or eight minutes and never reached full, devastating intensity. The point was, if the panic *did* reach full intensity, Ralph would probably be unable to lift an arm to look at his watch and time the seizure. And even if he *could* bring his watch into view, he would certainly be incapable of seeing the figures and working out duration, because his eyes and brain stopped functioning in an authentic, uncurtailed, bowel-deep, Ralph-type panic. So if, during an attack, Ralph could gauge its length, he would regard this as en route to a triumph, meaning he still clearly had basic limb control and sight.

But, if he installed a protective pod for himself at the Monty, members might conclude he was into a non-stop, grave, continuous breakdown, and would regard the need to insulate himself as symptom of pathetic, permanent collapse. Above all, though, Ralph considered this retreat into sealed-off safety as entirely out of tune with his project for soon giving the Monty a prime social and intellectual reputation. The metal plate might not be wholly effective as protection, but it did have a discernible quality as distinguished decor, because of the tasteful pix from William Blake's unique work. This suited the new profile Ralph sought, or must soon be seeking, for the club. A glass cockpit to preserve him could not bring anything of that aesthetic sort to the Monty. It would be merely an ugly, functional life-saver.

Ralph felt more or less certain that none of the Athenaeum's controlling board felt it necessary to cower away from members inside a bullet-proof carapace. True, Ralph despised the Monty membership pretty well en bloc, but thought that as long as they *were* members he had that continuing obligation to move among them with greetings and chummy conversation, not isolate himself in a turret, as if he considered them essentially different and lower and to be shunned. He *did* consider them essentially different and lower and to be shunned, but would think it inhumane and unstrategic to proclaim this yet.

Impasse, really. He needed a good barrier but disliked the means of creating it. As a matter of fact, the deadlock in his mind now actually began to produce one of his panics and when somebody knocked hard on the Monty main door he felt this funk start to colonize him absolutely at the usual merciless canter. The Monty did take some deliveries in the morning, but not via this door. No, they came to a side entrance in the yard, and only after 11.30

when someone would be here to accept them. Ralph disliked the coincidence that on one of the very rare days he was in the club alone and out of hours, this caller seemed to know. Had he been watched?

He felt the harbinger, generous sweat across the back of his shoulders, and those sudden difficulties in breathing that always signalled a jumbo panic. But, just the same, when he decided to try to walk to the door and use its security spy-hole to see who the hell might have trailed him here, he found his legs would do the job without any serious wobble and, obviously, without total paralysis. The fact that he could decide *anything* also heartened him. His mind managed sequence. He was not lost yet. He did his anti-panic breathing routine, emptying his lungs as thoroughly as he could and then pulling in a total refill, but doing that slowly and under major control, a stupendous example to anyone who suffered this kind of appalling upset.

Seeing Meryl Goss about to bang again at the door with her fist, he felt the panic really go fast into retreat – nearly as fast as it had begun to overwhelm him – and when he opened up he had a wholly serviceable smile on and easily enough breath to say intelligibly, 'Here's a surprise, Meryl, if I may call you that. Can I do anything for you?' He didn't let the smile get too much, knowing that some people thought he looked like a silly-ass-style TV comedian years ago called 'Cardew the Cad', acting a schoolboy twit, and not Chuck Heston at all. Ralph realized the gap between the absurd and the grand could be small and vigilance was crucial.

'I took a chance,' she said.

'Well, yes. But, anyway, here I am. Come in, do.' Ralph stood back for her, giving plenty of space. He knew it would be an error to rush things. This was a woman in pursuit of *him*, not the opposite. He would certainly be civil and genial, yet measured. 'I can do you coffee, or there's a drink, of course. The bar's at your disposal.'

'Coffee.'

He went back behind the bar and got the percolator

going. Now, for instance, away from his shelf-desk, he would be in an area where the shield did nothing for him. But, then, consider, he would have had to step outside his glass fortress to make coffee, so that defence would be equally useless. She said: 'I've been inquiring around.'

'Well, yes, I expect so. Very much a quest, as I understand it. All of us at Low Pastures were sorry we couldn't help. And we admired your tenacity.'

'I've come to recognize I'm not going to find Graham alive.' She seemed to want to make it sound matter-of-fact, untragic.

'Oh, that's terribly bad and sad. What's pushed you to this?'

'Time. And a feeling I have about Chandor.'

'What feeling?' he said.

'That he knows.'

'Knows about your partner?'

'Knows what happened to him – because he saw to it himself or ordered it.'

He poured the coffees. It irritated, hurt, Ralph that she had obviously come here, not because she realized he looked like the young Charlton Heston, and might be interesting to get private with on his own premises, but to discuss some aspect of her fucking obsessional search for another man altogether. Ralph felt a profound insult in this attitude. He'd said he and the others thought well of her tenacity, because that had to be said as politeness. It did not mean she should think of nothing else, nobody else, for God's sake. That was a kind of self-indulgence, the kind sure to get up his nose.

'Property, building work, is a handy front, isn't it?' she said. 'Handy in all kinds of ways. One is that a body can be easily entombed and a semi put over it.'

'Oh, that's a frightful notion,' Ember said. But he had thought of it a long while ago.

'Look, Ralph, I've talked to a lot of people and picked up plenty of rumour and hints.'

He regarded it as all right for her to use his first name,

because he'd used hers. 'As long as you realize that's what they are, rumours and hints, if I may say.'

'And now I begin to get the picture,' she replied.

'Which picture?'

'You and that character in the comical suit and mauve shirt, Mansel Shale, dominate the drugs scene here, and a very favourable scene it is, because Assistant Chief Desmond Iles seems to see peace on the streets as his chief objective. He doesn't give you trouble, as long as you can guarantee such peace on the streets – which you do, between you. Or have to date. My guess is Chandor heard of this sweet arrangement and came here wanting a very profitable slice of it, property speculation as his cover.'

Ralph had a considerable chuckle and wished he'd gone for an armagnac not coffee so as to take on this sharp, relentless cow better. 'There are so many vast and inaccurate assumptions in what you say, Meryl, that I –'

'Graham brought home a real whack of money, you know, in London,' she replied.

'Property, even when supposedly in the doldrums, still does produce.'

'I didn't know and didn't ask where it really came from, but I guessed it wasn't from normal, straight property dealing, or possibly not from property dealing at all.'

Ralph saw now why that weird word 'worldly' to describe her arse had come to him. She *was* worldly, a lot more than appeared at first. He'd sometimes thought you could tell a bit about a woman's character from her behind, in the same way as the shape of the skull could be a giveaway. Meryl Goss had almost a moll streak that she'd concealed so damn well until this morning.

The attempt at matter-of-factness, even of offhandedness, came back. She gave him some stare. He was facing her across the bar, the coffee cups between them. 'I'm not going to find Graham alive, and something should be done about it,' she said.

'Well, the police –'

'The police won't act. I had two daughters of Harpur with me off and on, and from them and him I gather a

198

missing adult is that, only that – a missing adult, entitled to be missing and of no real concern to the authorities unless the body is found, which it might never be. The reporter and I even told the girls we knew Chandor had us stalked so that, if they passed this on to their father, he'd bear down on him. It hasn't worked.'

'You shouldn't be certain of this. Harpur is –'

'I didn't hear of Chandor in London, but I suppose he and Graham had a grey area business connection. No charges, no convictions, for either, presumably. Harpur and Iles would have discovered this on the computer, wouldn't they? So, maybe another reason they don't act.'

'Things are not clear and –'

'Of course, I did meet *some* friends and business mates of Graham when we were in London, of a certain type, you know,' she said.

'No, which type?'

'Oh, crooked. Total unreconstructed villains. You can often read it, can't you?'

'Can you?' he said. Was her stare intended to 'read' him? But she didn't need to, did she? Hadn't she just done an accurate account of the drugs game in this city, *his* game?

'Oh, yes,' she said. 'It's in my mind to say to one of them that Graham has been done by Chandor and there's £15K on offer to knock him over. Knock anyone else around him over as well, if necessary, but make sure and finish *him*. Listen, Ralph, I can't let the sod live after this, can I? The bank account is joint, Graham's and mine. I insisted. I'm very solvent. I can buy help.'

Ember chuckled again in a calm fashion, a quizzical fashion. 'You're saying you know hit men?' he asked.

She wrinkled her nose. 'Fair enough. No, I'm not sure I do know hit men, not absolute, experienced pros. That's why I'm here this morning, isn't it?'

'It is?'

'I know shady folk who were Graham's friends and might – might – want to do something to even things out for him and for me. But, you're right, they're probably not proven, accomplished contractors. That's a select and confidential calling, isn't it? And so, yes, I hesitate over asking any of them, in case they fuck up, or take the money and don't do it but bugger off on holiday to Mexico, or start blabbing about it, and I'm in bother.'

Ralph thought he began to cotton the astonishing, contemptuous, outrageously unsexual purpose of this morning visit.

'A lot of the talk I've listened to lately here is appraisal talk, Ralph.'

'Appraisal of what?'

'Of people here – figureheads. You come out pretty all right. Not perfect, but pretty all right. Gifted. Well, I'm not going to approach someone like Shale who picks such a suit and shirt, am I, for God's sake?'

Still with his face quite close to Goss's in this empty club, Ralph felt hopelessly distanced from her. He was conscious of enormous, warranted rage growing in him. This he reckoned as a magnificent positive factor, chasing out all remnants of the panic. A woman with that fucking razor wire haircut intended offering him, *him*, Ralph W. Ember, £15K to kill Chandor, because she fancied a bit of vengeance for the probable death and special burial of a lover. He'd had a thought to kill Chandor, yes, still had the thought, but just as a pure and necessary kill. He didn't take commissions, was not purchasable, as one of Trove's gutter London pals might be. Her talk of the money sickened him.

He'd very reasonably thought she arrived here today because she carried away from Low Pastures a recollection of him that sparked an understandable yearning she could not dowse. In fact, she came not driven by such admirable, natural desire but to buy a sniper. Just the same, he found his rage centred not so much on her as on Chandor, who had created this vile situation. Ralph would reject her foul proposal, yet his own project for Chandor grew stronger.

'He's threatened you, hasn't he, Ralph? I've spoken to people who were in the club when he mocked the fine, elegantly collaged steel shield as farcical, and said you were wide open to a bullet or two. You'll want to give him an answer to such abuse, won't you?'

'I don't recall anything like that, not in the least,' he replied, 'and I can tell you it wouldn't make any difference if he did say something of the sort.'

'You should give him an answer and get paid for it. I could probably go to twenty grand for you, taking account of your experience, as long as it's a definite wipe-out.'

'Look, I –'

'And among other gobbets of chat I heard was admiration for the way you might – I say might because there's no proof – that's the brilliance of it – the way you *might* have seen off awkward fuckers in the past – Alfred Ivis, for instance? These are the kind of credentials I'm looking for if I engage someone.'

Such an awkward fucker, Alf Ivis. 'I don't think it suits to engage in slander of that sort, even though you may be emotionally off balance,' Ember replied. God, the only time she could sound really enthusiastic about him was as an executioner – nothing to do with his unquenchable glory as a man.

'Up to £20K,' she replied. 'Old notes, obviously and no fallible fifties.'

This genuinely grieving bitch thought she could get his services for cash, his thug skills, and not his more comforting and attentive flairs. Would she be able to comprehend the degree of affront in this, even if he explained it to her? He wouldn't, of course. That would be so much beneath him. Did any woman ever go to the head man at the Athenaeum and offer him a bag full of notes to flatten a business rival? Good God, something like this would most probably not even happen in that London media club, the Groucho.

However, Ralph recorded another present triumph. He was able to convert his revulsion and disappointment into a further restrained chuckle. 'Turn assassin?' he remarked, in one of the best wry tones he thought he had ever uttered. 'Not quite my line of things, I fear.' He continued to aim his reproaches and loathing at Chandor, the dirty fountainhead of all this, responsible for causing such a grotesque, soiling interview.

She stood, as angry as himself, but showing it. 'So, I will have to try a London mate or that fancy dress grammarian, Shale,' she said.

When she had gone, Ember went into the loft at the Monty and looked out a Heckler and Koch pistol, new, of course, and able to fire untraceables. Almost everyone had switched to H and Ks these days, including the police.

Chapter Ten

Harpur read the front page of the *Evening Register* to Iles in the Assistant Chief's suite. He liked being read to sometimes and would sit contentedly listening with one eye shut. A while ago, he'd told Harpur that this took him back to childhood and his mother going through the *Uncle* elephant story books for him at bedtime.

'A very flattering comparison, sir, if I may say,' Harpur had replied, '– your mother.'

'Oh, I didn't much like her. The tales were good, though. Not everyone likes Uncle, the elephant. They find him arrogant and vain. For myself, I loved him. Yes. He warred constantly against evil, as represented by the Badfort Crowd. Perhaps that won me. Did *your* mother ever read to *you*? What would it be, form articles from the *Racing Times*?'

Now, Harpur began: '"Marina Murder and Mayhem, by crime correspondent Kate Mead.

'"A prominent local businessman was shot dead yesterday near his luxury home and only a few hundred yards from his marina office complex. Two of his associates, with him at the time, were severely injured and rushed to hospital where they remain in a critical condition. Because of its ruthlessness and expert planning, detectives believe there could be a gangland element to the shooting.

'"Police were today examining a burned-out car possibly used in the attack. Marina residents and office staffs are shocked by the outburst of violence in a normally quiet, prestige area. Detective Chief Inspector Francis Garland, who is in charge of the case, said: 'This was an appalling crime in one of the city's most sought after districts. It is essential that the attacker or attackers are detained very soon.'

'"Hilaire Wilfrid Chandor, 41, the dead man, had recently arrived in the city from London to establish a property business, H.W.C. Developments. The two men injured are executives of the company.

'"The shootings took place at lunchtime yesterday. Mr Chandor usually left the office at a little before 1 p.m. and walked to his home in Cape Matapan Terrace, which he occupied with his partner, Fiona Raegi and their son, Lance, aged seven, who attends Mayflower Preparatory School. Ms Raegi has a part-time post in H.W.C. Developments.

'"Neighbours say Mr Chandor was almost always accompanied by at least two members of the firm, as if for security. Police are investigating whether he had received threats, possibly from business rivals and perhaps with a London connection.

'"A near neighbour who did not wish to be named told the *Register*: 'I heard a car outside at about 1 p.m. and then the sound of what I thought at first to be fireworks. I went to the window and saw Mr Chandor lying on the pavement. There was a blood patch on the pavement near his head. Two other men lay close by. One of them attempted to get to his feet but fell back. Mr Chandor and the other man were totally still. The car I'd heard had disappeared. I went to the telephone and dialled 999. The police arrived within five minutes.'

'"Although business rivalry is regarded as one possible motive, DCI Garland said he was keeping an open mind at this stage. Nothing was taken from any of the men and robbery has been discounted. Police would not disclose the make of car found burned out. DCI Garland said the efficiency of the attack could suggest a professional hit man or team.

'"Ms Raegi and Lance were being comforted today by relatives and neighbours. A member of the family said Ms Raegi was too upset to talk to the Press at this juncture.

Cape Matapan Terrace is a quiet side road of red-brick, marina-style town houses. It is believed Ms Raegi was in the kitchen at the rear of the house when the shootings took place and did not know of the attack until neighbours alerted her.

'"Although police would not comment on the nature of the injuries, the *Register* understands that Mr Chandor was killed by two bullets in the head. The two colleagues injured are Mr Rufus Vincent Esham, 37, Personnel Manager for H.W.C. Developments, and Maurice Spencer Corl, 43, Director of Strategic Planning. Both are in Intensive Care at Paston Hospital. Mr Esham was hit in the abdomen and Mr Corl in the chest. Paston confirmed today that both men remain critical.

'"Police say they have little to go on at this juncture except the abandoned car but are conducting house to house inquiries on the marina. It is likely the attacker or attackers switched vehicles in their getaway and that the torched vehicle was stolen.

'"It is not clear whether property was Mr Chandor's only business activity. It is believed he might have wished to diversify and that this could have brought him into confrontation with established local firms. Mr Chandor had previous business interests in the Eltham district of London.

'"The local business community were shocked by the incident at Cape Matapan Terrace. Because of his comparatively recent arrival in the city, he was still not very well known, but one prominent local businessman who also wished to remain anonymous said: 'He had seemed to be settling in very well. This is a very regrettable setback and will cause all members of the commercial community considerable anxiety.'"'

Iles, back to two-eyed mode, said: 'Hint, hint. But, OK, she's doing her best to tell what has to be told, yet can't be, because there's too much unknown. Someone hires a marksman, or marksmen, to take out Chandor and those guilty by association, Col?'

'"Someone" being Trove's woman?'

'We have no Trove body, though.'

'Chandor does some genuine property and building work. Classic.'

'Ah,' Iles replied. 'Then again, perhaps Ralphy or Manse don't like the potential opposition as Chandor tries to "diversify", and act themselves, or put their people on to it. Plus, Chandor might have already given all kinds of actual, infuriating offence.'

'What are you thinking of, sir – Manse's staircase as glimpsed from Matilda's little bedroom?'

'Chandor could be the kind who dishes out plenty of disrespect and threats,' Iles replied. 'And then there's Manse's new chauffeur, isn't there? Eldon. He looked capable and short-fused to me. I don't suppose the girl herself can use an automatic, can she?'

'Goss?'

'She's probably got a rough side. How else would she be with Trove?'

'You, personally, thought Chandor should be removed, didn't you, in the interests of order?' Harpur replied. 'The Forensic people say H and K shells, but everyone has H and Ks these days, haven't they, as well as you – I mean, us?'

Iles glared, *very* two-eyed, across the desk. 'Do I see a news pic of that fucker Garland?' he said. 'Yes, the word – *fucker*.' Harpur was holding up the *Register* as he browsed the inside pages, accidentally and foolishly giving Iles a view of Page 1. There had been a time when Sarah Iles seemed to panic in her marriage and turned for a while to Garland and, of course, to Harpur. The ACC transformed himself into anguished shouter once more. 'Garland – that smug-looking, lesser-breed sod. He's another of your atrocious sort, isn't he, Harpur? Tell me this, was he before or after you with my wife?'

'Ralphy has a letter on Page 6 of the *Register* that –'

'Sarah and I can smile together about those incredible, grubby episodes now. Oh, yes, we smile. Episodes. *Episodes*, Harpur. And you can tell Garland the same.

That's how we regard them. We are civilized, we are adult. We are strong. We have come through.'

'That's a quote, isn't it, sir?'

'But I don't understand what in God's name she could see in either of –'

'Ralphy has a letter on Page 6 criticizing the water authorities for still not doing enough about river pollution and a heavy decline of trout population,' Harpur said. 'This is despite previous published appeals by him on the subject. He goes as Ralph W. Ember when writing to the Press.'

Iles nodded economically and swam gracefully back to the present, like a very hale fish. 'Sometimes, only sometimes, Harpur, things work themselves out satisfactorily without too much involvement on our part,' he said pleasantly, patiently, the voice of masterful overview – civilized, adult, strong, having come through.

'Francis Garland believes it's going to be very tough to fix these shootings on anyone.'

'I believe it. If Francis can't crack this, nobody will,' Iles said. 'He's a very gifted officer.'

'Oh, certainly, sir.'

'I feel badly about Chandor's woman, and the son – that kind of violence on our ground, Col. So sad.' Iles paused. Harpur always worried about Iles's pauses. Ferocious egomania and galloping self-pity could set in during even a very short break. The ACC re-upped the volume: 'But, then, relationships are always liable to bring suffering as well as pleasure, aren't they, Harpur? Aren't they, Harpur? Aren't they? Think of the pain you and that scheming lech, Garland, brought me through your despicable –'

'On the other hand, perhaps Meryl Goss's suffering will be a little less if she believes the people responsible for her man's death have been adequately dealt with now,' Harpur replied.

'One dead, and those two so thoughtfully named lads, Rufus and Maurice, perhaps on their way out, or uncorrectably maimed. A primitive reaction by Goss, Col, perhaps via Goss's bravos? Comfort from a kind of clever savagery? Yet, understandable? Understandable, I think. What's your opinion, Harpur?'

'Well, sir, I –'

'The way I see it, too. Enforcement of the law has to be in good hands, of course, or society will founder. But occasionally those good hands should stay, at least as far as can be seen, wisely idle.'

'And washed, like Pilate's?'

'I would never endorse *fait néantism,*' Iles replied.

'Oh, hardly, sir. I can't see you going for anything like that. They wouldn't know how to spell it on your CV.'

'Which historical figure was it who advocated a policy of what he called "masterly inactivity", Col?'

'I don't know whether the new Chief would accept that as the way to run his domain.'

'No, you *don't* know, do you, Harpur?'

'He's not like Mr Lane, easy to browbeat and –'

'How about leaving *me* to educate the new Chief?' Iles said.

'You've had so much practice.'

'*His* fucking domain? *His?*'

'Well, he's –'

'Things are in goodish hands, Col.'